THE FACE IN THE MARSH

A TALE OF TERROR

BY ELIZABETH HIRST

This is a work of fiction. Any similarity to any events, institutions, or persons, living or dead, is purely coincidental and unintentional.

Cover and interior design by Nathan Frechette. Edited by Natalie Cousineau, L.P. Vallee and Vicki Martin.

Legal deposit, Library and Archives Canada, April 2019.

Paperback ISBN: 978-1-987963-50-2
Ebook ISBN 978-1-987963-42-7

Renaissance Press
http://renaissancebookpress.com
info@renaissancebookpress.com

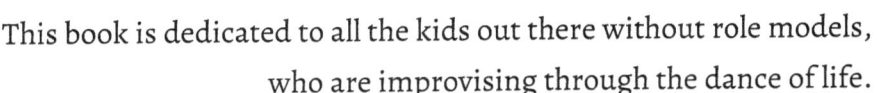

This book is dedicated to all the kids out there without role models, who are improvising through the dance of life.

I see you.
Keep dancing.

THE GAMBLE

The driving rain of early spring pattered against the sliding doors to Kenzie and Maria's apartment balcony. The wind rattled the doors in their casement, making it feel as though a truck had just driven by the eleventh floor. The shifting light left shadows on Maria's otherwise perfect cheeks.

This was their favourite place to look out on the world, standing at the balcony doors in bad weather. They shared an obsession with light. Maybe it was that they were both trained as museum curators, thinking about displaying things to their best advantage, but Kenzie thought it went much deeper.

Even though Maria's back was stiff and her hands trembled, Kenzie still enjoyed looking at her beautiful thick eyelashes and eyebrows. She was stunning, even when she was angry, a mixture of high cheekbones and soft curves, and body language that spoke of hard-chiselled masculinity. Kenzie put a hand on Maria's back, half expecting an elbow to push her arm away. None came.

"Did you see a box in the bedroom closet," Kenzie said, her voice soft, "labelled 'Kenzie's Private Stuff?'"

Maria sighed, raising her chin. "Hall closet, top shelf. You couldn't see it because you're too short." She turned from the window and headed for the hallway with heavy steps.

Kenzie followed her, feeling useless as Maria reached up high, pulled the box down from the shelf, and held it out to her.

Kenzie crossed her arms. "Why was it up where I couldn't reach?"

"Because you hadn't opened the box in two years and I needed space for the dehumidifier," said Maria. "For something labelled 'Kenzie's Private Stuff' it sure doesn't seem like you thought about it a lot. So, what is it? Still too private for me?"

Kenzie fled into the bedroom, where suitcases and boxes had bred like rabbits over the past few days. Maria followed her and set the 'private' box down on the bed. She gave Kenzie a quizzical look, as if waiting for permission to open it.

"Go ahead," said Kenzie, "It's just the stuff I saved from art school. The little worth salvaging, that is."

Maria opened the box, reached in and brought out a lopsided 3D print of a cartoon duck. She turned the figurine over in her hands, then read off the bottom: "Canooie?" she said, giving the first smile Kenzie had seen all day.

"Yeah," said Kenzie, busying herself in the closet. She picked up an armful of clothes, hangers and all, and brought them to the bed, where she began folding them into the suitcase. "That's his name."

"Just yeah? No artist's statement?" Maria teased, grin growing wider.

"I'm not an artist," said Kenzie, "I'm a curator. I just want the pencil that's in there. The one with the special grip on it."

Maria's smile faded. "Oh. Okay. Here you go." She groped in the box and held out an old, weathered pencil extender, the kind with a little slide mechanism to grip the pencil nub so that you could draw until your pencil was down to a centimetre or so. Painter's tape held the slide onto the wooden handle, which had been dyed a variety of colours and shades by dirty fingers.

Kenzie took it, unprepared for how sour her stomach would turn at the feel of it in her hand. She put it in the shoe pocket of her suitcase, trembling as she did so. A long silence passed between her and Maria as she folded clothes.

Maria burst forth on her like one of the rain clouds scudding by the windows. "This is still a shit idea! After everything you've been through, I can't believe you'd even consider...I mean...uuuuurgh..." Sometimes, when she was really worked up, Maria's English failed her. She gesticulated and accidentally struck the box of art school stuff, knocking it off the bed.

Kenzie pushed the box aside with her foot and tossed a dress into the suitcase, where it crumpled. "They're offering me the curator position, and it's not a small museum either. It's my only job offer with potential. If I can stick with it for a year, I'll have my pick of jobs back here."

Maria sat on the bed and crossed her arms, bouncing a little. Her big brown eyes begged for no bullshit.

"And where have I heard this one before? This is what you said after co-op, and with the start-up, and you were probably whistling that same tune when you sailed into grad school, although I didn't know you then."

Kenzie tossed a hand in the air and went for another armload of clothes. "Those things should have resulted in a job. One of them, at least. Co-op worked for everyone else. It worked for you." She gestured at Maria's T-shirt, with its screen-printed logo of the South American Museum and Cultural Centre.

Maria blew a strong breath out of her nose and stood up from the bed, fingers pinching the bridge of her nose. Kenzie knew she was sick of having this conversation, but it had never been settled.

"I wanted better for you. You know that. But I can't force people to like you. I have no idea why others react to you the way they do, and even if I did, would it help our relationship for me to tell you?"

"You were always hanging out with people from our year in grad school," Kenzie said. "They must have said something, sometime that would indicate what the hell their problem was with me."

"We've been over this," Maria said. "It was just hanging out. It wasn't all about you. 'Oh yes, Maria, let me spill out my deep philosophical differences with your girlfriend while we prepare dioramas for design class.'"

Kenzie felt her cheeks flush. She paused in the center of the room for a moment, her toes digging into the carpet, swaying and holding her bundle of clothes. The closet looked so empty. The room would be so empty when she left. How could Maria not want to fill that space with someone else?

"I think I'm cursed," she said.

Maria came over and took the clothes. Kenzie felt the warmth of Maria's skin for just a moment, and longed for her before even leaving. Kenzie's eyes teared up again. Maria put an arm around her and pulled her close. Kenzie sniffled, in spite of herself.

"If you've got any bad luck, it's all radiating out of that family of yours," Maria said. "They never let you live. You're just catching up to everybody else. You have to stay away from them. They'll just fuck you up, and this time, it could be permanent."

Kenzie's tears flowed thicker. "Why shouldn't they give me a hand up?" she said. "And what's my alternative? Stay here and live with the consequences of having failed. Keep running into the same old people and tell them I'm not working, or worse, working in retail or some call center?"

Maria kissed her forehead.

"Or, you could stay here with me, work part-time, and volunteer for museums and historical societies until you get something permanent. Lots of people in lots of programs have had to do that. You wouldn't be the first, or the thousandth."

"Those people usually have connections," Kenzie said. "I can't think of one person, other than you, that I can count on to recommend me for a job. All the hotshots look down on me, and the people that are struggling would try to take it for themselves."

Maria let out a breath which played across Kenzie's cheek, making the trails of her tears go cold.

"And how impressive is it going to be when your only two references are Mom and Dad? They want you to go to that little town and work with them, so you'll stay forever," Maria said.

Kenzie pushed away then, her indignation stoppering her tears.

"You don't think that I might make an impression on one or two people before I'm done there? Or maybe you don't think my work can speak for itself?" She pitched a felt cloche hat into a nearby box labelled 'fragile', hearing the tinkle of glass underneath. Her heart had sped up.

"Oh come on, don't do this," said Maria. "You know that's not what I meant! New grads need mentorship and guidance. How are you going to grow as a curator when you're wading through the muck of your past, with the same old people and the same old problems? You've worked so hard to get here, in school and in therapy. Don't throw this away."

Kenzie trembled. "And you don't think, for one minute, that I might be able to make things right?"

Maria threw up her hands. "You know what? No, I don't. But not because there's something wrong with you, like you seem to think. It's because you don't have a fucking time machine. Or a mind control device. Or anything that can make your parents be anything but what they are. People are going to be how they're going to be, Kenzie. All you can do is choose how to react to them. This obsession you have with rewriting your childhood, with taking it all on and making it work, is what's going to take you far away from anything you want in this life."

Kenzie slammed the lid of her suitcase. She clamped down on the urge to say something hurtful.

"I'm not trying to rewrite the past! I just want to think that the future can be better, all right? That change can happen."

Maria went to the nightstand and picked up the photo sitting there in a decorative metal frame. She looked at it, sadness playing across her features.

"No, you want to think that you can force change to happen," said Maria. "And yet, you've barely given *me* a second thought in all of this. How often am I going to get to visit you? And even if I do, am I just going to be a 'friend'? Did you even think to ask me to go?"

Maria plopped back down on the bed and held out the photo for Kenzie to pack. Kenzie didn't even need to look at it. They smiled goofily at the camera as they lounged on a crocheted throw Kenzie had made. It was summer, and the ground was strewn with a picnic basket, a wine bottle, and a variety of sandwiches.

She had met Maria at the campus LGBT club, at Halloween in first year archival studies. She had been dressed as Rambo and Kenzie as a gingerbread woman, complete with sparkly foam jujube buttons. Kenzie had showed up there, despite her nerves, despite being terrified of being seen by her classmates, out of hope that there might be one place in the world where she could live without her secrets.

Maria had been honest. Blunt, even. Maria's blunt honesty had struck the hard rock of Kenzie's defenses and brought forth a refreshing spring of authenticity. Soon, Kenzie was answering questions that she never thought she would answer truthfully and falling in love with someone that she swore she never would. In the beginning, she'd dated around, dabbled with a few guys, but it soon became obvious that Maria was her person. They'd moved in together in third year and built a harmonious life of cozy couch time and forever making new pictures to put on the walls. Kenzie might have trouble with other people, but she'd never doubted Maria.

Kenzie took the picture from Maria. She buried it under her socks, deep in her suitcase where not even Mum would snoop. She felt a surge of nervous energy run through her as she assessed what it would take to keep this photo hidden.

"You're not making this any easier for me," Kenzie said.

Maria rolled her eyes and tossed her head, turning away. But even without seeing her face, Kenzie could tell that Maria was blinking back tears.

"You expect me to make it easy for you to leave me?" she said.

"I'm not leaving you."

"Yes, you are." Maria's voice was low. "And I like you as you are now. Big, bold and bisexual. If you throw that away, you're an asshole."

"Judge me all you want. It's hard to stop loving your parents, even when you know they don't love you," Kenzie said quietly, out of tears now.

She felt the mattress shift as Maria got up.

Her lover's voice rose steadily as she said, "You know what? Go. I see it now. You've got to just keep repeating the past until it destroys you. You don't love yourself, Kenzie. I thought I could fix that, but it looks like someone else holds the key."

Kenzie searched for a reply but found none. Instead, she sat frozen as the door slammed and Maria's angry footsteps faded down the hall.

The sick feeling in the pit of her stomach, the one that made her feel broken from stem to stern, crept outward until it consumed her whole body. She walked around to the clear side of the bed and collapsed onto it, her back to the door. She was tired, so tired, of fighting. Going back would just be easier. She wanted everything to be easy and simple again... No more tough choices, no more emotional anguish about whether she'd done the right thing. Just black and white, approval or exile.

It seemed like everyone else around her took care of themselves effortlessly. They paddled through adulthood like ducks through water, navigating situations that would break Kenzie in two.

Enough with the pushing of rocks uphill. Everything was going to be easy again for a while, because after all she'd been through, she deserved a rest.

And rest she did, eventually, as rain tapped against the windows. In her sleep, however, a much deeper part of her felt great regret to be leaving this cozy place and the woman who understood her. That part, which had only just begun to breathe properly, felt a great fear and trepidation at the return of the past. And so it was, under such tension of the self, that Kenzie embarked upon the strange and terrifying journey that would define her life.

ETTENBY'S LOG PALACE

Kenzie watched the river curve along beside the car, the sun dancing off the ripples of dark water as it splashed, shallow and carefree, over the stones. Oh, to bathe in that river naked or, better yet, be a creature of the river and just float, with neither a care nor a responsibility in the world other than feeding oneself and occasionally following the inborn instincts forged by nature. Surely that was happiness, being in a state of blissful, cool suspension and never knowing guilt, or shame, or duty.

Her phone buzzed.

MARIA: Text me when you get there.

Kenzie scanned the message, careful not to linger for too long, but it was no use. Mum had heard the buzz.

"Who's texting you?" she said.

"My old roommate," Kenzie replied.

"You never did tell me where you met her," Mum replied.

"Yes, I did. We were in the same research methodologies class." *That should be boring enough to shut her up*, thought Kenzie.

Nope.

"Why have you never brought her for a visit? You're always so secretive with your friends."

Kenzie didn't answer. She leaned toward the window, hoping Mum would take the hint. Why did she have to come instead of Dad, or maybe an intern? Oh, yeah, because Mum didn't know enough to actually help run the gallery, so she had to do something to feel self-important and included. Kenzie wondered how someone could stand being as much of a third wheel as her mother was most days, without ever having the impulse to strike out on their own, learn something new, or do *anything* different. Perhaps she refrained from busying herself elsewhere because it would leave her less time for insinuating herself amongst those far more qualified and standing on their accomplishments.

Mum started in on something else. Something about washroom renovations and the way they picked the tiles and the nice young man at the tile store and he's a rugby player for charity in his off hours...I just thought it was so cool! And Kenzie let her go on with an occasional um hum or yeah?, all the while consumed by the scenery as they rode along.

The stunning, sparkling river grew wider, shallower, slower. Islands cropped up in the middle, along with tumbled rocks from nowhere, carried there by the glaciers eons before man. They stood like mossy monoliths to forgotten gods. The trees were everywhere, poker-straight, strobing along beside the car and populating the distant hills. Amongst the pines were some birch and some maple that had managed to be almost as skinny and abstract in shape. In the late spring breeze, their new leaves shone, tender and waxy. A tiny island, made from a fallen rock, had at some point accumulated some soil and a twisted little pine tree had even popped out on it.

Travelling upriver, they eventually met a place where the river made a sharp fork; or perhaps a meeting place would be more accurate, as the waters flowed together there. The side of the fork that ran along the road remained wide, and shallow, and visibly flowing, but the other side of the fork, which stretched into the interior of the forest, grew sluggish and turned to marsh within a hundred feet. Reeds sprung out of the water and grass, and an algae-like substance floated on the top, along with water lilies and other such adornments of still waters. *The water must move beneath that cover,* Kenzie thought, or else the river would run out of fuel very quickly, but how odd and slightly disturbing that one could not see it move, nor did any of the plants sitting atop it seem to drift in any way. It was as if the river wore a mask.

A green sign up ahead signalled the way to Ettenby's Log Palace Museum and Art Gallery, with an arrow pointing right. Mum swung the car into the little laneway leading to the bridge that took them across to a flat island covered in trees. A little sluiceway lay under the bridge, the green water cascading smoothly over the man-made embankment.

The house sat on the island at this corner of the two rivers. A log mansion built to mimic Tudor architecture, its main gallery hung over the bottom floor of the building, lined with square windows with rippled glass. It was a large, sprawling place, shaped like a U: one large central building with wings jutting off on either side. In front of the house, a lawn stretched down to the pointed end of the island between the rivers, perfectly manicured and bearing a flapping Canadian flag. The island became lawn, became stones, became water. Across the bridge, a large wooden sign welcomed them to the museum and art gallery. A parking lot, well screened from the road by twenty feet or so of pine forest, took up most of the rest of the island. A few cars and well-laden vans sat in the spots closest to the museum, but it was too early in the season for the place to be packed.

Mum pulled onto a gravel track and the car bumped its way to a staff-only, five-car lot beside the right wing of the Log Palace. The shadows of pines waved overhead here, and the tarmac was littered with needles and pine cones.

Kenzie got out of the car, her backpack swinging from one shoulder, and breathed in the beautiful, fresh air. Thin cloud cover amplified the sunlight, and she could smell the fresh earth of spring all around. In the distance, she could hear the constant seashell sound of the river, bubbling over the rocks on its way south to the great lakes. Perhaps she could schedule time in every day for a long walk down to the riverside.

Mum popped the trunk and immediately began dropping things unceremoniously to the ground and stacking them in ways they shouldn't stack. Kenzie hurried over and pulled her duffel bag out from under her book box.

"I told you my cloche hat was in there! Would you please just let me do this, or at least listen when I tell you what's fragile? And that other box you just dropped on the ground had a vase and a picture frame in it!"

"Oh, get over it. That wouldn't have hurt anything," Mum said. "You're always so sensitive about everything! Miss Fashion Plate. I try to help and all you can do is criticize!"

Kenzie gathered up as much as she could and walked away with her arms full, her face hot.

"It's not *help* when it's not *helpful*," she said over her shoulder. "Helpful would be taking anything I said into consideration when throwing my bags around like an orangutan at the airport!"

Kenzie balanced a box on one knee, pushing down the bar to open the staff entrance. She emerged into a hallway lit with flat, institutional LED tubes, a coat rack on one side, an opening for the break room ahead on the left. She went ahead and dumped her stuff in the break room on an empty table.

A few more runs of grabbing things up and swatting Mum away like a puppy trying to pee on everything, and her stuff was inside. Undeterred by the recent dust-up, Mum followed her in and regarded the boxes and bags sitting on and underneath the table.

"You should load that stuff up into the apartment right now. Then you'll have it done," she said.

"I'd prefer to do it later and take a tour right away during operating hours. The sooner I get a feel for the place, the better," Kenzie said, feeling another battle coming on.

"Nobody really expects you to figure everything out right away. Suppose you took a week to—"

"Dad was clear. I start tomorrow," said Kenzie, struggling not to roll her eyes in frustration. Why did her mother have to make everything so hard?

Mum straightened up and tried to look imposing. She was a lot shorter than Kenzie, so it never quite worked out for her. "Well, I don't want this stuff here. I'll sit and worry about someone coming along and stealing it unless you take it upstairs!"

"Then by all means, sit and watch it. I'm looking around," Kenzie replied, pushing open the door to the main atrium. Mum followed her, slinking behind. Her coral-coloured floral shirt and Bermuda shorts made her look more like one of the tourists than staff. She'd dyed her hair again, this time a mousy brown colour that did nothing for her skin tone. She kept her hair short, wore little make-up, and yet constantly complained that Kenzie never made an effort to look good.

In public, where the tourists could see her, Mum gave off a generally friendly vibe, which tended to spill over into a kind of hyperactive toadying that made Kenzie cringe inwardly, especially when she did it with extended family and virtual strangers at the store. Now, as they came into the atrium, a museum patron passed them by on the diagonal, and Mum inquired as to how their day was going with an insincere little laugh. She offered them a tour they had already taken, then made a joke that wasn't funny before she realized that Kenzie had gotten as far down the atrium as possible so as not to be associated with the display.

Kenzie saw Dad sitting at the visitor's information booth, like a beacon in a storm, rifling through some files and speaking absent-mindedly to a dark-haired young girl with a volunteer badge on. He spotted Kenzie and stood, with open arms. He strode around the desk to meet her.

"Kenzie! You're here!"

Kenzie hurried to him and hugged him tight.

"It's been too long. We've got so much to do!" he said.

"I'm excited to get started," Kenzie replied, smiling.

Dad's motions were emphatic, his speech excited. He gestured around the atrium.

"Look at all this! Finally, you're getting to see what we're bringing to the community! We need a good curator to make sure that we keep this place the best it can be, and serving the local people that made it great!"

Kenzie did look around now, ignoring the area where Mum stood almost by reflex. The main hall of the palace was large and open, comprising most of the bottom floor of the main wing. What had once been a reception hall and ballroom was now a beautiful, modern space with comfortable chairs, shelves of brochures and reading material, and a small resource reading room and gift shop on the end opposite the staff rooms, encased in glass and staffed by more volunteers. Everywhere, signs pointed to the different exhibits. There was Historic Living, Folk Art, Community Space and Archives, along with Touch Our Heritage! A Hands-on Exhibit for Kids. The ceilings were low, kind of like an old-style theatre lobby, but large, plate-glass windows at either end of the room let in plenty of natural light and reminded guests of the beautiful, untamed forest beyond.

"This is incredible," Kenzie said. "What a victory for the Society."

"Indeed it is," Dad said, "It was worth the ten years of fundraising, and legal battles, to see this final outcome." She could tell he was tearing up a bit.

"My life's work," he said, "I can finally feel like it all came to something."

Kenzie put her arm around him again.

"I'm so proud of you, Dad. I tell everybody about the work you've done, uncovering the history of this area. You're one cool dude."

"He certainly is," said Mum, jumping on the bandwagon, "I picked a good one!"

Everybody let that comment slide into the bin, where it belonged. Mum would probably try to steer the conversation in her direction about once every two minutes, but it looked like she was coming along for the tour, whether Kenzie and Dad liked it or not.

THE GRAND TOUR

Facing the info desk, with his arm around Kenzie, Dad began.
"I'm sure you can see that we're starting at the hub of this
operation. Everyone who enters the building purchases their
admission here, and then they can either carry on to the Folk Arts wing or
the Heritage Living wing. The crowds often overlap, but we do also get many
specialized visitors who are thankful for the clear organization of the art and
the heritage," he said with a dry chuckle.

"To your right and behind are the reading room and the gift shop. Other
than keeping an eye on the till balance throughout the day, you shouldn't
have too much to do in the shop. Mrs. Myers down in Hillscroft loves to do
the buying and merchandising (she's a retired marketing exec), and we think
she does a pretty good job of it."

Kenzie nodded. Hillscroft was the nearest town to the Log Mansion,
nestled in amongst tall clay hills and thick forests. The bus had dropped her
there. The place had a homestead-y feel, and she knew from her father's
phone calls that it contained an odd mixture of executives from Toronto
who'd had nervous breakdowns, retired organic types who wanted to do
crafts and live off the land, and drug users who wanted to do their thing in a

place where nobody gave a shit. Overlap between the three was common, and often came in surprising combinations.

The town had won 'Small Town of the Year' five years running for community engagement and arts activities, so it was the perfect place for Dad to find a host of wealthy busybodies looking to run a non-profit. They were also close enough to Peterborough that they were never short of history interns from nearby Trent University.

In that regard, the Log Palace would probably run itself for a while. Volunteer recruiting could be minimal, and she could focus on the collections and activities. An ideal position to be in, especially for a newcomer. Usually new curators ended up jogging uphill for quite some time in their first placements, with tiny organizations that the executive had trouble getting anyone to care about beyond making a donation once a year. Some new curators would make progress, and others would be fired within a year for not making enough headway with the public and be stuck in a very bad position indeed, resume-wise. Although accepting this post had made her uneasy, she was starting to feel like perhaps she had been savvier than she had initially given herself credit for.

Dad pointed out the reading room as they passed.

"This area will likely take up some of your attention. We change the reading material every week and very careful attention must be paid to the transfers. We've got anti-theft tags on most of the documents, but you can't tag everything. Watch the amateur historians especially, or people writing books. They're the most likely to make things disappear, or worse, make them re-appear on the Internet. And we tend to keep the really sensitive material in the archives, where we have greater security, not to mention better humidity control."

They reached a blocky, modernized room with a cantilevered staircase leading up on the left, and another hallway beyond it, leading to a set of glass doors with 'Archives and Community Activities' printed on the glass in white. Inside, Kenzie could see a row of security scanners. Beyond that, she spied a large, open space with a stage, complete with old-fashioned velvet curtain, and several stands and wall spaces holding amateur paintings, sculptures, and photography that Dad explained were from the local community. Another door at the back of the room led into the archives, and Kenzie could just make out row upon row of tall bookshelves, descending into the haze of distance. Dad went on about the events that happened here once a week or so, but Kenzie could tell he was eager to get up the stairs.

Dad had been talking about the Folk Art wing for months. Every time she phoned, they had found something new, or someone had donated something extraordinary. The original owner of the property, George Ettenby, had been very eccentric and had not been known as a lover of art, but when the Hillscroft Historical Society gained possession of the property after a long legal and fundraising campaign, it had been Dad, poking around in the attic and the maintenance passages, who had found the current trove. He had said many times that the finding of these pieces felt like the most important re-discovery of his career. According to his research, there was nothing else in Canada of the kind, and he was hard pressed to find anything like it in the entire former Commonwealth.

Dad was leaping up the stairs as they headed to the Folk Art wing.

"I knew as soon as I saw this art that, besides being my daughter, you would be the woman for the job," he said, "Seeing as you've always been so interested in art galleries and the avant-garde. I've never seen folk art like this. I'm saving the dolls for last, because I'm sure you'll be floored."

Kenzie followed him upstairs. The gallery beyond the fire doors was well-lit, white, and clean. As they reached the top of the stairs, Kenzie could see the main gallery stretch away on their left, the pictures for the moment hidden behind the angle and the sheen of the lights on the glass.

On the right was another hallway, perpendicular to the other, stretching away into shadow.

"We've got the lights on motion sensors," said Dad, "It conserves electricity and guarantees that the works don't spend too much time in the light." .

They moved into the first gallery, on the left. It contained four works, hung in a neat row, all fairly large, square pieces. The first thing that struck Kenzie was the predominant pumpkin-orange-and-brown colour scheme; the second, that the works were all mottled and pitted, as though they had an aquatic quality to them.

They were not paintings, as she had suspected, but rather woodcuts, some of which showed cracks at the top or bottom, or evidence of joining several boards together. In bas-relief, someone had chipped out of the wood scenes of the surrounding area at different times in history. The first one, at the far end of the gallery, showed a peaceful river fork, looking up toward the wilds further inland, with an abundance of water lilies and rushes. Off in the distance, a pair of Native people strode along the far bank.

The second showed a man in the garb of a sixteenth-century explorer, standing proudly on the bank. His eyes were inlaid with what looked like bone, and they were disturbing: almond-shaped and staring, with perfectly round, perfectly black pupils. Behind him, a woman's head and shoulders protruded from the same water, her hair slicked back so far as to almost render her bald-looking, her eyes staring too, boring into the viewer. The menace emanating from that woman was palpable, and Kenzie suspected that she would emerge only to drown the explorer. And why did it all feel so documentary? Was it because the first carving had seemed so plausible?

Kenzie frowned.

"What the hell *is* that?" she said, forgetting her father's feelings for a moment, "When was it made? What is it supposed to depict?"

Her dad gave a little conciliatory chuckle, the kind he made when he was giving a presentation and someone had a question that was just a little bit ahead of him.

"We're working on that," he said, folding his hands and then rubbing them together. "Based on how long the house was locked up in legal limbo, they can't be any later than the 1950s. But judging by the type of paint used, and the fact that the artist used bone inlay, we're thinking that they're at least a hundred years old. They probably date back to when Ettenby himself was living here."

"So, who do you think made them, and why?"

"At the moment, we just don't know," Dad said, with a sigh. "But we know that they belong here, and they're a part of the area's history, so we're going to display them and keep investigating. They're not even signed, and we've been unable to find anything like them so far in art history texts."

"I think they look Dutch," Mum chimed in.

Kenzie forced herself to stop making eye contact with the second carving and move on. The next one was nearly as bizarre, a carving of tree trunks, only tree trunks, with some slight impression of grass beneath, with little differentiation between one and the other, all fading off into chocolate-brown darkness.

The last carving at the end of the line was the Log Palace, as it must have looked when brand new. There were more and different trees around it, no bridge in the distance, and only a rowboat moored to a small dock at the river fork, where the pebbled beach was now, to allow passengers access to the mainland. A person, small and seemingly female but generally androgynous in form, peeped out of an upstairs window, close to where they would be standing now, her eyes those same staring bone almonds, striking against the dark chocolate tones of the rest of the carving.

20

"Do you get many visitors to see these things?" Kenzie asked, wondering who would come back for a second look.

"Not yet, but we think with the proper advertising campaign, we're going to start attracting attention from the big city in a few months. This is something that people have never seen before, with major historical significance. Academia abhors a vacuum, after all, and once we get a few art students up here writing papers, creating a dialogue...the rest will come."

Kenzie nodded, glad to be back to territory she understood. Her heart slowed down a bit, and her breathing relaxed.

"True enough," she said. "Everyone's looking for a new angle for their thesis, and we've got it. It's a ready-made marketing strategy. We'll have to talk later about university outreach."

Even as she said it, Kenzie felt the heaviness grow in the pit of her stomach. She pictured going back to U of T, where she'd done her Masters, knowing the professors were judging her, thinking it was only nepotism that had gotten her the job, because how else could she have gotten a serious position? Or worse, maybe none of them would show up at all. Everyone staying away from the museum except for outsiders like herself because people were whispering about her nerve in coming back. They had hoped that she'd fade into a service job somewhere and be forgotten, become worthless the way they had tried to make her worthless. Would Dad want to keep her then, knowing that she really was hated by her peers and not just making it all up?

Kenzie squared her shoulders, grounding herself against an invisible foe. She'd cross that bridge when she came to it and hope that the trolls underneath would respond to a good, solid kick in the teeth.

They retraced their steps to the other gallery. The lights snapped on in the second hallway as they cascaded off in the first. They entered through a set of fire doors with security glass frames, into a high-ceilinged area featuring more typical nineteenth-century landscapes, work scenes, and portraits.

"These were the works that were hung around the Log Palace when we opened the place up," said Dad. "These we identified fairly easily; most of them were imported from England and France. The exceptions, of course, are the portraits of the family, which were painted by artists from Toronto."

"You mean York," Kenzie said. "It must have been York at that time."

"Yes, indeed," said Dad, "But no one gets excited or self-important about the name York, at least not in this country."

Kenzie chuckled. She gravitated first to a very large portrait on the right, taking up almost all of the wall from floor to ceiling. Still in its original, ornate frame, with its original plaque, it declared its subject in an elaborate script today wholly unknown to the Internet.

"George Ettenby," she said. "So this is him."

Even in a large, imposing portrait, he seemed a timid man, especially for one of his biography. The George Ettenby of fact and legend had struck out into the far edge of the English settlement, taken charge of an island nobody wanted at the fork of two streams, and built an elaborate mansion of logs, using a style of construction hitherto unknown in the Western world. The mansion had been considered a wonder of architecture for its sheer rusticity combined with the luxuries of English life, and the arts and crafts movement had gone mad for it. Ettenby had consulted on a number of other buildings in Ontario, New York State, and Detroit, now all pulled down, and had made quite a name for himself as an independent thinker, artist, and general Renaissance man. His children had gone on to become some of the first major urban planners in the area.

And yet, for all his genius and renown, this man looked afraid. Wide of eye, with dark shadows beneath, sandy blonde hair and a posture hovering between confidence and submission, he reminded Kenzie of a rabbit pretending to be a gentleman. She felt as though at any minute, he might bolt from the world behind the canvas and disappear. She wanted to come back and look at this painting later, longer. Perhaps it was more appropriate than she knew that she'd come here. Here, in this painting, she felt as though she had connected with a kindred spirit across time.

"Why did he come here?" Kenzie asked Dad, "You've never mentioned that, and I can't seem to find it in any of the histories."

"His family sent him here to manage their forestry holdings," Dad said. "He was a younger son, and chances are that they wanted to keep him busy and give him a trade. Unofficially, though, some say that he had trouble with his father. George Ettenby, Sr. was a man's man, always on safari or riding or gambling, and by contrast young George was bookish, artistic, and retiring, by all accounts, and not too fond of the idea of marriage. Some speculate that his father saw him as an embarrassment and thought that living in the wilds of Canada would man him up."

Kenzie cracked a little smile.

"And yet he came here and did it his way. It seems like Canada may have been the place for him after all."

"It certainly was," said Dad, "And we're proud to have him. But enough about old Ettenby for now...I want to know what you think of the dolls!"

Dad placed an arm around her shoulder and guided her across the hall and down, to where a large, glass-protected platform sat against the wall. Mum had been prattling on the entire way but Dad silenced her with an upraised hand.

"These are an even greater mystery than the wood reliefs. Of course, we wonder if Ettenby himself could have created them, but why?"

Truly, the first question Kenzie had upon looking into the long case was 'Why?' as well, but for far different reasons. She would not have had the courage to pull the figures before her from whatever murky depths they had

23

dwelt in for so many long years. She stared into an old doll's face, with eyes made of coins battered and beaten so that they resembled staring pupils. Short hair of a beaver, or perhaps of a bear, sat on top of its head. The bottom half of its face consisted of the back portion of an old shoe-size ruler, the metal kind that some of the better shoe shops still had. It formed a gaping, makeshift jaw, attached to rings at the back of the head. This one had brown butcher's paper for skin, torn over the torso to reveal ribs made of barrel strapping. Its legs and feet were old railway spikes, cunningly blacksmithed to have rings on the ends of them.

A profusion of these figures sat crowded in the little glass space, some made with more modern materials. Another doll at the front had the head of a cherub made from milky glass, cracked with age and sporting brown dirt veins. Its body was a large oil can, banged into the shape of a corseted torso; its arms a pair of funnels. The hands were china as well, with dirty fingernails. Several had tin cans or pots for heads, banged, dinged, and augmented into eerie faces. Even in their makeshift state, they all looked strangely...complete. They all had joints and a full body. Some of the ways that everyday items had been modified were ingenious. And yet...

"You're right. I'm wondering why," Kenzie said briskly.

"We're thinking that they're folk art," Dad said. "Crafts made by someone locally to stave off the boredom of living on the frontier. And yet, some of the artifacts date to the early twentieth century. Ettenby died before the turn of the century."

Kenzie nodded. One of them had an early car headlamp as the basis of its head. Others were strapped together with old, insulated, appliance cables.

"Perhaps his heirs bought them for some reason and stored them here?"

Dad cleared his breath through his nose, as he often did when struggling with a real problem.

"If they did, then they got misplaced somewhere along the line. Come along and see the rest of the museum, and then I'll show you where we found them."

Kenzie followed, reluctant to turn her back on the dolls, not because she feared they would move, but because she feared that she would move before figuring out why they existed in the first place. She was overcome with a fascination of the most dreadful kind, the kind that made her want to stare and stare until some sort of sense came out of staring at them, accompanied by the feeling that perhaps there was no sense to be made and it was all just a spiral. Did dolls feel like the right word for them? Not really. She would have to think on it.

Think on it Kenzie did, right through the rest of the museum, thoughts rolling through her head, fascination mingling with revulsion and a steady ebb and flow of inspiration. The dolls were shocking, truly shocking, and although it might take time to adjust to them, they were precisely the kind of thing that put museums on the map. Add in the mystery of their provenance and history and, within a few years, National Geographic could be knocking on their door. Strategies climbed through Kenzie's head, like towers of Tinkertoy, only to be knocked down by the latest and greatest idea that had just then presented itself. She hoarded a few, which she was sure Dad would approve of, for later use. Pushing the mystery would be key. Not knowing would draw people in, and those creepy little faces would keep them there. Think of the Halloween tie-ins...

They breezed through the library, redolent of old paper and well-stocked with reading nooks and old granny volunteers to point people in the right direction and shush them appropriately. In the next wing, Dad showed her through a series of rooms on the upper floor that had been preserved in their original state, complete with period furniture and accurate home accessories. Here, mostly younger volunteers shuttled through, getting their summer experience for high school transcripts or college degrees by explaining the history of the Log Palace and talking about life in the nineteenth century. It was all pretty standard stuff, available at most historical estates these days.

The lower floor held a white-walled, sanitized children's exhibit where specific replica objects and things that could not be hurt (mostly stone objects and some bricks) were laid out in colourful settings with little picture quizzes and push-button games alongside for those who were waiting. A large-screen TV in a darkened room at the end of the hall played a video about games and songs for nineteenth-century children.

At the end of the tour, Dad brought them back to the stairs leading up to the Folk Art wing. Underneath the staircase, there was a fairly large hatch in the floor. The top had been covered in linoleum, and the handle had been painted, but Kenzie could tell from the pitting of the handle, and the shape, that it was actually very old. Dad pulled his keys out from his pocket and undid the lock on the hatch. He squeezed the flashlight on his keychain and flickered it at Kenzie in a playful manner. Right in the eyes, of course. She held her hands up to stave off the glare.

"We'll need this!" he said. "It's dark in there."

The hatch was about four foot square, big enough for someone to descend into without too much claustrophobia. Would they be going down into some drafty, low-ceilinged sub-basement? She hoped not, at least not without masks on.

"Watch out for the edge, Daniel," said Mum.

Dad ignored her and pulled the trap door up, toes practically teetering over the lip of the shaft.

Kenzie crept forward, leaning over it. A shaft it was, and a deep one, at least fifty feet, perhaps seventy-five. Interlocked limestone flagging lined its walls, and the bottom, only just illuminated by the power of Dad's tiny, little light, looked dry as dust. Odd for an island in the middle of two rivers, on a very shallow piece of earth. Much odder was the fact that it went nowhere. No evidence of blocked-up doors, spur tunnels, or cave-ins. It was simply a very deep, very dry hole. It felt like an oubliette, where you dropped things you wanted to forget about.

"The dolls were stuck down there in a pile," Dad said. "Like prisoners with no hope of escape. Still, it seemed as though they reached for the light. It's odd how alive human-shaped things can seem, isn't it?"

Kenzie felt a draft of dry, stale air puff up at her from the hole, as if it were sniffing her and found her too strong. She backed up, startled, coughing.

"I think it was a way to gauge flooding," Mum said, "If the water levels were high, then they would know something was wrong, to get on the boats."

"Mandy, we've been through this before. There is no evidence that this shaft has ever been underwater," said Dad, clearly irritated not only with this comment but also her half-baked running commentary throughout the tour.

"I know," she said, taking one last look into the tunnel before it was shut. "You've told me, but I just feel like it has been."

Kenzie kept quiet this time, but was surprised to find that she sided more with Mum than Dad. All logic aside, it did feel as though there had been water in that tunnel once. She pictured water flooding up through it, menacing the residents of the house from right below the floorboards. She pictured the hatch bumping against an unseen chop from below. Bump, bump, bump.

She shook her head. Stupid, hormonal, brain games. Of course, she would come here on her period. It was giving her woman-think. That was her word for weak, feelings-based decision making. If she had followed her woman-think, she would have gotten married right out of high school and never pursued this higher course, would never have done the public any good.

And still, the trap door in her mind bumped in an unseen current, unifying her with her mother. Time to haul some luggage and forget about the past.

HUMAN-SHAPED THINGS

Simulacra, she thought as she threw the last of her luggage onto her new bed. *That is the word I've been searching for all afternoon.* They are not dolls. They are simulacra.

This she knew very well, without knowing exactly how she knew it, except that dolls usually had some social function. Dolls were rounded, meant to be pleasing more often than not, or meant to represent something identifiable. The things in the Folk Art gallery were all mechanics, hollow and bony, shells of human things that thought they looked human. You could not hug something with skin of paper, nor play with it. Mechanical skeletons made of junk were not meant to be displayed anywhere but a museum. It was as if someone had decided to mimic the human form with no other aim than to make a copy in its own particular style, like a cave painting of a buffalo or a cubist still life.

Kenzie looked out the windows. Her new bedroom was dry-walled and modern-looking like the rest of the museum, excluding the historical wing, but the windows still showed the rough-hewn logs forming the walls, and the glass and frames were original. A century-and-a-half of bumpy paint coated the wood, holding the six panes of wavy glass together. Outside, she could see the visitors' parking lot. The staff quarters were at the front of the building, on the second floor through a door leading from the back wall of the Folk Art gallery.

She did not relish the thought of passing those staring carvings every day, but she had handled the stares of her classmates. At least these eyes were inanimate. Then again, she wasn't so sure a lot of her old classmates weren't made of wood either, with the way they behaved. Five years with almost no hint of human kindness to help light her way...an existence drier than that old shaft, indeed.

Outside, she could see that all of the museum patrons had gone, and the parking lot was a wide-open expanse of tarmac littered with pine needles at the edges, the trees swaying in the early spring breeze. The winds at the change of seasons always captivated Kenzie in a way that she didn't quite understand. It was as if the powers of the earth and sky were blowing one season away while another entered.

The wind signalled transition, a cleansing of the old ways and bringing in of the new. It even cleared away much of the physical evidence of the previous season. A strong, cold winter wind could dry out the leaves of fall and banish them to deep ravines and hidden corners where nobody raked. The warms winds of spring melted the snow drifts that had collected all winter, filled with road grit and debris. There was something spiritual about the wind and the way it heralded change.

The swaying of the trees was hypnotic and comforting. Maybe soon, the wind would bring her some change as well. Maybe her old ways of being would be blown into a corner, or melted, and something new and green and lovely would be left in its place. Perhaps the dead leaf-mould of her life would fertilize something vital and alive, the way she had always wanted to be.

Kenzie set about unpacking her clothes and possessions. The room was well-appointed, with a nice, comfortable double bed on the right-hand wall, a work desk by the window, two IKEA chests of drawers and a closet on the left wall. A small ensuite bathroom opened next to the head of the bed. Down the hall was a shared kitchen and living room space with a TV and stereo, much like a dorm would have. She didn't expect to be watching much TV there. Mum had terrible taste in shows and tended to hog the remote. Kenzie's computer would supply all of the entertainment she needed.

As she laid out her clothes on the bed, she found herself thinking, as she often did, that the person that owned these clothes must be frightfully boring. Grandma prints, sensible slacks, and nondescript sweaters ruled. She had a couple of interesting concert tees in there from events she'd gone to with Maria, but that was about it. Even her jeans were crappy, elastic-waisted mommy numbers, inherited from relatives who were cleaning out their closets. Ah, the joys of living on the student loan system. Good thing Maria knew how little money she had...sometimes she wondered why Maria was even attracted to her. Kenzie wouldn't be attracted to herself.

With everything folded or hung up, she sat on the bed. There was more to do, but right now the only item she cared about unpacking was the computer. The books could wait, and Mum had taken care of her kitchen stuff. She hoped that she could find it all when she needed it. Mum had a bad habit of purposely misplacing things that she knew Kenzie liked.

Right now, Kenzie just wanted to talk to someone about what she had seen and done today. It seemed like a lot, and she wanted to share the weight of it all with someone else.

She pulled her laptop computer out of its bag and set up all the cords. While she was at it, she heaved her scan-print-photocopy-fax machine, a huge brick of a thing, onto the desk with a large clunk. She arranged a small lamp, an antique ceramic piece Dad had given her with a chunky body and irregular glaze. She plugged it in and turned it on. Now it felt like home. Home is where your Internet connection is.

As her computer flickered on, blaring the Windows music, Kenzie jumped. She had forgotten to change her desktop. How had she forgotten to change her desktop? That's right…living in Toronto, it had all gotten too natural for her. Behind all of her icons was a picture of her and Maria, kissing at the Ex. It had been taken by one of those professional photographer guys that events pay to go around and take photos on commission, and it was spectacularly well framed, the sun just going down with the midway lights in the background like a modern fairy land. She loved that picture. It was magical. And like most of the magical things in her life, it was now going to have to live buried deep in her hard drive, in a folder labelled private, within a folder labelled art, within a folder labelled ENGL 2597 Course Materials. A place where even the most well-meaning person could lose it. Maybe by hiding it, she had already lost it.

She heard the latch just in time. She closed the laptop, with just enough time to make it look like she was getting up from the desk when Mum barged in.

"I just wanted you to see everything I did in the kitchen!" she said.

"Okay, let's see." Kenzie was reluctant to leave her laptop, but also happy that Mum was willing to disclose where she'd put the cheese grater.

The tour of the kitchen turned into a movie, which turned into eating cake and drinking tea, all of which were also welcome after the long day. By the time she got back to her room it was 11:30, and she was exhausted from all of the hauling and lifting, both physical and emotional. Maria would have to wait. She popped onto her phone to send her a quick good-night text and an apology.

dont worry about it, Maria texted back, without her usual care for grammar or punctuation.

Kenzie changed into long pyjamas, sadly one of the cuter items in her wardrobe with little smiley owls on them, and then got into bed. The mattress was nice, but it was still going to feel like a hotel for a few days while she got oriented. She'd probably wake up confused a couple of times, thinking her bed was the wrong way and wondering in the dark where she was.

She woke up by the hole. The hole was open. Why was it open? Cold air puffed up out of it, but this time, the dusty smell was gone. This time, it smelled like a dock on open fresh water. She heard water below, lapping against something, causing it to bump. She looked down, unsure why she could see, but the hole was lit as if the moon shone right through the roof. Down below, standing in three feet of water, Kenzie stood. Eleven-year-old Kenzie. Kenzie in a white night shift she had been given by her grandmother, that had been ruined when she was fifteen and experimenting with hair dye. Her long, brown, straight hair spilled over her shoulders. Her eyes were tired, as if she had been kept up far too late and run laps during the day.

"You're going to kill me," the young Kenzie whispered, a tear spilling down one cheek, "And I deserve it." The words echoed up the tunnel, causing them to hiss and bark off of the stones.

Kenzie should have screamed. She should have run. She should have cried, or fallen to the floor, or anything, but another power was in control, within her and yet not created entirely by her. Totally numb from head to toe, she averted her eyes from young Kenzie, closed the hatch, and walked, smoothly and evenly, up the stairs toward the Folk Art wing.

A knife of cold fear stabbed her, however, when she realized that she would have to pass through the darkened gallery with the staring carvings. She padded up the stairs as quietly as she could, feeling like she had at eleven, when she had been eavesdropping on adult things that she longed to know but could not ask about.

She reached the picture gallery. The moon shone in through the skylight, illuminating the path to the door along the rear wall. She edged into the gallery, her eyes on the wall but not focused.

There were more than three sets of eyes in the carvings. The Native people on the far bank now turned and stared at her with those ivory-coloured almonds, and they glowed in the dark. The waterlilies had formed into faces, also staring. In the woods, nothing stared. A simulacrum slumped at the base of the tree, its half-broken body both naturalistic and completely unnatural.

Kenzie could feel her hands trembling, her knees shaking.

She stared back at the eyes the way a rabbit stares at a looming snake, watching for the strike. The eyes had changed, but still nothing moved, at least not that she could see. Her bare feet hit the cold floor, again and again, and she felt every sensation heightened, especially the cold. The eyes glowed, and stared, and she inched excruciatingly before them. Finally, her hand hit the knob for the door to the dorms. She opened it, ducked inside, and closed it as quickly and quietly as possible.

A flashlight beam flicked on, shining out of the pitch black. She blinked and swore.

"Kenzie, what are you doing out of bed? We thought there was an intruder," said Dad. "You're lucky you didn't trip any of the alarms. Rahul down at the fire department doesn't take too kindly to false alarms this far out of town, you know."

Kenzie shook her head, feeling suddenly very heavy and off-balance, like an old silo with too many bricks missing.

"I think I'm sleepwalking again."

SETTLEMENT

K enzie's eyes sprung open, this time in the right room, in the right bed that still felt wrong and would for some time. Her stomach twisted within her, and for a moment she thought that she would throw up. Then she realized that there was nothing *to* throw up. The mattress was a touch too hard, which didn't help. Her face felt flattened and one sinus had filled in nicely. Never mind that her hair, like goose fluff on the best of days, had formed an anti-gravity pancake on the side of her head that itched like crazy.

Her memory had been gone while she slept, but now that she woke, she remembered the sleepwalking and the things that her younger self had said to her.

You're going to kill me, and I deserve it.

Kenzie felt raw, flayed of skin. This was usually the time when she would make notes to tell Dr. Maissen, but with a year to go here and the Students' Union and their free health care hours south, what was the point of writing it all down? It would take another year just to work through it all when she finally did get back.

That is, if she went back.

She would just have to learn to be her own Dr. Maissen for now. Even if she could find another free therapist in Hillscroft or Peterborough, the referral would take ages and then she would have to explain everything all over again. She had already done that with three therapists before now and had sworn that Dr. Maissen would be the last one. That was when she had thought of the city as her final destination. When she had wanted to stay forever, assured of her ascension into something better—into someone better. Sometimes getting help felt like processing a criminal case, testifying over and over and over, trying to get someone to believe you and make the charges stick.

She sat down at her laptop, flipping up the lid and turning it on. No one would be awake now. She could change the desktop so that she could work. Maybe she could even put up another shot that included Maria, where they could be construed as friends. Something from before they were dating. Photo opportunities in university were myriad, and she had saved every Facebook tag and attachment from club newsletters. Photos reminded you that other places and times had existed. Sometimes, when you're adrift and awash in ideas—identities—not your own, that reminder was a vouchsafe that you were not crazy.

The screen lit up. She signed in. The picture reminded her of a tenuous sort of home, the one made from the longings of her heart rather than genetics and history and expectations. The kiss. That sunset. She could still remember their warmth, how it had reached into her bones until she felt at one temperature with the universe, like a soft bonbon melting into a pot of stirred chocolate.

Something stared at her from the far background of the photo. She could swear it had not been there before, although she had a tendency to misremember (or be mis-believed, she could never tell which). It hung from

36

the rafters of one of the midway games, a limp toy body with stark white, almond eyes, staring eyes like the kind on those creepy cheap seventies dog stuffies. But this one was not a dog, it was a man. A man dressed in the clothes of a settler.

She shut her eyes, hard. She focused on her breathing, on her feet touching the floor. She concentrated on the solidity of her butt and legs touching the chair.

I am here now. I am here now.

She opened her eyes and it was still there. It held much less menace now that she was breathing properly. It was just a toy knight at the balloon darts stand. It had a smile on its face and a bouquet of roses in its hand. Next to it was a rounded, over-stuffed toy horse. Play till you win 'em all. Not a junk doll. Not a settler with a water woman behind him. It had been a horrible nightmare, but it needed to stay where it belonged.

Kenzie closed the laptop. She grabbed some paper from her printer, then rushed to the underwear drawer. No type on a computer screen would describe what she had seen last night, in the shaft. She would have to draw it.

Kenzie pulled the pencil and extender from the bottom corner of the drawer where she had buried it last night. The tool burned in her hand, sending all of her nerves aflame. She was not worthy to wield Excalibur. But she shoved her laptop aside and put the paper in its place anyway, then tried to shade in the dusty blackness of the shaft, the stark square shape in the floor and the vulnerable little girl below.

She could not draw herself. Her face melted into a puddle of isolated features whenever she looked into a mirror or tried to see herself in her mind. Even with photo reference, she had never been able to draw a self-portrait that wasn't hideous. The shading was all wrong. She had made the strokes go in the wrong direction and instead of looking raw and slightly scribbled, they just looked messy. The perspective wouldn't work on the little girl either, and she ended up looking like a disjointed pile of shapes.

Kenzie accidentally smeared the shaded area, further confusing the crisp square of darkness. Tears rose in her eyes, and a great frustration beat at her rib cage from within. She crumpled up the drawing and threw it into a corner. The pencil, she saved. She had other plans for it.

She pulled on some comfortable clothes. The air in the room told her that it would be nippy out there, with the dewy chill of early spring. She opted for a grey hoodie and brown, comfy corduroys, with her old sneakers, the ones that had been with her since she started applying for archival sciences programs.

In the kitchen, she scarfed down some canned peaches, then made her way to the apartment door. She focused in again when she reached the doorknob. Was it normal to not remember coming up to the door? Did other people forget things they'd just done?

She flushed as she remembered the last time she had used this door, during the dream. The disorientation. The fear. All of it driven home and layered upon like old paint by her parents' staring eyes. What the fuck did the staring eyes want with her? Staring eyes just followed her around everywhere. She felt staring eyes on her as she turned the knob, heard the security system beeeeeeeeeeeeeeeeeeeeeeeeeeeeeeeeeeeeeeeeeeeeeeee

She punched in the numbers that Dad had taught her and all was silent. Lights blinked in several corners, then went out. The gallery was dark again, but a different kind of dark. Rather than the light of the moon, the cool, filling light of early morning filtered in through the high windows and cast itself on the walls.

Kenzie looked at the carvings furtively, as a bullied child looks at her tormentors when their backs are turned, hoping not to be noticed. They looked exactly the same as they had when she had arrived yesterday afternoon. Dead. Brown. Nothing but old boards and bone and thick toxic paint. Her fears had painted those other pictures, and for the first of many times, she marvelled at what a great and fantastical artist her fear really was. The lizard brain was capable of some truly stunning work. Her nausea came back a little as she thought about how powerful her own mind could be when fighting against her.

Still, she thought, If I could paint the way my mind does in my waking hours, I could fill a gallery all my own. Too bad my hands don't match my heart. Or whatever it is that sends imagery through my brain.

She jogged down the stairs like one chased. She did not look into the simulacra gallery. She did not want to see them move. Why did she think they would move? They didn't have muscles. They didn't even have organs or brains. Why would they move? Perhaps because they had earned it. Because being created hurt. Weird, weird morning thoughts. Time to get out into the air.

Out the employee doors she went, banging her forearms on the push bar. No one would hear her upstairs. She was too far away. Immediately, the whoosh of the wind soothed her ears from the sound of cloistered silence. It was an overcast day, the kind where the clouds scud by like race cars made of loaf cake and things drip on you from above when there is no sign of a tree or a rain gutter anywhere. Off in the distance, she could hear the honk of some waterfowl. The leaves whispered tales. The other birds were silent.

She picked up a pine cone. It was slightly damp and smelled of earth. A pair of pine needles stuck out of it at a funny angle. Kenzie wondered how it would roll. She threw it, and watched it tumble down the slope to the distant river, dislodging more pine needles and wiggle-wobbling its way over a few times before its own ungainliness stopped it. Already something inside her loosened its grip.

The lawn was very nice once she was on it, and surprisingly well-maintained. Most lawns had divots and tiny little hummocks beneath which toads sheltered. This one was straight, and level, and covered in as perfect a grass as one could reasonably expect in rural Ontario, where seeds drift around as readily as the common cold, and lawn-care people had realized long ago that the fight against dandelions is about as effectual in the long run as the campaign at Gallipoli, and about as helpful to human life.

She wondered how accurate the wood carving had been, the one from the perspective of the river. She turned around to check out the vantage point she was at, curious to find the exact place where it had been carved, if she could. She did the thing she always did, that she could not stop doing. She put her hands out and made the little picture frame with her fingers.

She remembered the first time she had learned that the finger frame actually worked, that it was not just a thing that directors did in hackneyed old films when they were saying stuff like 'Baby!' and "I can see it now. You're gonna be a star!' Her layout teacher at animation school—the program she'd failed at before she switched to archival studies—was an old-school import from Eastern Europe. He had introduced them all to the finger frame as a way to gauge real-life subject matter and learn about shot composition.

"Think of your fingers as a camera. Much cheaper than a real camera," he would say in a thick Polish accent. And yeah, on a student budget, fingers were much easier to come by than a real camera.

She was too close to the museum, this much was obvious immediately. The carving had been done much closer to the river. Looking behind her every few steps, she moved backward, toward the water line, until she got it just right. Almost there...

Something cold trickled into her shoes, startling her out of her compositional trance. She was standing in five inches of water, which had happily soaked into her socks and the soles of her shoes just as quickly as it

40

could manage. Kenzie squish-squooshed out of the muddy bank area, upbraiding herself for losing track of the water. Funny... the water must have been lower when the carving was done. Not surprising, with all of the extra rain and melt going on these days.

The area she had just sloshed out of was a muddy mess, her feet having disturbed all manner of dirt and debris on the river bank that had remained undisturbed for eons. She walked down the bank, toward the deep forest, called by the abundance of lilies in that direction. The water there looked deep, and blue, and surprisingly clear. Many areas with water lilies had a mucky brown or green tinge, but this water was as clear and deep and inviting as the river in which Ophelia drowns in the painting by Millais. Maria had told her on several occasions that she had a long and shapely neck, like those women in the Victorian paintings. That didn't count for much, in her opinion, when her chin had absolutely no definition. Of course, your neck looks longer when it's hard to tell where your neck ends and your face begins.

Kenzie found a spot along the bank where she could see pebbly rocks lining the bottom of the river, small weeds trickling up through them. A little arch of water lilies protected this area, bumping against one another in just such a way that they held each other back. Kenzie spotted a little minnow at the bottom, then another. It reminded her of the little round entrance areas to swimming pools, where the steps led you in deeper and deeper until you were up to your neck.

She knelt on the last dry bit of bank before the water began, noticing that even here, moisture soaked into the knees of her pants. She dunked her hands into the water. It was cold, but pleasantly so, in that way that makes water feel very clean. She cupped her hands and brought the cool water to her face.

She remembered the day when she had learned that, in a scientific sense, water counts as a sticky substance. It was a matter of minor revulsion and great fascination. Things that are normally described in common parlance as 'sticky' are the opposite: dirty, easy for kids to get into, hard to clean off of furniture, clothes, and dishes. But, when water gets on your hands, it sticks and runs down your fingers. The dissonance between fact and perception fascinated her. Water got a free pass not to be sticky, because it was useful, and liked, and pure.

The water dripped and beaded on her skin, but offered her no new perspective on what to do about the pencil. She was still thinking about the pencil. It didn't help that in her pocket, it dug into her leg while she crouched.

The pain clarified her thoughts much better than the water ever could. This pencil had never belonged to her. It had always hurt her and felt wrong in her hand. With it, she had done nothing but screw up all her drawings, be last in her class, and fail to realize any of her visions on paper.

She stood, pulling the pencil out of her pocket. She held it out in her upturned palm and looked at it one last time. That was a mistake, because she could feel her face crumpling into tears. Her vision went blurry.

Now was the time to decide. She would curate, not create. She raised her hand and flung the pencil as hard and as far as she could. It disappeared between the lilies without even a splash. The metal slide must have weighed it down. She stifled a sob.

Movement on the other shore and a honk. A large goose shuffled its wings and took a few slow steps to come up level with her on the other side of the river. A large, grey goose, with an orange bill. Kenzie concluded that it, or a few of its ancestors, must have gotten loose from a farm somewhere. It was almost the size of a swan, and it regarded her with one large, black eye which never left her, even as its neck and body shifted.

Kenzie looked around for a nest or some reeds, wondering what caused the intensity of this creature's gaze. It made a little chuckle in its throat, the kind that geese at petting zoos often give when they are feeling chatty and want a piece of bread. She slowly backed away from the bank. Her business was done here. If the bird lunged for her, she would run.

The goose regarded her for another few seconds, then ran toward her, its feet flapping against the wet bank. In one of those strange, surreal moments where all of a sudden, the worst is happening and you're not doing the thing you thought you'd do at all, she crouched down, covering her head. The bird skidded across the water, its bulk chopping up the surface, and then lurched into the air at the last possible second, skimming over her head with a patter of dirty droplets. Kenzie trembled, and rebuked herself, and trembled some more.

Its going was like a cloud lifting off of the sun. A single, downy feather drifted back to earth, and as Kenzie watched it fall, she noticed something, back in the woods. Stones piled on top of one another to make a foundation. Half-formed windows that had once been part of a basement. Leaves and dirt had in some places reduced it to hummocks, but in others, she could see what had been there. It had been a barn, or perhaps a long, low sort of house.

Kenzie touched her cheek, feeling the cold and damp left there from when she splashed her face. The water had a surreal feeling after her recent musings, and the goose hadn't helped either.

How sticky is too sticky? She thought as she reluctantly turned her back on the river.

Dad immediately made a joke about Hobbits when Kenzie arrived back at the apartment. He bustled around the kitchen, cracking eggs and sizzling bacon in a pan, inviting her to sit at the island and grate cheese for an omelette.

43

The cabinetry was all covered in that white matte linoleum stuff that gets dirty really quickly once it reaches a certain age, does not tolerate food colouring of any kind, and always, always starts peeling at the corners.

The center island in the kitchen invited more comfortable thoughts. Kenzie hopped up onto one of the bar-style chairs and watched the trees wave in the breeze through the open-concept living room.

"I appreciate the gesture," Kenzie said as she ran some mozzarella over the grater, "but I already had some peaches this morning."

"Perfect!" he said, sloshing some batter as he gesticulated, "Second breakfast! I wonder what we'll have for elevensies!"

Dad had obviously been planning this for some time, for her first morning at the site. So, she let him continue. What else was there to do? And he would make pancakes, and crispy bacon, and quite a few things that Kenzie lacked the energy to get up for herself. After cooling off in the breeze and the frank light of the early morning sun, her feelings of the previous night had faded, as dreams do in the light of day. A certain sense of unease stayed with her, but she likened it more to the electricity of starting a new job or school program than the terror of a deep nightmare. She grated the cheese with renewed vigour, and even grabbed a few small pinches and ate them.

After she had a few minutes to get into the rhythm, she said, "I took a walk around the grounds today."

"Good," said Dad, pouring several large pancakes onto the griddle. "The landscapers did a good job, didn't they?"

"Yes, it's lovely." She took a deep breath. "What are the ruins on the other side of the river? I was exploring by the shore and noticed that there were ruins of a barn, or another house. They looked older than this one."

"Oh yes," said Dad, "there were other settlers on the river fork. Some wanted to farm, others to work in the logging and hunting trade like

Ettenby. Several generations tried to make this location work for them, but between the stony soil and the trickery of the river, they all eventually moved on. By the time Ettenby staked out his land for the Log Palace, there was nothing on this island but a few dilapidated timber houses. The Native people were spooked by the site, and the best guess we have about that is that it was too settled, and perhaps the people here were not the friendliest to folks unlike themselves. Perhaps that was why the settlement died! After all, the most successful settlers always worked with the Native people. They knew ways of surviving, and lore about the little nooks and crannies of the land, that Europeans just didn't store up. In their home countries, they never had to."

"How much information is there on that old settlement?" Kenzie asked, smelling a historic village in their future.

"Not enough," Dad said, transferring the finished pancakes to a plate. "We know who lived there, and what they did for business, but it was a tiny hamlet with nothing going on. There are rare mentions in the Hillscroft *Gazetteer*, but nothing of real note. If it were all on the same piece of land, we'd spruce the ruins up and let people wander, with some well-placed fences to keep the little ones off the rocks. But in order to get people over there, we'd have to build a bridge or send out boats, and both of those are out of our budget right now. We've got enough on our plates just keeping the Log Palace afloat, as you'll see."

He shook some tongs loaded with bacon in her direction, and they flopped like a tasty, salty mop head.

"Come on, don't make me whack you with these! Have some!"

Kenzie did not make him smack her with bacon. She loaded up her plate and went to town.

THE SOUND OF MS. WINTER'S ANKLES

The ink glided out of the pen so easily, and sunk into the page with such finality, that Kenzie wondered if she had just made a deal with a cartoon sorceress or something from a movie. The contract sat before her, type so regimented, controlling her for the next year. She was now committed to twelve months of work at the Log Palace, come hell or high water.

High water. The trap door bumping in the night. Sticky water rising up the lawn, toward the manor when the rains got bad. It was a very flat little island. Who knew how bad it could get?

The people under the trap door knew.

She stopped herself, blushing a little from the knowledge that she was sitting here, in front of her first real contract, in the small office down by the employee entrance, in the harsh fluorescent tube light, embroidering stories and making sketches in her head. She had chosen her new path, and it did not involve either embroidering or sketching. The only thing that she would sketch now would be the date, right above that perfectly straight, little line made by a computer somewhere.

"All right," said Dad. "Now that the formalities are out of the way, let's get to work! There are several big jobs that we've been saving for you to oversee. I tend to corral the volunteers, so that is what I'll be doing today. I can also take closing duties and show you those later in the week. Our biggest priorities right now are the plans for our debut social media campaign and the backlog of materials in the archives. Ms. Winter works there most of the week, but she's so busy with the re-filing and assisting the researchers that come in that she could use an extra pair of hands. She's also crafting a database and, as I'm sure you know, that takes time."

"Okay," said Kenzie, "Let's start with the archives. I don't want to miss anything when we go to the public. I want to know what we have."

"Perfect," said Dad, opening the door. "Let the findings in our collection support the social media campaign. That's why you're the curator! I've got enough work corralling the teenagers (and the seniors)."

He leaned toward her in a conspiratorial fashion with that last comment, nodding toward the gift shop where Ms. Myers fussed with some snow globes on the cash counter. Kenzie held in the comment that Dad was getting close to his brand of 'senior' himself in his sensible golf shirt, khakis, and white, goose-fluffy hair. He'd managed to keep most of his hair as he aged but it behaved as though it wanted to leave anyway. His beard did the same thing, sticking out at all angles, as though it couldn't stand to be close to him any longer. He'd tried shaving it all off once out of frustration at its behaviour and colour, but he had ended up looking like a sad turtle and grown it all back. Weak chins ran in the family, as well as bad hair.

When they reached the archives, through the auditorium that gave the echoes of their steps that ping-pong quality that only empty gyms can achieve, Kenzie breathed in the smell of the old papers and books. It smelled like adventure and learning in here and, like all libraries, it was just the perfect temperature, with a crispness in the air from the humidity controls. Yes, a good library was a thing of beauty, like the old used book shops she used to dive through like an otter in her youth, one of various boyfriends in tow. She had wanted then to take all of the books home, to give them a safe place to exist. She didn't really care if they were out of date. Out-of-date books were a glimpse into history, into how people thought, different fashions, different cooking styles. In fact, she liked some of the out-of-date ones more than the slick offerings at her local mega-bookstore or online. When she read them and learned from them, she felt like she was learning from another era, and doing things in a way that no one would do them now. It felt unique and different and good.

When everything went crash in animation school, she had decided that if she could not make great art, she would work for the rest of her life to keep great art safe, so others could find that joy too. So she'd started all over again, this time in archival sciences. That's where she'd met Maria. It had taken her until twenty-seven to finally start her career, but better late than never, she supposed.

An alarm bell over the door said 'Bee-oo,' bringing an enthusiastic voice from the back of the room.

"Hello? Can I help you?"

A middle-aged woman strode out from between the stacks. She wore sharp yet well-worn secretarial garb consisting of a houndstooth pencil skirt and a frilled blouse. Her hair was greying, but still mostly a chestnut brown, and wavy, reaching to her shoulders. Her smile, and her eyes, were young, even if her skin couldn't quite keep up. She wore a badge.

Dad affected his best Victorian English. "Ms. Winter I presume, tamer of documents, explorer of darkest libraries. Guardian of the written word."

"Underpaid old biddy, you mean," said Ms. Winter, shaking a finger. "Every library needs an old biddy. Community centers, too!" Her voice was vigorous, with a slight squeak to it. She turned her young smile on Kenzie.

"And you must be Daniel's daughter. It is such a pleasure to meet you. You have been all he talked about since we decided to hire a curator. With your credentials, how could we say no? You were a shoo-in, my dear. And we're lucky to have you."

Kenzie felt another pang of grief constrict her chest at Ms. Winter's compliments. Yes, she wanted to say, I have the piece of paper from a school with a good reputation. Heaven forbid you ever find out what that school actually thought of me, because I guarantee that piece of paper only happened because I paid the money and put my butt in the seat for four years. They don't fail people anymore, Ms. Winter. People can't fail. And yet they still do, all the time. More so than before.

What she actually said was, "It's an honour to be here. I can't wait to get started. Do you have time right now to show me the backlog and familiarize me with your filing system and database?"

"No," said Ms. Winter with a laugh. "But for you, I'll make time."

Dad said goodbye and left them to it. Kenzie looked around. The archive was a rectangular room, about the size of two good-sized living rooms put together, with nothing much to recommend it but some good, stout, cream-painted drywall and a dehumidifier in one corner that hummed away like the dresser from *Beauty and the Beast*, rumbling slightly every now and then and draping a large, white, ribbed tube around itself like a boa. The foundation had managed to find a number of sturdy steel shelves with chips and dents here and there that gave away that they weren't entirely new. They had probably gotten them in a hospital sell-off somewhere, once the records went digital.

Kenzie looked up at the ceiling as Ms. Winter led her through the stacks.

"Well, the lighting in here kind of sucks," she said. "Does the board have any plans to replace the tubing with something more efficient and more conducive to reading?"

"Believe me, I've said it," said Ms. Winter. "But if you planned on making it a priority, I'd be much obliged. People don't tend to linger when the lights bother them. Not if they can help it."

"I will definitely do what I can," Kenzie said. One of the inevitable challenges of running a large non-profit, especially a museum, was that everybody had a stake and everybody had their own idea of what would be best. Factions formed easily, and often the directors and curators would end up mediating amongst volunteers, donors, and the board. At her co-op with the medical museum, she had become the uncomfortable hypotenuse of a triangle of interests—the folks on her team, who wanted to keep her indefinitely due to the overload of work on their plate, and the board, who wanted to do things as cheaply as possible and place the job (if a job there was) to the most political advantage. Kenzie had tried to keep her head down through the whole thing, hoping the quality of her work would shine through. In the end, the board and her team found a compromise. They let her contract expire and hired a bilingual woman whose family had just immigrated from Iran and who held a degree in medical terminology, to do the exact same job that she had been doing readily and efficiently for the better part of a year. So much for establishing a track record.

Ms. Winter led her through the stacks to an open area at the back, with computers and microfilm readers lining a long table. A man sat poring over one of the readers, back hunched, turning the crank ever so slightly every few seconds. He wore a battered, black T-shirt, and Kenzie wondered if what he wore on his head counted as a hairstyle. There were so many buzzed areas and overly long patches that perhaps he had just gotten in a fight with an electric razor.

"Talynn," said Ms. Winter, "I'd like you to meet Kenzie Glaston, our new curator."

Talynn's age could have been anywhere from thirty to fifty-six. He had a strange baby face, punctuated with eyeliner and shot through with a profusion of unflattering piercings. When he looked up at Kenzie and smiled, she noticed a number of weird symbols tattooed under his hairline.

Kenzie had seen punks and goths before, living in the city. They were usually fun people and she envied their courage. This guy was neither punk nor goth, but something stranger, created by a whole lot of isolation crossed with equal measures of weird and clueless. His handshake was firm but clammy.

"Hello, Kenzie," he said, like the narrator of some cheesy horror show. "It's good to see a fresh face in here. Perhaps with some new leadership, we can throw off the stifling mantle of the oppressor left over from the Burning Times." His smile was unsettling.

"Uh, thank you?" said Kenzie. Behind her, she could hear Ms. Winter shift her weight.

"I can see that I make you uncomfortable," said Talynn, "But don't worry. Soon you'll brush right past me like another artifact in a case. I won't turn up nude, although that is my preferred state." His smile was still unsettling, and Kenzie had the vague impression that she had offended him somehow. He seemed determined to make her uncomfortable.

She struggled with how to respond. They hadn't covered this in library school. She paused a moment, while he continued to wax poetic about getting naked.

"Good luck to you," she said, when he took a breath.

He raised his metal-laden eyebrows. "Thank you, my darling. Now back to my microfilm I go! The witch isn't going to research herself!" he added with a wheezy chuckle.

51

"No, indeed," Kenzie said. She turned to look for Ms. Winter, who had left her with Talynn and was now standing at the open door of a small closet. Kenzie hurried over. Inside were rows of pantry shelves, all covered in boxes, portable file folders, and stacks (and stacks, and stacks) of books. There was even some clothing hung in the corner, covered in cheap garment bags from what was probably a long-defunct dry cleaners. Another small dehumidifier chuffed away in a corner.

"My goodness," Kenzie whispered once they passed the threshold. "What was all that about?"

"That," whispered Ms. Winter, slinging herself in the doorway like a tired jazz dancer, "is the biggest pain in the ass I have ever encountered in all my years of doing this work. He snarks at the staff, deliberately makes everyone uncomfortable, and he won't stop going on about the most disturbing parts of pagan history. He's following some urban legend about a witch, without a scrap of evidence. The board *and* I would love to ban him, but he's just the type to go on about religious discrimination and give us loads of bad press. Just help me to contain him, and I'll be your friend forever."

Kenzie nodded, her brows drawn tightly inward. Then, realizing that Talynn might think their silence suspicious, she said, loudly, "So, Ms. Winter, what do you have to show me in here?"

Ms. Winter gave her a tight-lipped smile and nodded.

"This stuff is the last of the collection that was left in the Log Palace by Ettenby's heirs. Most of the stuff is his, but some could be theirs, as a few of them stayed here for brief stints when it was convenient for them. We found it in the attic, in crawl spaces, packed away in old bedrooms. It was murder to find everything before the demo started for the renovations. At least one thing is helpful about a log palace: you're unlikely to find anything squirrelled away in the walls. The Victorians were terrible for that. Hide something away in a dumbwaiter and the next thing you know it's bricked up, or the item falls into the walls to get eaten by rats."

Kenzie nodded. "Did you have a system? Where did you leave off? I plan on picking it up and getting as much catalogued as possible."

Ms. Winter looked down at her over her glasses, as if that was the question she had been waiting fifty years to hear.

"*Well*, let me tell you. We'd better sit down, it could take a while."

Take a while, it did. Ms. Winter had been taking the items out, one by one, and carefully reading and cataloguing them based on whom they belonged to, subject matter, and whether they were part of a set. The letters were the hardest, because she found pages here, and pages there, scattered amongst the other documents, some wedged in books. Ettenby's handwriting also left a lot to be desired, being a loopy, long script with fewer distinguishing bumps and lines than one might hope for. Some of the letters were written in pencil, which also made things more interesting. Hopefully the archives had a light desk stashed away somewhere. Any good animator knew that a light desk would expose a world of pencil lines that strained the naked eye. They were fantastic for finding errors, deciphering lines from one another, and generally making things accurate on a multi-layer basis. Then again, Kenzie was not a good animator, designer, or anything else, but she had been taught. Yes, the money that was missing from her bank account and the technical knowledge that she had accrued would certainly testify that she had been taught.

The filing system itself was rather standard, once she learned the nomenclature. The database, too, had been well-constructed and was easy to add to. Ms. Winter had organized it all to be understandable and searchable. Kenzie concluded that she probably was underpaid, considering the museum's budget and the fact that this was a start-up.

As she started in on another stack of letters, collected into plastic binder sleeves for protection, she addressed the librarian, who bustled about with a cart of books that needed re-filing. Her shoes made that comforting tock-tock that teachers' square heels often made in grade school.

"So, what brought you to the Log Palace? Do you live around here?"

"No, I moved. I'm from Toronto originally. I'm retired, and I was looking for someplace where I could do the most good. Working in a big university is fascinating, stimulating work—until it isn't. One day about twenty-five years in, I woke up and realized that I was spending all my time just preaching to the choir. The only people who came in were those who were already educated and just looking to back up their research or gain new ground against other scholars. I wanted to do something for regular people, help to found a library that taught local people about their history. Toronto is so over-studied that it had all been done. Out here...this is where the real frontier is for this kind of work. It excites me every day, and I don't have to worry about what they pay me. I have a good pension and the rest is just gravy."

"Sounds like you have a real vision for the place," said Kenzie. "I guess we'll have to do lunch, so I can pick your brains. You like picnics? I was wandering the grounds today, and I have to say that this would not be a terrible place for a picnic."

"Ahhh-ha," said Ms. Winter, knowingly, "so you saw the other buildings across the creek."

Ms. Winter was at the corner of the next shelf over, looking down her glasses again in that wily way of hers. Kenzie decided that she liked Ms. Winter. She was outspoken, driven, educated, and best of all, not passive-aggressive in the slightest. Not like Mum and Dad.

"I take it that you and Dad differ on the subject of the other buildings?" she said.

"That we do," Ms. Winter said with a nod. "I think we should be working on building a boardwalk or a float bridge over there. They don't cost much— I mean, the bottoms of them can be plastic oil canisters, for Christ's sake. A little bit of rope, some wood and some floats, and we've got another 500 feet on our attraction for people to explore! All the property for another two miles up the slope there belonged to Ettenby anyway. We bought the property when we bought the Log Palace."

"Dad seems to think that the educational value would be minimal for the outlay, and I have no doubt he's got insurance on his mind as well. After all, what if some little kid takes a nosedive into the marsh?"

"So what if he does? There's no quicksand, the water is shallow, and they'd have him hauled out of there in no time. It's a scrape or a tetanus shot at the very worst. People these days! Always so paranoid about kids hurting themselves. Maybe they'd learn something. And as for the educational value of the place, any education we could give people, and any protection we could offer to that building, would be better than what's going on now. Down in Hillscroft there's some stupid urban legend about the building being a witch's house. We've got teenagers trespassing in there every other weekend, getting drunk and lighting fires and doing stupid devil chants they saw on TV. Real winners," she said, looking over at where Talynn was scanning. Kenzie could tell she didn't particularly care if Talynn heard them.

"At least if we fixed it up," Ms. Winter continued, "we could get rid of all the stupidity surrounding the actual history and tell people it was a barn or whatever."

"Oh wow," said Kenzie. "Have the cops been called?"

Ms. Winter leaned on her cart, clearly exasperated. She had had this conversation many times, with many different people. Stories got a feel about them when they had been well-worn.

"No," she replied with a sigh, "I say stupid about the teenagers, but maybe they're stupid-smart, you know? Seems like as soon as someone notices them, as soon as the lights go on, they cheese it to God knows where. I swear to God, nuisance people are like spiders. You see one, you get your husband to come smack it, and it's disappeared into some cranny. I don't even know how the heck they get over there. There's no road, and where are these idiots going to get a boat?"

Kenzie nodded. Clearly, there were a lot of emergent issues connected with the museum start-up, and she would have to sit down and assess priorities soon. Ms. Winter's assessment made sense, and she would have to continue this conversation with her parents, much as she dreaded Dad's famous stonewalling tactics. She had come into the job knowing that there was the potential for her and Dad not always to be allies; she just hadn't thought it would come up so soon.

In front of her was a very delicate newspaper. Its intense yellow colour and warm yet dusty smell told her it was very old indeed. The date on the top confirmed it—August 19th, 1826.

"The Hillscroft Gazetteer," she said. "Are we scanning any of this?"

"That was the next planned phase," said Ms. Winter. "Your dad planned to do it in-house, to avoid any of the documents getting damaged or 'walking away.' Those big scanning companies are really meant more for businesses and hospitals than museums. And by the time someone goes through all the work to check it, you've spent just as many hours on checks and revisions as if you'd just done it yourself in the first place."

"I'm inclined to agree," said Kenzie, pulling the next document from the stack. "It saves money and ensures accuracy…hey, speaking of which, did we get any donations from other collections yet?"

"Not yet," said Ms. Winter, "but give it time. We've got a few estates in our sights."

On the front page of the old newspaper was a pen-drawn political cartoon skewering some local politician of the time. Not bad for a small-town paper. The highlights on the front page were mostly a who's who of the local citizenry, advertising who had gotten married, who was going to get married, who had turned an old age and who had just celebrated a strawberry social, along with the headline of 'Troubles in Stony Forks.' Kenzie wondered where Stony Forks was. With so many tiny, failed hamlets dotted around this area, it could be hard to tell. Everywhere was stony, and a fork was wherever you made two roads, really. The founders of that town could have used a little more creativity.

What was particularly of interest to Kenzie, however, was the little serial number pasted on to the front of the paper, which had also yellowed with age. Below the little label was a rubber stamp, in see-through red ink that had developed a pleasing ochre tinge over time. Kenzie had always thought that rubber stamps didn't get enough love in this day and age. She loved their solidity, the way they bled a little around the edges, and the way they could be customized to anything and then reprinted as many times as you cared to smack them against something.

This rubber stamp said, in lovely vintage lettering, 'Property of the Hillscroft Town Archives and Public Lending Library.'

"I think either Ettenby or his heirs had sticky fingers," said Kenzie. "Come look at this."

Ms. Winter leaned over her shoulder, still holding a few volumes she had been in the process of re-shelving.

"Well, well, if it isn't the volumes of the Gazetteer that we're missing from the microfilm! We've got a reciprocity arrangement with the Hillscroft Public Library. They've been really good to us in the fundraising effort and with the sharing of resources. Those must have been here for a while, if they didn't get them on microfilm."

Kenzie nodded, understanding where Ms. Winter was going. "We'll need to get these scanned right away and sent back to the library for their collection," she said, "or they'll wonder why we were sitting on them. I'll do it tomorrow, after I get some momentum in on this cataloguing."

"Fantastic!" said Ms. Winter, clapping her hands together silently, the way only a practiced librarian can. "Linda down at special collections is going to be thrilled."

Kenzie spent the rest of the afternoon riffling through brittle, old papers and assigning them numbers based on their position relating to other brittle, old papers. Nothing terribly compelling surfaced after the newspapers, and she pushed her way through a crowd of business letters, uphill, on the hottest day of the year. Other than a quick lunch break, she and Ms. Winter spent the rest of the day doing what good archivists do best—categorizing and filing things in their proper place. She made sure to wash her hands often. Old paper could be astonishingly dirty.

She got a head rush when she finally stood up from the chair, bleary-eyed and achy-backed, like she had just trudged out of some forced march in a dream world. There was something about consuming desk work that made one forget how to breathe, how to eat properly, how to do anything but float in that place where things just aren't quite done. Ms. Winter stretched her back as well. She perched on her desk, pulled her feet out of her shoes, and rolled her ankles. Kenzie could hear the pops from the door.

"The sound of another day in the bag!" Ms. Winters said with a smile.

Kenzie smiled too, although she knew her smile could only reach a small fraction of the radiance Ms. Winter displayed.

"We did good work today, I think. Tomorrow... the scanning."

Ms. Winter raised her coffee mug.

"The scanning!"

THE NUISANCE PEOPLE

K enzie lasted only two hours and a shower past closing time before she got into her soft flannel owl pants and pulled on an old U of T shirt that she had bought at the campus bookstore. Comfy pajama time.

No sooner had she gotten into bed, determined to read for an hour or two, than the last of the twilight faded from over the tops of the trees, fading from a cut-out silhouette of shapes without names to a velvety blackness as deep as the forest itself.

Off in the distance, ever so faintly, with the air conditioning off and nobody stirring in the living room, she could hear the water rushing over the stones of the river fork outside, like the distant shell-tongue sound of waves crashing on a beach. Water sounds always carried, or perhaps humans were just conditioned over centuries and millennia to hear them. After all, a person could live for forty days without food, but only three without water.

A bout of shame washed over her when she realized that she had not contacted Maria in almost two days. In the dark, with her blanket a cozy tent around her, she texted Maria's number, the green screen of her phone making her blanket cave a dragon's lair. She tried to picture where Maria would be right now.

It was a Tuesday, so tonight...Maria would just have come back from her LGBT crochet circle. Kenzie could picture her sitting with a good book, reading by the patio doors as the city darkened around her.

Miss you, she sent out into the night. And waited. Too long, she waited. While waiting, she thought about the goose from earlier and Googled 'farm goose types.' She discovered it was a greylag goose, an ancestor of the domestic farm geese found in Europe. According to the articles, greylag geese did not exist in North America. They lived only in Europe and Asia.

"What are you doing here, then?" she grumbled. "That is definitely what I saw." Of course, her first day would bring stolen library materials and impossible geese. She was cursed Kenzie, the wonder failure.

Her phone buzzed, finally.

Miss u2. 2morrow night, video chat?

Kenzie did the sort of complicated mental calculus that only closet cases and dedicated people-pleasers are capable of. Maybe she could convince Mum to go out tomorrow evening. If she chatted with Maria right after close, Dad would still be bustling around doing the end-of-day stuff and there would be no one in the apartment. Despite the museum's outer walls being thick, made of stacked logs covered in drywall, the apartment's interior walls were just as flimsy and sound-porous as any dorm room.

I'm free around 7, she typed, hoping it would be true.

Lookin forward to it, Maria replied. *Luv u.*

Love you too.

Truth there, although she doubted herself all the time. But that habit was not just limited to Maria. When reality seemed to slip away from you like water through your fingers, when identity was transient, it was hard to hold onto things, even things you liked. Even things that you loved, that had made a powerful impact on you as a person. She never talked to Mr. Brunelleschi anymore, even though he was on her Facebook. Even though he had taken a great interest in her and said to keep in touch. Once she had moved on from the artist part of her life and had become someone new, her art school acquaintances became like articles in a history book—only the history book was Facebook. This had happened to Kenzie so many times that she appeared to have hundreds of online friends, but talked to only two or three.

When she was young, she had enjoyed this aspect of herself. The other kids seemed to be able to do two or three things really well. She didn't excel at anything in particular, but she could mould herself to different situations—at school, or in after-school activities, or when playing around with her friends—better than the other kids could. She was bad at actual gymnastics (her cartwheels were more like fancy flop-and-drops) but inside, she was so flexible she could put her soul's legs up over the back of her head, or fold over backwards until her butt touched the back of her neck. This adaptability had earned her a ton of praise from adults back then. The praise had convinced her that she could literally do anything in the world. That was why she had been so convinced art would work.

Until the first day at animation school, that is, when the professor had pointed out that to be an artist, one needed to have an authentic self. "First and foremost," he had said, "animators are actors with pencils. Know yourself, draw from your authentic voice, realize that this is only a race with yourself, and you will do well."

That was the exact moment when Kenzie had looked at the hole in her gut and known she was in trouble.

And she was right. Being an artist had required something more, a well of experience to draw from that she never had access to. The only person she could act like was herself, and herself was nebulous.

She had wanted to find that person inside, like all the other students seemed to have found theirs. But her drawings were flat and lifeless, and everybody knew it.

Now, sitting on the bed under her blanket, she felt odd. Odd like something was wrong. She had been staring at the screen, green and glowing, with an addictive wet citrus-skin pattern on it that she liked to contemplate sometimes when she was feeling spacy. This odd feeling had fallen over her many times, but this time there was something minuscule in the background that itched at her. Something was actually touching her senses in the present moment and twigging her unease. It was a beat in the bubbling of the river outside. Like castanets playing a syncopated rhythm. And, underlying it, an organ playing long, low, unsettling notes, not quite in harmony with the jangling of piano keys that played above it.

Mum was probably watching some trashy late-night show. She had done that a lot when they all lived at home, and often times the volume got away from her when she started to doze.

"Mum, are you watching TV? I can hear it in here," Kenzie called out.

No one answered. Phone still in hand, she crept out of bed in the pitch black, thinking that the carpeting felt weird and dangerous between her toes. What if she had dropped something? What if Mum or one of the renovators had dropped something, and it was now up to her foot to find it? And she would, too. Cursed Kenzie, and all that.

To her right, the window was a blue square in the black of the walls, with little white sparkles moving around in the parking lot below, as the wind blew through the trees.

Kenzie reached the door and blew out a breath that she had not realized she was holding. She grasped the doorknob and opened it. In the living room, the television was off. Only the blinking green lights from the entertainment unit, the glow of her phone screen, and beams from the parking lot lights coming in through the windows kept her company. Mum and Dad must have tucked in early too.

Kenzie closed the bedroom door behind her. The strange music simultaneously got louder, going from a whiff of a hint that tickled her ear drums to the menace of a booming sound system in an unknown parked car. The organs, especially, grew louder, creating an uninterrupted background hum.

Irregular shapes twisted in the corner of the living room window. At first, Kenzie could not distinguish whether they were a distorted reflection of the light from her phone in the bent and warped glass, or whether the shapes actually danced, black figures around a green glow.

She crept closer to the window and gasped. The view she was seeing would only be possible from the end of one of the Log Palace's wings. It should have been impossible to see from this side of the building, but she saw it nonetheless, and knew that it was happening. There was the river, the swampy area in front of the log palace lawn, and the ruins across the river, rocks rising like teeth from the undergrowth. In the ruins, under the green glow that flickered like fire, shadows licked up and down, people caught in a frenzied dance like the Night on Bald Mountain.

The dancing filled her with a revulsion that made her stomach ache and her head become light. She was in danger of 'zoning out,' the way she sometimes did, and had to force herself to concentrate. The dancing was so vulgar, all shaking of tits and slapping of ass and wiggling of things not worth mentioning to oneself, all combined with leaping and punching and biting and—

The cops. She had to call the cops. This was getting out of hand. This was a fire hazard. What if these devil worshippers decided to break into the museum? What if they torched the place? What if they wanted to sacrifice the tourists—or worse, her family?

Kenzie raised her right hand, feeling the weight of her phone like a brick. Her finger creaked with effort, but her eyes never left the fiends down by the river.

A loud jangle of piano sounded, as if it were right beside her, and she smelled old, rusty metal. Kenzie screamed as a dark shape flew up suddenly into the window, striking the glass with a brush and a smack. It was large, with feathers, gone almost as quickly as it came, but it left her heart pounding through her ribcage. A faint honk echoed out into the night.

When the shape left the window, the dance disappeared, along with the strange view of the ruins. She stared out into the parking lot, the white, haloed lights flickering occasionally with the blowing of wind through the trees.

PUT OUT A SIGN

A second day with little sleep compounded the first, as Kenzie knew well from years of taking exams and working odd hours at crappy jobs. She woke up encased in slowly drying cement, which pressed on her head, her eyes, her lungs, her legs. She then ate a big bowl of oatmeal, which left her as nauseous as she had been when she was hungry. At least she'd been hungry. That could be a sign that she was settling in. New places were the worst.

When her parents had dropped her off for college the first time, she had begged them to stay in town one more night, to see a movie with her, to go out to dinner. Anything to ease her into the inevitable aloneness that would wrap around her like a suffocating cloak for the next six years. She and Mum and Dad had gone out to Chancey's, a local roadhouse with crazy crap on the walls, and eaten mozza sticks and arugula salad while her parents chattered on about all of the fun they had had in college. Actually, neither of them had had any fun in college, it seemed. But their friends had done things that they remembered with fondness, and that seemed to be enough. Kenzie had wondered where all their friends wound up, what jobs they had. They never came around anymore. She was their friend now, she supposed.

All the more pressure on her to have adventures they could remember fondly, the kind that stirred a laugh and maybe some kudos but no real controversy. Those kinds of adventures required real skill and a lot of thought. Polite adventures, performed for everyone's benefit to convince them how fun you are, how much promise you have.

The kind of 'spontaneous' actions that actually took a lot of building.

Actually, what took building was simply her ability to stay taped together long enough to make it home on the weekends—home, where they served your food and you didn't always have to cook it.

Worse than the extra hassles that dogged her as she tried to succeed, and have adventures, and show everyone how many adventures she was having so that she would have the requisite amount of fame before leaving school, was the emptiness. The tape she used to keep herself together was holding back emptiness.

The cracks in her surface had been there a long time. For instance, things would just fly out of her skull, escape her memory and not return. It usually got worse when there was a change, or when she felt insecure.

And then there was the anger that would leak out sometimes, when she lost control, coating her in loathing and bitterness and envy when she had a quiet moment, telling her that every other person in the world was a measuring stick, and if she did not manage to be higher than everyone else on that measuring stick, then she would have to cut others' sticks by any means necessary until they were shorter than hers.

The other cracks in her surface came from outside. Every dent of perception, every rock the cosmos sent at her, every layer of pressure that stress laid on, sent painful, vulnerable cracks through her—like the spiderwebs that tick through glass when you step on it, or the random yet organized smashing of an eggshell when you tap it against a counter.

When she wasn't at home, in the place she had grown up, among the people she had grown up around, like a vine on a trellis, she felt like she wasn't really anywhere. Not all of her, anyway. She was just in a holding pattern, waiting to go home.

Part of her had struggled against it. Part of her had woken up, seen each new day and said, 'Say, it's a new day, and you're a new person today. Let's make it better. Let's forge a new path. Let's really live this day and see what it brings.' Unfortunately, every day that voice would be smothered by a much stronger voice, one that she controlled less. The one that was the voice of everyone else that she had made up in her head so that she could always please them.

Over time, the floating feeling had lessened. She learned to take care of herself, somewhat, although she often still felt paralyzed. Once she left art school for archival sciences, once the stakes had been lowered and her tears had carried away the idea that anyone would ever think her impressive, or dynamic, or creative, let alone a creative genius, she had slept better, at least. And coming out had helped. Maria had helped a lot.

But she still struggled to care for herself when things changed.

Kenzie washed her oatmeal bowl and wandered into the hallway. It was funny how her fears shifted with the days, the winds; like the changing windows or the carvings that added characters when their backs were turned. Perhaps she had been dreaming, but dreams could still show you real things. She thought things up in her dreams all the time. Whole paintings materialized in front of her, and she knew how to do them. They were beautiful. She designed clothes—breathtaking clothes that would bring Instagram to a halt. She wrote stories. And they moved her, and she remembered them. She wanted to take them to people, and then remembered that her vehicle was broken. Cracked.

She pushed the pressure plate on the door leading to the main art wing as gently as she could, feeling a sort of reverence for the silence and the stillness itself. It was home now, yes, but still a museum. She made her way to the case containing the simulacra. There was one that had bubbled up to the surface of her mind since last night, one that she remembered when all of the others had mercifully faded into jagged blobs of rust and butchers' paper in her memory.

There, the one with the glass doll's head—or was it porcelain? It could have been either: a thick gloss glaze over white porcelain, like the kind sometimes found on old lamps or dinner plates, or solid glass with a lot of weathering. Cracks lined its hands and face. Dirt had made its way into her. Her heart, in the beaten tin can made to look like a corset, was shapely but hollow. Kenzie felt almost as though she could cry, staring at the simulacrum (doll) simulacrum (child) *thing*, as though she wanted to take it out of this hideous trap where people stared at it all day. It had failed to become a doll, or a human, or anything but an interesting configuration of junk, and now people gazed at it all day, their eyes sliding right over it as they meandered in and out without a particular care for its provenance, history, ambition or dreams. They knew it was there, and holding an interesting shape in space and time was its only function now.

Kenzie stared and stared at it, growing sadder and sadder. An impulse zagged through her to break the glass, right then and there, to hug the doll-child thing close and never let it go, to let it sit on her dresser and be inconsequential with her. They could be ignored together and would never ignore one another.

She leaned forward and put her head on the glass, her weight pressing her into it. She sighed. Another day of this. Could she do another day?

The lights snapped on, one by one, and Kenzie heard footsteps. They were solid, definite, and just a shade faster than most people normally walked. She would know that gait anywhere. It had left her and Mum behind at innumerable fairs and hiking trails.

"Dad," said Kenzie, only now noticing that she had made a forehead blob on the glass, "sorry, do you know where the Windex is?"

"I'll get it," he said. "Were you sleepwalking again? This late in the day? I thought you were up already."

"I was up. I must have just dozed off a little. I came in here to look around. I feel...like I'm starting to get an appreciation for all of these artifacts. They take some getting used to, but maybe that's a good thing."

Dad's look of concern faded into a soft smile, turning him from a jowly hound dog into a generous old monk welcoming the poor.

"I know you don't sleep well after moves. If you need another hour..."

"No, the museum opens in an hour, and when the museum is up, I'm up," Kenzie said, rubbing her eyes. "I'm sure it doesn't take infinite energy resources to scan old newspapers. I've seen ninety-year-olds do it all day long."

Dad nodded. He headed for the left-hand wall, just past the case with the simulacra in it. The doll-faced figure still called to Kenzie, but she tried not to stare at it, not to give away their secret. Dad turned a key in a section of wall and pulled it back to reveal a hidden broom closet. He grabbed a large bottle of Windex with a 'now 20% more!' sticker on it and came over to spritz the forehead mark.

"When do I get my keys?" Kenzie said. "At some point, I might need to access the James Bond broom closet of doom over there. Not to mention just about anything else after hours."

"I'll go down to the hardware store today or tomorrow," said Dad. "The only problem is that it's not like the key cutters in the city. One hour, guaranteed—that's a myth."

Inspiration. More than one hour. Busy work that Dad didn't want to do. Time bought.

"Why don't you send Mum, then? She's not exactly holding up the roof."

"Ah, but she thinks she is," Dad said, putting away the Windex and shutting the camouflaged door. "She'll never leave the museum during operating hours. It gives her a feeling of control, I think, like she's doing something. She always wants to be watching everything as it happens. All I can really do is try to keep her from damaging anything—artifacts, or the relationships with our vendors."

"I wish she's get a clue...or a hobby," said Kenzie.

"Well, she's come this far. I don't think she's ever really interacted with people the way other people do, and I'm not sure she could change. I'm not sure she could even realize what needed to change. So just let her alone, and re-steer her when she's headed for something fragile."

Kenzie rolled her eyes, but said nothing more. She headed back out toward the security doors at the end of the hall, remembering the things she had to do. The scanning would take up most of the afternoon, but there were always housekeeping items to be done. Something had happened last night that she needed to address...what was it...

Oh!

"Dad," she said, turning back around at the door, "did you hear anything odd last night down by the river?"

"No, I slept like a baby log. Why?" he said, with his most charming, 'everything is perfect so why are we talking about this' smile.

Kenzie took a deep breath.

"I think those teenagers Ms. Winter is worried about came back to the ruins across the river last night. There were lights, and dancing, and a lot of weird music. It was pretty creepy, and I think that we should do something to roust them out before something bad happens. That area is our property, right? It sets a bad precedent."

She needed the parties to stop, regardless of whether they ever escalated. If she was going to live here long term, she needed to feel safe, and that was never going to happen with a bunch of satanic hoodlums shaking their tits every night across the river and wishing death on the world.

Dad gave a little grunt and tossed his head.

"Not this again. Look, if Ms. Winter wants to be a nervous old biddy, it's her right. She's old. But don't you fall for that crap. 'Oh, I don't like the looks of those teenagers' is not a basis for sound policy. I thought you knew that much. What the hell have they been teaching you in that school of yours?"

Kenzie's eyes stung briefly.

"They *taught* me to protect documents and artifacts, to oversee their preservation and care for future generations. And that is what I intend to do, unless you want your life's work burned down by a bunch of stoned trailer trash! I am the curator here, whom *you* hired, might I remind you, to be a moderator between the staff and the management, among other things, and I am calling the police," she said, marching through the door.

"And the fire department!" she called back over her shoulder as a final punctuation.

Kenzie sat in the office on the ground floor, tipped back in the too-bendy office chair brought from somewhere else and marvelling at just how bad the lighting was in here. The hold music at the police department sounded like someone had taken a repetitive 20s jazz loop, translated it badly to midi, and then re-recorded it on one of those crappy recorders kids used to buy in the 90s that played fart sounds and called people losers.

She'd been on hold for nearly twenty minutes. The museum would be opening soon, and she had wanted to get started on the scanning right away. Come on...

"Hillscroft Police Department," said a younger man's voice. "This is Officer John Brocklebank. Who am I speaking with today?"

"Yes," said Kenzie, putting on her best grown up, no-nonsense business lady voice. "This is McKenzie Glaston, the new curator at Ettenby's Log Palace. I'm so pleased that we're finally able to talk, although I'd rather it were under better circumstances."

"What's your complaint, ma'am?" said Officer Brocklebank, as though he were stifling a sigh, or maybe a yawn.

"Well, it seems as though we've had some kids throwing parties and lighting fires on our property across the river from the palace. They're making a lot of noise, and we're honestly a bit worried about break-ins. I was wondering if you could come and investigate, perhaps put up some tape around the area to scare them off."

Another stifled sigh.

"Unless you call while they're there, we have no way of making an arrest. My advice is to put up a no trespassing sign, and maybe set up some hidden cameras. From there, there might be something we can do."

"Doesn't that seem a bit lax? They are coming onto our property, and it's only a matter of time before they damage something!"

"In case you haven't noticed, there aren't a lot of movie theatres or skate parks up here, ma'am. Kids go looking for things to do, and that property was abandoned for a very long time. Just put up the signs and do your best to scare them away, and if it doesn't work, call us when they're actually on the property and we'll call some parents."

"Hokay," Kenzie said, feeling her face go beet red.

On to the fire department.

It rang immediately, and a chipper-sounding girl picked up.

"Hillscroft Fire Department! If this is an emergency, please hang up now and dial 911!"

Kenzie summarized the situation again.

"It's a pretty wet year," said chipper Skipper. "I'm surprised they can even manage to light a fire that close to the river...have you tried putting up a no bonfires sign?"

"No, I'll be sure to do that. Thank you," Kenzie said, as politely as she could manage.

"Rrrrrrrrr!" she said as she hung up the phone. She left the office and paced up and down the library, thankful that no patrons had arrived yet. "There is such a thing as being too laid back! They're going to lie back and watch the apocalypse! Anarchists on bikes could be swarming the town hollering for human flesh and they'd be telling homeowners to put up a 'No cannibalism' sign!"

"Yeah...I did forget to mention that part," said Ms. Winter, with an embarrassed stretch of her lips. Today she wore a calf-length, burnt orange pencil skirt and cream blouse, with a handsome large, blue, teardrop pendant on a long chain. Kenzie had found her much as she had left her, leaning on her desk, drinking a coffee, and drinking in the moment.

"So, what do we do now?" Kenzie said. "We've got a problem, obviously, but the Keystone Kops aren't going to fix it for us."

"You could put up the signs," said Ms. Winter.

Kenzie put two fingers to her forehead. Jumping through these inane hoops felt like admitting the police and fire officials had been right. And they were most definitely not right. But her foremost duty was to protect the museum, and she would be neglecting her job if she refused to take the first step toward potential prosecution.

"Fine, let's put up the damn signs. I'll have to figure out how to get across the damn river. But first, I'm going to scan some newspapers."

STONY FORKS

Working with the giant scanners in the back corner of the room was fun, when the locals stayed out of her hair. There were three scanners, all identical make and model, but old people sometimes took a proprietary interest in one or the other and she did receive a few rounds of, "But you're going to be on *that* one? All day?" and the covertly jealous, "Well, you picked the right scanner. That's the best one in the whole place!"

Perhaps the regulars liked it for the same reasons Kenzie liked it. The computer had a large, clear swatch of desk on one side, perfect for arranging things flat before laying them out on the scanner, the keyboard was the least clacky, and, best of all, it was in the corner farthest from Talynn, their constant hangnail.

She monitored him out of the corner of her eye, far down the row, his black clothes making him easy to track against the archive's tan walls. No matter where he was in the room, she was listening to his footsteps, gauging where he was and what he might be doing. He had wanted to show up here naked—had he been in that horrible group last night?

The process of scanning was twofold. First, she would open to a full, unfolded page. Then, she would document what issue it was and list the articles that were contained on that page for the database. For every issue, she also planned to make an index of all of the articles contained therein and a short summary of the contents. This would put them in very good stead with the library, who would then just have to convert the information to their own filing system. When it was all done, the Hillscroft Public Library would have a complete set of the *Gazetteer* again, at long last.

She liked the rhythm of scanning, and the first issue in the pile (August 19, 1826) was in good condition for its age. She still wore cotton gloves, of course, because any document of that age, made of cheap pulp paper, could be significantly weakened by skin oils. But, unlike many documents she had worked with both at school and in her internship, this newspaper did not feel like it was imminently falling apart. The library had obviously taken good care of these papers for whatever length of time they had kept them, and then they had lain somewhere in dry storage and thankfully had not run afoul of any nasty beetles, millipedes, or rodents. They did not smell of mould either, only old, dry paper, a delightful smell for the bookish.

Page one went on the scanner, and she checked the scan. She entered the data, then moved on to the next page. Page two came out crooked. She nudged it a smidge, then scanned again. Time to enter the data. Page three, the rhythm continued. Articles about the local harvest, parties that had been held, one significant arrest of a man who stole a goat and would not give it back, claiming it was a different goat with similar colouration, local politics, some national politics, some poetry...

And an etching, most likely a wood block, but well done for a local paper. It showed a treed island at the fork of a wide, shallow river, which came to a point in a beach of stones. One fork was bubbly and active, and one sank off into a marsh in the deep forest. The picture looked like it had been drawn from the vantage point of a road (*the* road, still the only road there was) looking across the water at the island. Only, instead of a log palace, there was a little timber homestead on the island, with grazing cattle all around it and a chicken. The other side of the river was cleared, and there was a little semicircle of houses with a blacksmith's shop and a British flag running high on a rustic flagpole.

Trouble at Stony Forks, the title read.

One Samuel Corkstone, a cattle farmer of good repute, has reported incidents most unsettling in the vicinity of the small hamlet of Stony Forks, which stands some twenty miles from here along the river Croft. Mr. Corkstone reports that his house has been pelted with rocks, and beset with frogs of which no man from the town can seem to find the origin. More unsettling than this are the floods and storms of rain which regularly assault the house—from the inside! Corkstone's wife testifies that she once opened a door to find two feet of water inside the house, which stood there without pouring out for nearly a full minute before finally running out and down to the river. The Corkstones have ceased leaving their baby alone in the house and call on anyone in the community who might be able to shed light on these recent disturbances, to the tune of offering a reward of a full ten pounds and a hen.

Kenzie re-read the article numerous times before it all sank in. There had been people living here before. They had troubles with the water. They were not here anymore. Something had happened before Ettenby had bought the land. Kenzie felt ankle-deep in that same cold water, standing still when it should move, threatening to drown her childhood self. She pulled a pad of lined paper over and noted the page, subject matter of the article, and the number assigned to it by the database software. If there was a thread here, she would record it.

Nothing more turned up before lunch. She had scanned a few more days' worth of papers, and Stony Forks had not been mentioned, as she was sure it had never been mentioned before, or after, except as a side note, perhaps, about cattle deals or logging or hunting. As long as no scandalous crimes broke out, and no one lost their shirt in agriculture, and the place was too small to really have any arts or culture of note, what was there to write about? Those kinds of places were lucky if they showed up on the surveys, let alone in the newspapers.

She and Ms. Winter sat at the librarian's desk, sharing a cup of peeled carrots and munching on their respective sandwiches.

"You ever want to say something but don't want it to fall flat before you can prove it?" said Kenzie.

"All the time," said Ms. Winter. "I'm excitable when it comes to books, although you've probably already guessed that. Bye bye, Ms. Thomas," she said as a lady in a purple print dress, sun hat, and fringed purse shuffled out the door.

"Okay then, I'll tell you, but don't get disappointed in me if it doesn't pan out." Kenzie ventured a glance at Talynn and lowered her voice. "I think there might be something to all of this witch business that's floating around town."

Ms. Winter raised an eyebrow, her mouth full of ham, cheese, and spinach. She flipped a hand that said 'go on.'

"I found an article in that first newspaper about the old settlement that was here before Ettenby. Apparently, in August of 1826, Stony Forks started experiencing poltergeist activity. Enough to bring in a journalist from the Hillscroft Gazetteer. They're claiming in the article that the whole town saw the manifestations."

"Such articles became popular from time to time," said Ms. Winter, gesturing with her sandwich. "I'm not sure one newspaper article from 1826 an urban legend makes."

"You might be right," said Kenzie, "But I'm going to keep an eye out for more articles. If the hauntings continued over time, that's the stuff of urban legend and there's no two ways about it. The kids do it. Think of the nursery rhymes and schoolyard chants that have survived among children sharing secrets on the playground for generations, long after most books and movies have faded into obsolescence."

Ms. Winter gave a grin like the cat that ate the canary.

"What?" said Kenzie, wondering if she had dropped mustard someplace embarrassing. She glanced down. Nope, no extra condiment nipples today. "Seriously, what are you grinning about?"

"I just like having a lunch buddy who isn't afraid to say 'obsolescence,' is all."

They laughed.

Kenzie scanned two more papers and catalogued their very pedestrian and small-townish contents, socking away more scandals involving the shared town wheelbarrow and a loose donkey that would not stop eating anything it could get its jaws around and was evading all attempts to get it back into its paddock.

It was on the front page of the August 25 paper that she spotted the next article. There, in the boldest and most eye-catching typeface that the printer could muster, were the words,

Internationally-Renowned Spiritualist Vows to End Stony Forks Mystery

The devout reader of this periodical may remember our article of August the 19th of this year, wherein we documented some of the many strange and unexplainable phenomena plaguing our good neighbours to the North, in the town of Stony Forks. Never in the history of this newspaper have our readers shewed such interest in what we had originally deemed a story of minor interest and intrigue. Our offices have received visits from well-wishers and letters from the same, all concerned for the good people of Stony Forks. Indeed, it seems that nothing more has been talked about in the town square since the article ran.

Now, we have on good authority from the household of Mrs. Dorothea Johnston that her pen friend and close associate, the Reverend Dr. Davis Olbom, world-

renowned spiritualist and man of inquiry into all things strange and mysterious, is on his way to Hillscroft from England presently, bringing his associate and assistant of many years, the medium Miss Peggy Sands. Mrs. Johnston and her household anticipate the good Doctor's arrival within two weeks and respectfully request no visitors or well-wishers at this time.

Dr. Olbom, as reported in many fine newspapers worldwide, has investigated purported hauntings in Canada and abroad, using the latest science and the ancient art of the medium to bring peace to man and spirit alike. Mrs. Johnson has informed the Gazetteer of the contents of one of the good Doctor's letters, in which he vows "By God as my witness, I shall find the cause of these strange events at Stony Forks, and enact His peace upon them, whether through the comforting of the citizenry that there be no ill spirits and only the acts of Nature, or by banishing any evil present by the power of our Lord and saviour."

Standing out amongst the crowd of well-wishers and excitables is our very own Reverend George Smith, who has this to say regarding Dr. Olbom's upcoming visit: "People of Hillscroft, hold steadfast to thy God and turn away from things of the Devil, of which ghosts and spirits surely count among that number. The work of witchcraft, which this surely be, cannot be banished by further witchcraft. The faithful must bend the knee and pray to the good Lord that the people of Stony Forks be freed from their sin, and heed not the ramblings of some foolish rogue who believes that he may stand in the Lord's place."

Although many respect the good Reverend's sincere and devoted attentions to our Lord and saviour, that has not stopped a party from forming to travel to Stony Forks and see the manifestations first-hand. All who may travel without fear for their health and can manage their own room and board are welcome to meet in the town square this coming Thursday morning at the crack of dawn to begin the journey.

Kenzie wrote frantically on her notepad as she read, once scratching the paper right through in her zeal. She could feel her pulse thumping inside her neck when she finished. There was more to the story. There really was something that had gone on here in the 1820s. Which led to the question...why had someone stolen these papers specifically from the Hillscroft library, and why were they here at the museum? Perhaps they were trying to cover things up, to pretend the poltergeist activity—and perhaps even Stony Forks—had never existed. She imagined that even before cars, strange and legendary spots probably attracted their fair share of teenagers trying to test their mettle. Ettenby had been reclusive in his old age. Perhaps he'd hidden the newspapers here because he just did not want the unwanted visitors, the frustrating young bucks trying to take on an entity that didn't exist.

It didn't exist. There was no poltergeist, only her disrupted brain waves. Kenzie had night terrors and sleepwalking incidents all the time when she was a kid, and periodically now, especially around times of change. It was too easy to believe the things you saw while half-awake were real. That was why she had shaken Maria so badly a couple of times when she had gone to the door of their room and started screaming to be let out, or claiming that there were tarantulas on the ceiling or goblins at the window.

They had nothing to fear, now. With today's technology and (hopefully) policing, no one would have to fear trespassing or nuisance. They could turn these papers back in to the library, and people could learn the truth about the supposed witch. She took a deep breath and scanned the first page of the paper into the system.

She only had time for the rest of August 25's paper by the time six PM rolled around. This time, Dad came to collect her, looking a tad sheepish.

"Hallo, Shelley. Ready to pack up for the day?"

Ms. Winter was just wheeling the returns cart back into position, blissfully empty.

"If you can tear Kenzie away from the scanner!" she said, smiling. "She is making major headway with that database."

"Just a minute," said Kenzie, mentally running through the save procedures to make sure her work was backed up. "I'm just double-checking my entries."

Dad continued to make small talk until Kenzie had everything put away for the day and made her way up to the front.

"John was in again today, regaling us with tales of his country club novel," said Kenzie, "and Ms. Thomas shushed more people than either of us could hope to in a year."

"She's a shushing machine, that one," said Dad, nodding and grinning. "So, I've sent Mum off to the hardware store in town to get the keys cut. Since you're getting them, you should probably know how to use 'em. Want to come with me and learn the lockdown?"

Kenzie agreed right away, but inside she felt hesitation, nerves tightening. It was a big museum, with relatively few employees. They would need to do a sweep, to make sure nobody was still inside, then lock all of the entry doors and exits. They would have to check the exhibits for signs of vandalism, theft or damage, and then, finally, turn on the alarm systems. All that time would bring Mum closer to getting back to the museum, and her closer to the time that she said she would call Maria.

She followed Dad around, listening to him prattle on about his process, taking notes on the notepad she had adopted from the library. This was important, but she knew that with anxiety humming behind her ears constantly, she would never be able to remember the procedure later if it was not all written down neatly, in order. So her hand flew across the page, and her ears let things fly in one and out the other, as her brain kept going back and back to Maria, and what she would say, and Mum, and what she would say, and the excruciating tension between whose opinion mattered more.

Finally, they finished the walk-around. Nothing had been stolen or vandalized, and all stowaways had been evicted from the premises. The place echoed and smelled of old paper, dust, and floor cleaner once again, rather than of churros, children, and shoe rubber.

She and Dad stopped in the atrium, right in the middle, evening light cascading down through those beautiful church skylights.

"It's a beautiful thing, isn't it?" said Dad. "It never hits home more to me than on these little walks at the end of the day, when I look at everything we have in one sweep and see how much there really is. Finally, in my retirement, I can do the work I'm meant to do. And the icing on the cake is that my family can share it with me. You were the last piece I needed to fit into place to make my dream come true."

"Well, I needed a job, and this is so much better than anything I could get in the city," she said, feeling unease wriggle inside her like a tapeworm.

"But how many kids would have taken it if it meant coming back to live with their parents?" said Dad, walking back toward the stairs to the folk arts wing. "People today lack the sense of family that the Victorians had. People stuck together back then, lived on the same farms for life, working with one another to build something greater than themselves. Families belong together, not drifting apart, chasing careers around the world and never seeing one another. It's not natural, and it's not healthy."

Except when it is, thought Kenzie. How many people were crippled or killed by their family's constant expectations, or worse, cast out and forgotten because their family could not deal with who they were?

No, if Kenzie had learned one thing in the city, it was that the concept of family she had grown up with was warped and had warped her. Maybe in another time and another place, people had made it work, but not in this modern world. She hated listening to Dad going on and on about how they should all do everything together. If they were all that close, Kenzie would never get a spare moment of sanity. She thanked God that she had retained what autonomy she had, that she had even been able to question things. Because what do you do when you've grown up feeling like family is your life, but your family would hate you if they knew you? You self-destruct.

She had self-destructed spectacularly when she quit animation at Hallidan. She had blown the one dream she had ever had for herself. And Mum and Dad had done nothing while she crashed and burned, because they had warned her that she didn't work hard enough. They had tried to dissuade her from the archival sciences program too—from paying any more money for education.

No, sometimes distance was a good thing. She would take more distance after this contract, when she could get another museum job closer to the city. Because if Mum and Dad ever found out how she was different, they would beat and batter her with their words, apply so much pressure to her life that she would either snap, run away, or die. It had happened before.

FROM THE INSIDE

Kenzie reached her room and tip-toed apologetically across the carpet to her laptop, feeling perhaps not as though she were walking between shards of glass, but more shards of ceramic. She flipped the laptop open. She still had not taken down the shot of her and Maria at the Ex. Something inside her just would not let her do it.

The summer when she turned sixteen had been the most confusing. Boys started to want more from her than just kissing and holding hands, and the very idea filled her with shame and terror. She could not stay in school. It wasn't that she couldn't handle the work. She couldn't handle the people.

They made her take anti-depressants. Mum dropped her off at school every day and refused to come back, because the social worker said that was good for her. Most of the time, she ended up in the learning resource room or reading a book or drawing in an empty hallway somewhere because she still could not sit in classes. When she got especially out of hand, she was to take the tranquilizers.

Things started to get better with the drugs and, as she challenged ideas about her behaviour, so too did other challenges shake loose, some revelatory, some frightening. The tranquilizers often exacerbated the issue and made thoughts come spilling out of her head that she would not have otherwise said to anyone, lest she be cast out.

She and her boyfriend at the time, Jamie, had agreed to attend a concert put on in the basement of an all-ages club by her sometimes-friend from guitar class. Lolly Janssen was there and a crowd of about six or eight well-wishers. The basement was damp and close, with ugly, semi-matte brown tiles that lay on the walls and reminisced about the seventies. You had to take a staircase up and down that zigzagged along the back wall of the venue and felt like walking into a serial killer's secret lair. The lighting was dull, and the chairs were uncomfortable, and everyone would notice if you left. Add to that, the band was trying to be Nickelback and failing horribly. Let that one sink in for a moment.

She had felt odd all night. They had all sat in a circle in the corner before the show: her, Jamie, and Lolly. Lolly was being bright and chipper, as usual. She started talking about the party she'd had at the beach the weekend before, and she mentioned that she had made out with another girl. Her mom was a strict, born-again Mennonite, formerly an alcoholic, and she would put her in a nunnery if she found out (if Mennonites had nunneries, that is). Lolly had just buzzed her hair at the back, and her hair was this beautiful, natural, German blonde, and she had big eyes that Kenzie struggled not to look at too long, lest someone get the right idea. But look at her Kenzie did, only for an acceptable length of time, only when Lolly spoke, polite and unassuming and certainly not looking at her boobs. The struggle not to cast her eyes downward at Lolly's boobs was the hardest thing.

That was always the hardest thing. Liking boys and looking at boobs too. Who did that? Freaks did that. She would not be a freak anymore.

She had felt uncomfortable when the concert started, not wanting scrutiny, wanting to get away from the situation but not wanting to be seen leaving because that, too, would tell people she was a freak. A mental freak.

She needed to get through this concert and not stand out at all. So, she took one of her tranquilizers, hoping for camouflage.

The pill relaxed her in a way she had never been relaxed before. Instead of helping her clamp down harder on her feelings, it released them. Suddenly, for the first time since she had learned that bisexuals were all promiscuous porn stars or AIDS carriers, she felt okay to be herself. The fear and control tried to assert themselves and couldn't. The drugs made her feel okay about it all. Maybe she could finally come out. Maybe she could finally be real with people.

The first person she told that night was Jamie. She had expected him to be overjoyed, obsessed as he was at the thought of threesomes and open relationships and harems. Instead, his face went stony, and he said he would talk to her about it the next day. She went home afraid, and she slept afraid, but the drugs made her resolute to stay with this aspect of herself, to not let it go and to face whatever would come. Doing so felt like it would solve a lot of problems and clean up a lot of gunk inside her.

The next morning was not so easy. She told Mum before anything else. At that time, Mum was her foremost friend and confidant, and her worst critic. The first thing Mum said was, "you're just confused." The second thing she said was "don't tell your father, because he'd be disappointed." The third thing, the thing that scared her the most...

"Do you want to have sex with a woman? Could you have sex with a woman right now?"

Kenzie, of course, had answered no. What she had not realized, under the barrage of all that criticism, was that she did not want to have sex with a man at any nameable point in the future either. She was terrified of both, terrified of what it would mean about her as a person. But she had returned to her room troubled, wanting to hold on to the feelings she had felt so keenly the night before but realizing that no one was going to support her.

Then Jamie had killed it for good.

"If you want to be bisexual, you're going to have to come out to the whole school, right now. I won't let you stay in the closet with everyone except me. I'm not sure I could stay with you, either. I'm going to have to think about things. I don't want to get cheated on."

Kenzie had curled up on herself then, like a dying flower that has hit frost, and learned to fear herself once more. If she had had just one role model then, rather than seeing only alcoholics and genuine perverts identifying as queer; if there had been one place for her to go other than the seedy gay bar in the part of town that had thirteen-year-old hookers, perhaps she would have reached out. But there was no one to reach out to then, and she rose or fell on her own power. Always on her own power.

When she had gotten to the city, she started to meet people who had effortlessly flown out of the closet at fourteen, surrounded by supportive organizations and school professionals that talked them through the process. They had no idea what it was to be awkward, and intelligent, and alone in a bigoted country town. They looked at people like her, people who had had doubts, and problems, and who had come out of the closet at 24 or 25, as somehow deficient. Like they weren't brave enough, or confident enough. Like they had no excuse for what had happened to them. Kenzie hated those people and their privilege and the ideological time warp they lived in. The way they brushed off her opinions on the need for mentorship of queer youth. The way they implied that her aloneness was her own fault and her own doing. She had been a child. She had been at the mercy of her environment. She had been taught to hate herself in a way that city kids could never really get because they were raised to believe themselves masters of the universe. And she guessed, in some ways, they were.

Maria had never been like that. She had listened. She had shared stories of her own strict Catholic upbringing, and her mother who had told her that the flu was a demon trying to get her to stay away from confession. Maria had told her about the parents she had cut off for now, and the cousins she loved forever that helped her to thrive on her own. She and Maria had held each other many a night when the ache of their past, and the aloneness, pressed down on them again. They shared the sweet parts of their early lives with one another, so that they didn't have to feel like those parts of their lives were lost. Maria taught her about Argentinian food, and samba music, and little things about farming that Kenzie never knew she never knew. Kenzie taught Maria about roller coasters, and how to do Canada Day right (the answer: roasted marshmallows until you can't eat any more), and canoeing.

And now, Kenzie's hands trembled as she clicked the mouse to open chat. She feared swimming in aloneness again, and desperately hoped Maria would tether her to the shore.

The program rang once, twice, three times. Kenzie's heart beat faster, and her stomach clenched. A window popped up on the screen faster than a blink, and Maria was there, just at the tail end of sitting down.

"Hey, sexy, what took you so long?" she said. "I got tired of waiting and started to do the dishes."

Kenzie took in Maria's new hairdo. She had gotten a mohawk again in anticipation of summer, a shorter one, just a strip running down the middle of her head. Kenzie wanted to jump through the screen and tackle her, especially since she was wearing those arctic camo pants that made it impossible not to squeeze her butt, and a practically-see-through white tank top that showed the outline of her bra and her more-than-ample breasts.

"Mmmh, you're the sexy one, *Mama*. I'm in grandma clothes and I know it. Are you trying to tempt me home? Because it's working. I'm already contemplating when my paid time off is gonna happen, so I can come up there and rip those clothes off you."

"You wouldn't rip these clothes. You want me to wear them again the next time."

"You know what? I can't argue with that," said Kenzie, with half a giggle.

Less than one minute, and Maria had pulled a weight off of her that she hadn't even known was there. Kenzie floated free, relieved. She knew what was good. This was good. Maria was good for her, and so was inhabiting her real place in the world.

Maria leaned forward on both elbows, smooshing her boobs together in a most tempting way.

"So, how's the job?"

"You know I'm not going to be able to concentrate when you're teasing me like that."

"Be thankful you're not here. I'd be teasing something else, and you would not be talking in straight sentences then, I guarantee it."

Kenzie took a moment just to blush. She bit her lower lip. Maria pointed at the camera, her body language saying *mission accomplished*.

"Ohhh, there it is. There's that blush I love so much."

Kenzie blushed harder.

"I love you," she said, quiet now.

"I love you too," said Maria, "Now seriously, tell me about this job!"

Kenzie shifted her weight.

"It's...it's actually been pretty good. I've been having my usual moving nightmares, a little bit of sleepwalking, but that's not anyone else's fault. I've been scoping the place out, helping them organize the collections in the archives. We've already found a bunch of old newspapers that the Hillscroft library doesn't have, so I'm scanning those in and we're going to share them. Oh, and there's this really special character who comes in on the regular looking for evidence of a witch on the property. What a freaking creeper."

Maria rolled her eyes.

"A witch? Seriously? Why do some people have to turn everything into a bad horror movie plot?"

"I know," said Kenzie, "As if they have to spice up the real history. Real history is plenty spicy, if you know where to look."

"Is there a witch, though? Is there any basis in fact at all?"

Kenzie had been dreading that question. But, she was always honest with Maria. Lie to everyone else, but not Maria, Kenzie's official keeper of secrets.

"Fuck, maybe," Kenzie said, easing the tension within herself with a dry chuckle. "I've just found some newspapers that might pinpoint the source of the rumour. Now I don't know how I'm going to keep them away from him.."

Maria giggled too. "Come on, Kenzie, we curators are supposed to encourage the free flow of information and empower the general public to educate themselves. You owe it to society to put up with this asshole until the heat death of the universe. Don't you remember the ethics course?"

They chuckled again, and then a small silence escaped between them, in which Kenzie enjoyed Maria's presence again after all these days of confusion and nightmares and passive aggressive hoo-ha.

"The librarian's nice," said Kenzie.

"Good," said Maria. "Always easier to manage a place when the librarian isn't building forts out of books and chucking pamphlets at you."

Kenzie rolled her eyes, recalling Maria's rocky internship at a very, let's say passionate, refugee liberation organization. The librarian there had undergone some sort of meltdown when they'd decided to change the focus of the reading room from radical politics to statistics, and there had been some barricading and some very eccentric non-violent resistance that the woman thought was incredibly significant and metaphorical. People tried not to laugh, because honestly, a mental health episode of that scale was not *supposed* to be funny. But nobody could really go along with her assumption that this showdown was the library equivalent of Tiananmen Square.

"Nope, it looks like the staff are all pretty competent. The collection is solid, and we've still got more to discover and promote, and the facility is new and in top shape. There's this weird hatch in the floor that nobody knows what to do with, but I'm sure we'll figure it out eventually. My only issue right now, other than *Talynn*, is that we've got teenagers coming onto the property at night and starting fires across the river, and the cops and fire department are complete idiots." She raised up one hand and did a stupid face, in addition to a stupid voice. "Uhhhh, did you put a sign on iiiiit? Otherwise, how will they know to stay ooooout."

Maria laughed. "Seriously? They must send their third-stringers up there out of the way. What kind of advice is that?"

"I know!"

Kenzie smiled at Maria, and the smile felt warm. She felt warm. And not as frumpy. And definitely not as super fail-tastic as she had felt this morning. She needed Maria. Needed her here, even though work for both of them would make it impossible, even if her parents were not in charge of the whole thing.

"I miss you," she said, touching the screen.

"I miss you too," said Maria, her big brown eyes growing shiny. She shaded her eyes with her thick lashes and pursed her lips, turning her head away, "I don't know how we're going to make it a year without one of us just getting up and running to the other, forget about cars."

Kenzie smiled again. She forced herself to.

"Have you set up a friend yet? Someone to...keep you company? You know I don't want you to go without while I'm gone just because you miss me. You can miss me and still get laid. Hell, we managed just fine while we were together, getting other people into bed." She said it more quietly than usual. Unlike the bisexuality, this secret she hadn't even fully confessed to herself yet. She liked sex, and she needed and loved variety, but she also dealt with bouts of intermittent, crippling shame knowing that she and Maria were non-monogamous, especially when thinking about other friends knowing, or people in the community. She never questioned her devotion to Maria, or Maria to her. She just wondered how much other people would question, how much more they would invalidate their already-queer relationship, when they found out that one or both of them was also serious about someone else.

"Look at you," said Maria, blushing, "Just a big bisexual stereotype again."

"Yeah, but I'm *your* bisexual stereotype," said Kenzie. "So, who is it?"

Maria swerved her head in the air, as if shaking the admission out from between her ears.

"It's Lisa."

"Lisa? Like, Lisa Lisa? Stuck up Lisa?"

"She's not that bad. She's come a long way since U of T. We met up again at the opening for the new collection she's the assistant on."

"And why were you over there in the first place? Just to see her?"

"She invited me."

Kenzie felt a burning in her chest that threatened to make her lunch come up to say hello. Lisa Callery had been a study buddy of Maria's through the program, part of the group that somehow loved Maria but wanted to pretend Kenzie didn't exist. Lisa was one of *those* queer people. The ones who had burst out of the womb, perfect and courageous, with a rainbow spoon in their mouths, and subtly didn't talk to people who'd had a harder time with it. All Lisa had needed to hear upon meeting Kenzie was that she had come out at twenty-four, and she never talked to her again. She'd acted like Kenzie didn't exist, giving blank gazes over her head and always being on the other side of the room with the gold-star gays and queers.

"Of all the dykes in the world, you had to pick someone from our program? Someone that I hate? What are we going to do if you two start to be a thing? When I come back, how is that going to work? Are you just going to date her and tell her how fucking great she is, which she already fucking knows by the way, and let her ignore me and treat me like invisible dirt?"

Maria held both hands out.

"Calm down. It's just sex, and it's just for now. If anything else develops, I won't let her pretend you don't exist. She would have to apologize for how she treated you before she would get any further with me. I love you. I also trust you, and I need you to trust me."

Kenzie forced herself to breathe, feeling her diaphragm tremble as she did so. Anyone but Lisa. Lisa was *better* than her. Lisa was accepted and was in the rainbow flag club, and Lisa had gotten a real job after graduation. Everybody else thought Lisa was more worthwhile. How long before she got her claws into Maria, and Maria starting thinking the same way?

She pushed it all down. Maria was loyal. Maria was steadfast. She'd had lots of other chances to cheat or betray her, and she had never done it.

"The distance just makes it so hard, though," Kenzie said. "I want you to have company and fulfillment, and I don't want you to be celibate for a year, but I'm feeling vulnerable. I feel like I feel vulnerable all the time now, and I don't even have Dr. Maissen to vent to about everything."

"You can talk to me," said Maria, "You know you can."

"I know, but you're not my therapist, and treating you like one is not a road I want to go down. I guess it's just time for me to learn to handle my own shit."

"And what if you get sick?" Maria asked, her brown eyes earnest. "Eventually, everybody needs someone to wipe their ass for them sometime. If you get in trouble, you reach out for help. Promise me."

"Fine, I promise," said Kenzie, "and I just want you to know again how much I love you. And I miss you. I feel like running home, on foot, just like you said."

"Love you too, Baby. Get some sleep. You're gonna need it to kick ass and take names in the morning. Show those rowdy teens who's boss!"

Kenzie giggled.

"Okay, I'll get out my rocking chair and false teeth. Get off my lawn, you meddlin' kids!" she said, giving her best decrepit grandma voice.

Maria gave a warm smile, a smile that showed Kenzie how much she really did love her.

"'Night night, *Abuela*," she said, shutting down the chat.

Kenzie swirled around in her chair, blushing again and full of happiness.

Mum was standing in the doorway, just out of view of the camera, and from the look on her face, she had been standing there for a long time.

SELF-INFLICTED HARM

Mum just stood there, so Kenzie took the first shot. She always took the first shot. That was why Dad always blamed her, but there was a pattern to this shit and Mum was always the real instigator, with the way she behaved.

"I don't know what you think you heard," Kenzie said, like a cat raising its back, feeling the hairs on her arms stand up, "But it is none of your business. If you come barging into other people's rooms uninvited, you deserve to hear things that make you uncomfortable."

Mum put on her best innocent-and-offended face.

"At first, I was just listening at the door to see if you were napping, but then, I heard what you were talking about and I...I just froze because I was so shocked."

"Oh really," said Kenzie, getting out of her chair, voice rising but back staying hunched over, ready to strike. "That sounds so likely. No, you weren't eavesdropping at all like you *always* do so that you can bring trouble where there is none. No, somehow you managed, while shocked and appalled and frozen in silent agony, to open the door and step into my room and eavesdrop on me in complete silence. *Because that took no fucking premeditation whatsoever!* Why can't you just be honest for once in your life, you vile cow! You wanted to stick your nose into my life where it doesn't belong and harangue me for the next ten years about whatever you found that you didn't like. Or hey, maybe in your heart of hearts, you don't care that much about any of it. Maybe it's just fun to shame me and feel superior."

"You are so lucky your father isn't home," Mum cried, faking being on the verge of tears, like she did every time Kenzie got aggressive. She never really cried. "He would be so disappointed in you if he knew! You could just pack your bags right now."

"Oh really?" Kenzie said, "Why don't we tell him? In fact, why don't I just go on Facebook right now and tell the whole family? I'll tell them you inspired me to be this way! How about that? Pull the trigger, go ahead! I'm done with you holding Dad and money and the extended family and every fucking thing else that you can think of over my head. I'm never going to be a little copy of you—thank God for that because you're a fucking narcissist or borderline or something...I haven't figured it out yet because I haven't gotten you close enough to my shrink yet to be analyzed."

"Fine," Mum said. "Throw all of the mud at me that you want for finding you out, but I know my husband. He would never have hired someone who would want to—have orgies in here or something! What's next? Animals? Children? I thought we raised you better than to have no boundaries, like some kind of savage with a hareem."

"Harem, Mum, harem. Not 'hareem.' Why must you go out of your way to mispronounce everything? I know you're not stupid but you put it on, over and over. You act helpless and make everybody carry you and make stupid decisions. Maybe I'm your worst nightmare. Maybe I'm some Godless, boundaryless, babykilling, horsefucking monster. But you know what? I am smart, and I contribute to society! All you do all day long is harass tourists who don't really want to talk to you because you *add nothing.* You're not a historian. You're not an art specialist. You have put in exactly zero of the work to do any of those things despite, I might add, having all the money and the time in the world to do so. Typical boomer, expecting everything to be handed to you after putting in exactly zero work to get it. 'Oh, I'm here and I'm white and middle class, give me a job. Okay, take the CEO position, it's wiiide open.' I have worked my ass off, over and over and over again, and failed every time because the world is a pile of shit now, and what do I get for all my troubles? Stuck back here with you, having to put up with your bullshit and not being able to live my life, on my terms."

Mum gave a sarcastic little laugh, like she had just won. Perhaps she had. Dr. Maissen had told her not to rise to Mum's baiting. She told Kenzie that was what perpetuated the toxic little triangle they had lived in for so long. But every time she tried to ignore things, to deescalate, Mum found a way to hit lower. If she could just get away and not talk to her, maybe for a long time, perhaps things would get better slowly. But she was stuck here now, and the only thing she knew was to fight it out until one of them was too broken to go on.

"Can you even hear yourself? Saying these things to your own mother? Only a truly sick person would treat her mother this way after being given so much money, a job—"

"Dad gave me the job. You're just along for the ri—"

"Let me finish!" she screeched. "You continue to break yourself with these choices. Have you ever met someone who acts the way you do that has lived a normal life? Held down a marriage and a job and gained respect for themselves? Because all I see is bisexual gutter trash, porn stars and hookers carrying on the way you do with a million people at once. If you keep going down this road, your only legacy to the world is going to be a couple of AIDS transmissions! You'll never have a family. No man wants a woman that's been around the way you have. You'll lose the family that you have. No one would hire someone like you if they knew. They'd be afraid you'd sleep your way to the top or steal their husbands at the office cocktail party! You will *never* fit in with civilized people, and it will be all your fault. If you turn around now, hide it, forget about it, maybe in ten years we can all look back on this and laugh at what a fool you were. In the meantime, I'll be waiting for your apology."

Kenzie grabbed the pen off of her desk and threw it at Mum. She threw the pad next, and a few pillows off the bed. She advanced on her, murder in her eyes, and Mum drew back a few paces. Kenzie knew she was being led into the living room so Dad could walk in. At this point, she was so filled with rage she didn't care.

"And I know you'll never apologize, even though you're the one who needs to. What kind of a monster fucks up their kid the way you did to me? Tearing them down in all sorts of tiny little ways, making them fear having their own opinions, leaving them questioning the core of their personality because they can't separate out what is them and what is you and your brutal fucking conditioning? Who tells a child that they won't be loved if they don't conform? Who picks at them until they pick at themselves and make it bleed, and starve and bruise and kill themselves with work trying to live up to a standard they can never reach? You're the monster and, if you don't believe me, I've got a team of doctors behind me to prove it. Take a long look at yourself in the mirror, *Mum*. What you think is bad about me, that's the part that's actually me. All the shit I don't need, the stuff that's tripping me up? That's straight from you."

"People are sick in the city," said Mum, trembling. "It's not natural to live that way. You need to come back to the country and remember your responsibilities to your family, get all of that liberal brainwashing out of your head. You need to meet a nice man, and—and get married, maybe work at the local library. You have to forget that woman."

Kenzie advanced on Mum, getting within a few inches of her and hoping she felt the heat pouring off her.

"The only thing I plan to forget about is you. You are cancer!" She yelled the last few words, feeling her voice yelp like a dog ready to snap.

The door to the apartment opened and Dad walked in with a bucket of fried chicken and some salad in plastic tubs. His eyes twitched across Kenzie's, down to Mum. He had heard the last bit, no avoiding that.

"I thought we were done with this," he said, his words a staccato piano note. "I thought, Kenzie, that you had matured enough not to be constantly yelling at your mother all of the time. Is this what I get to come home to every day?"

"Okay, ask her why," said Kenzie. "Ask her about how she was sneaking around again, nosing in my things, listening with her ear to the keyhole like some pathetic old nanny goat trying to get the drop on her rival at the bridge club. She antagonizes me, and then you get mad at me for it. It never fails. Just once I'd like you to see the things that she does."

Mum put on her pathetic face again. God, she was good at that one. Kenzie was surprised she even had any other faces, given how often she wore that one.

"Daniel, I was just trying to check if she was asleep, and I happened to hear her talking, and now she's jumping all over me! Kenzie, you're so oversensitive. You get like this when you're overworked and haven't had any sleep. Maybe you should take the day off tomorrow."

"Can the faux concern. *Hopefully* it's not fooling anybody," Kenzie said, knowing spit was coming out of her mouth and not caring.

"Kenzie, slow down," said Mum, shielding herself with her hand. "You're spitting when you talk."

"Good! I hope it hits you and gives you AIDS. Because apparently I have that now."

"That is enough," Dad bellowed, throwing his hands down like a hockey ref. "Kenzie, there is no justification, anywhere, anytime to talk to your mother like that."

"If I had a tape recorder you wouldn't say that. Want to know what we were fighting about? Come on, Mom, tell him. You know you want to."

"I..." Mum hesitated, looking like a rabbit caught between two coyotes. "I don't like Kenzie's new boyfriend in the city. He smokes pot. I thought he might be running with a bad crowd. Kenzie blew everything out of proportion the way she always does, and I got carried away."

Dad's expression faded from the edge of rage to a paternalistic frustration. He gave a little shake of his head and a roll of his eyes, like someone would give to their three–year-old who had tried to enhance the pattern on the wallpaper.

"Jesus, Mandy, would you get with the twentieth century? He smokes pot. He's not working for some Colombian drug cartel."

"But...but he's Hispanic too," said Mum, looking over her shoulder at Kenzie in a portentous fashion, as though to say she would let it out little by little if she weren't careful.

"You're being ridiculous, as always," said Dad. "If you want to know if you should be worried, try asking."

Kenzie slept that night. All night. Without dreams, without nightmares or strange dances or dolls in dry wells. Most of her felt sick and wrung out, too tired to continue wasting any energy on low-level anxiety. But another more primal part of her felt like she had accomplished something. Not the standing up for herself, but the fight itself. That had been accomplishing something and now she could sleep. The fighting felt like home too. The injuries felt like home. Now to heal up for the next round.

DINGHY CROSSES THE RIVER

Kenzie stretched up on her tippy toes, leaning on the shelf with the tips of her fingers, and inched the giant box over the edge in increments. She sneezed once, knowing the dust must be coming down but unable to see it in the shadows of the utility closet.

Once she got the box into her arms she marvelled at how light it was. The boat, and the pump to fill it, weighed so little, and yet they would hold her up and convey her over the water. The box itself was dinged and scratched, even though she knew for a fact that the dinghy had never been used. A clearance item, probably one that Dad got for half price or less because somebody's kids had kicked the box, or it had gotten roughed up in transit, or accidentally scored with a box cutter during unpacking.

It was amazing how irrelevant packaging was, and yet how much people judged by it. All of the boats with pretty boxes had probably gone on to nice families who would tour them around the shore in Prince Edward Island looking at jellyfish, or run them down a stream somewhere, crayfish nets in hand. This one had been picked up last, out of a sense of duty, and stuck up on a utility cupboard shelf to be saved for a rainy day that may or may not come before its rubber grew brittle and its seams burst. Kenzie took a moment to balance everything before heading down the hall. In addition to the dingy dinghy box, she carried a backpack filled with signs picked up from the hardware store, nails, and a hammer. Although one would think that a large weight on your back and one at your front would provide some strenuous sense of balance, it did not. It only made her sway to one side, and then the other, depending on how she compensated. She ground the soles of her feet against the grainy canvas lining the bottom of her rain boots.

After disarming the alarm system, she picked up the box again and shoved the door open. The air smelled like rain. Cool damp was everywhere, a precursor to the cloying, humid damp of summer. But for now, it felt mostly refreshing, the occasional splash of water from the trees and the intermittent breeze periodically edging things from warm to cold. The sky was the colour of a mourning dove's back, the sun just shining through as a warm-coloured fissure in the clouds which cast a pale yellow and pink tinge over much of the sky.

Kenzie felt how early it was in her legs and arms. They felt rubbery and cement-y at the same time. Rubber cement then, maybe? Whatever she chose to call it, it was the familiar feeling of an early morning after too much adrenaline pumping in your system.

It had been three days since the fight. She and Mum had been avoiding each other as best as one can when living in a tiny apartment together in the middle of nowhere. Kenzie was enjoying the silence but knew it would not last. It was only a matter of time before Mum found some way of cornering her alone again so that she could harangue her. The silences never lasted long. Kenzie could tell that Mum was not sleeping well, which meant she was tossing and turning, trying to think of some way to come at things that would force Kenzie to do what she wanted. Mum would stay up all night if something was bothering her, thinking and obsessing, and as soon as she hit on something she thought would work, you'd be assailed with it immediately the next morning in her fervour to 'fix' whatever the problem was. Usually what she was trying to fix was someone's personality. She was like a pressure cooker right now, and as soon as enough steam had built up, as soon as she thought she had Kenzie pressed against a wall, she'd wait for Dad to leave the area, then the lid would blow off.

Kenzie still felt raw from the last time. She did not want to fight again. This was not helping her be a better curator and would only break her down. All Mum did was tug at things until they broke down and then act like a magnanimous philanthropist building them back up again.

Kenzie inched down the lawn sideways, taking little crab steps. The lawn was smooth, and wet, and sloping, and her boots had very little grip to them. She had bought them because they had a cute little truck with hearts floating out of it and said 'Carry Happiness'. Not because she had actually thought she would be slogging through a stream in them at some point. If they found you slogging through a stream in the city, usually someone called the cops.

She opened the box and hooked up the hand pump to the side of the boat. The connection broke the first time, sending a pathetic little pump of hissing air streaming back out of the spigot as fast as it had come, rejoining its brother and sister molecules on the outside.

"Oh no you don't," said Kenzie, locking it in place the second time. She had forgotten to wait for the click.

After a few more pumps, she threw off her jacket, making sure the lining stayed facing up. Nothing like a damp day to make you feel like you can't pull in enough air. At least her skin was already wet and gross, so the growing sheen of sweat had good company. Her rubbery arms strained at the work, and her knees trembled every so often. Eventually, though, she had a dinghy. It stayed firm, and none of the seams were singing in that high-pitched falsetto of balloons and covert farts. She looked at her watch. Two hours until work. She should have plenty of time to put up a few signs.

She found an area, almost directly in front of the Log Palace, that had fewer water lilies than the rest. She shoved the dinghy into the water, and watched the ripples spread around it. It felt strange to see ripples in that water, so calm and still it seemed, with the greenery on top hiding its movement. She had a moment of strange consciousness, where it felt like the ripples moved in a voluntary way, as if the water were reacting to the boat, and not just being water following the laws of physics.

She shook her head, hard, and told herself to knock it off. She'd stopped reading the old newspapers for the last few days for just this reason. She'd known she'd have to go across to the ruins with these signs, and she could not hear the end of the story before then. If she filled herself with sentimental hogwash about witches and poltergeists and haunted water, she'd never make it over to do what she needed to do for the museum. So, she'd busied herself with scanning other documents, and even taken a tour or two around with the volunteers. The historical wing was growing on her, and she was thinking she might just take over a tour now and then. After all the shadowing she had done the past few days, she had all but memorized the script.

She hopped into the dinghy quickly and without preamble, worried that she was getting to a depth where the water would top her boots. The whole thing sank down under the weight of her jump, letting about a half inch of water into the bottom of the boat. So much for staying dry. She'd have a big heart-shaped smooch of wet on her butt now, like a seafaring mandrill.

She reached the middle of the river and looked down. The water was so clear that the bottom looked close, even though she knew that at this point it was twelve to twenty feet down. She just drifted for a moment, the current being too sluggish to take her very far and the water lilies anchoring her like little green buoys, and stared down at the rocks below. The water was cool, and she had the sudden urge to plunge into it, to just go swimming, to do the backstroke all the way into the forest and see how far she could go. She knew, though, that in the shade and the slow current it was only a matter of time before leeches and mosquito larvae started sticking to her.

The boat bumped against the shore and she stepped out onto mucky and mossy ground. Worried it was quicksand-y, she stretched a little further, testing. Further up the bank, it still felt mossy but not muddy, so she grabbed a tree trunk and hauled herself to shore then pulled the boat up as far as she could, parallel with the bank so that it could not drift away.

The trees here were thin-trunked but thickly dispersed, a mixture of birch and oak and cottonwood. If it weren't for the stone structure looming in front of her like a boil on the land, she would never have known anything else had ever existed here but trees. The leaves alone would blanket anything on the ground, which was very damp with all of the cover afforded by the thick foliage. No wooden structure could have lasted here for more than twenty years, let alone twenty decades.

The long, low stone foundation sat before her, looking like many historical sites she had visited over the years, only without the care bestowed upon it to clean up the moss and straighten the stones pushed out by roots or dirt. Earth slouched up to it, half-submerging several old empty windows. She faced the outer wall from the river side and walked around to get a better view of the center of the structure. She picked her steps carefully, feeling every contour of the soil through the flimsy soles of her boots.

If the outer wall of the old structure looked like a bunker, complete with defensive earth berm, the interior struck Kenzie as a place where people went when they didn't want to be seen. The interior was scoured of moss in a rough way that spoke of pocketknives and flints. The floor had a thin coating of leaves on it. Someone had been clearing the leaves away periodically. Kenzie could see the remains of old cobbles dotting the dirt floor like acne on the face of a maladjusted teen. Unless there were sink holes nearby, there would not likely be any danger of falling into a disused root cellar.

The corner closest to her had completely fallen away, leaving a convenient gap through which to enter the structure. Kenzie walked through it, curious to see how much damage the teens had done and if there were any dangerous litter that would have to be picked up later—or could be shown to the cops as evidence of drug activity.

Inside, the place was surprisingly bare—no litter, just leaves. Whatever artifacts had been here had been looted or packed up and moved long ago. At the other end of the building, however, was a smear of what looked like red spray paint on what was left of the stone wall. Kenzie walked toward it, hoping, once again, that there would be some evidence that she could photograph and take to the authorities.

As she got closer, the paint solidified in her vision. The top line was writing.

Shes watching you

She stared at it. Off in the distance, and in the back of her head, she heard the echo of a goose's honk as it took off from the water. Below the writing, someone had painted a pair of eyes, sagged and bagged and looking so tired they could bleed (and maybe part of this was the colour choice), looking into her with an honesty that only street art and folk art can really manage, on their good days.

Kenzie, sensing that bingo was at hand and that these stupid kids had just daubed their way to juvie, took out her phone and snapped a picture of the graffiti. The little snap sound effect on her phone echoed a lot more than it should have. The echo was coming from below her feet.

She looked down to see that she was standing on a cast-iron grating, partially covered with leaves, over a dark shaft that led down and down, into nowhere, like the one in the folk art wing, dry and dusty and seemingly without a use. But she knew there was a use. She jumped back off of the grate, her nerves searing with electricity. How could she have missed something like that?

Because she was meant to. The graffiti was a trap. This whole thing now felt like a trap. She stepped backward, never losing contact with those red and bleeding eyes as she backed away. She did not catch a full breath until her feet hit the honesty of the layers of moss and leaves that blanketed the forest floor.

She rested against a large cottonwood for a few minutes. After catching her breath, she decided that leaving wasn't an option. Having to come back over here, even if she brought someone else, was worse than just toughing it out, getting the signs put up, and then, hopefully, prayerfully, leaving the rest to the police. This tree was as good to start with as any. It sat right on the corner of the building, within clear line of sight. She'd put some signs up here, and the rest on the other side.

She dropped her bag to the ground and rummaged through it, still facing the ruins. She had that feeling again—not like she was being stared at, necessarily. It was more that feeling that she would get in gym class when she had to change with the cool, skinny girls in the locker room. When she had to get naked in front of them, she had always felt a bit like a marionette, or a ballet dancer, trying to make every movement *cool* and present in such a way that convinced them she was graceful, and pretty, and was like that all the time. She even tried at home to practice being pretty and perfect and moving just so, because she thought that eventually, if she was effortlessly perfect enough, they would hand her the keys to some sort of secret clubhouse, or....well, she didn't know, it was childish. But she felt that way again now. Naked, stiff, trying to perform in just the right way for God-knew-what.

Good instincts. She had always had them. And right now, that primordial part of her brain was ringing like a school bell, calling everybody out to recess to run from whoever was it. Who was it, lurking in that hole, living in this ruin? The urge to run filled her legs, but she forced herself to turn her back on the ruins, wanting to scream the entire time.

She picked up the sign and straightened it against the tree trunk. She pulled a nail out of her pocket with the other hand, which also held the hammer. She set the nail into the little hole at the top of the sign, and held them both steady with her left hand, while tapping away at the hammer with her right. The hammering, rhythmic, with weight behind it and giving the feeling of impact, steadied her somewhat. The next nail was easier, with the sign already in place.

Okay, time for a No Fires sign. She would put that one up in the opposite corner. She found a likely birch, and got to work. First, the top. Tap, tap, tap, whack whack whack and it's in. Now, the bottom. Tap, tap...

Whack.

A loud honk from right behind her sent the hammer sailing into her thumbnail at full force. She let out a screech, wondering if you could just break off the tip of your finger or if it would maybe fall off. The world swam in her vision, and she lost her balance for a moment, leaning against the tree.

The goose was behind her, staring at her. It advanced toward her a step, studying her with one beady black eye. It gave a little grumble, low in its throat, like she had food for it and she wasn't paying up.

Kenzie's knees shook, buckled. She knew she was breathing wrong, but she couldn't stop.

"I can't walk...I can't walk!" she said, out of breath.

Something moved by her along the left side of her vision. It was blue, and moving faster than the river moved.

The boat! It had come unmoored from the bank and was rapidly floating downstream. The current had increased and the bank was gone, leaving only clear, cold water, seeping slowly up the grass and moss.

Kenzie's fear rose and she bolted after the boat, stumbling over a log and hitting rock after rock with her thin-soled boots. She headed for the delta, where the two rivers met.

Her mouth felt dry. All of a sudden everything was closing up. Lungs, nasal passages, diaphragm. She lurched, and not from a rock this time, but from reality swirling around her like water down a drain.

The dinghy sailed smoothly down the river now, unencumbered by water lilies, which were now under the water, their stems straining but too short to bring them to the surface at such short notice. It glided down toward the fork without her, the paddle lounging about on its deck like an idler drifting down the Thames.

She ran to head it off. The trees grew thinner and the light grew brighter as she reached the obtuse triangle of land that marked the end of the river fork on this side, fading from trees to dirt bank, and from dirt bank to stones and pebbles.

Kenzie climbed down the end of the dirt, eroded by the spring thaw with veiny roots hanging down from it. How strange, she thought fleetingly, that roots surrounding the earth and arteries surrounding the heart looked so similar, and both could be uprooted from their natural state of being by the impulses of water.

She ran across the rocks just as the dinghy rounded the bend and came into view. The left fork of the river, and the united river that sprang from it, was about two to three feet deep at the center, bubbling downhill at a fantastic rate along the road for many kilometers, and bottomed with not much more than smooth rocks of varying sizes, with the occasional boulder jutting out from the center. It was now or never. If the dinghy got going on that current, she'd never catch it, nor would she want to go with it.

Kenzie grabbed a long stick that had washed up on the bank. If she was careful, she could catch the stick on the edge of the boat as it went by, apply gentle pressure so as not to pop the rubber shell, and guide it back in to shore.

The boat rounded the bend between the rivers, faster than Kenzie expected, already speeding up even more. She stuck out the stick, straining from the shore to get far enough as the dinghy bumped a rock and drifted toward the other side. She caught the stick on the dinghy's side and applied gentle pressure, hoping to pull it back toward herself, but the current pulled so hard on the boat that any sideways movement was nearly impossible from her angle. If she put any more pressure on it, the jagged stick would puncture the inflated side.

Kenzie did some quick mental arithmetic—maybe a bit too quick, and she had never really been good at math. She stepped into the shallows, hoping to pull the dinghy closer to her using leverage. It worked. The boat drifted closer now that the stick was at a different angle, but she needed to get even further out. She waded into the river, now almost up to the tops of her boots.

Then her right foot skimmed off of a rock and she plunged into the chilly waters, her teeth chattering almost before she fully submerged. Her back whacked against a large rock. The dinghy was gone, sailing away down the torrent, and so was she, sliding over the smooth rocks with just enough buoyancy to keep her going.

She tried to put her feet out and catch something, but water was flying into her face, she couldn't see, her glasses were totally coated and her eyes flooded. She slid downriver, gaining speed like a kid on a waterslide, only her scream was real. Her hair flew behind her, around her, whipping in her face. Her shirt flew up. She flipped over, clawing for anything to grab on to. Her boots flew off at some point, having filled with water until they grew too heavy and left her feet.

Kenzie sailed by a spidery, grey-green blur and grabbed for it. It was a little skinny tree clinging to a large boulder. She hauled herself up, heavy with water but light with shock, and used the rock to trudge her way back to the shore that led, via a gentle slope, up to the main road. She'd come out on the bank closest to the museum, thank God. Ga-loomp, Ga-loomp, Ga-loomp. The most undignified sound in the world. Stomping on water.

Back on dry land, she sat on the bank for a moment, hugging her knees and trying to stop shivering long enough to get walking. With no boots. She was going to be late for work. Very late. And she would probably have to volunteer to donate another dinghy. One way or another, this would be coming out of her paycheck.

The river from this angle looked rather flat. It didn't really slope that much at all. How had she started sliding, and gotten pushed along like that?

Because it's me, she thought, it's always just me.

DWIGHT STOMPS ON HOME

After Kenzie emerged soaking wet from the river, she walked in a straight line on the road toward the Log Palace, staying on the pavement unless she saw a car coming. Single file, Indian style, facing traffic all the while, nothing in the old Girl Guide rhyme matched with 'suck' or 'dumbass' so it didn't stick in her brain for very long even as she remembered to stay on the proper side of the road so cars could see her. This put her on the forest and rock cliff side, with many charming little friends buzzing in her ears and trying to take drinks out of her arms and neck. Her dip in the river had washed off all of her bug repellent, and the mosquitoes had a long and exciting season to prepare for.

She debated taking off her socks and going barefoot. Everything stuck to the socks anyway, which negated a lot of their protective value. Then she saw headlight glass shattered on the gravel shoulder and thought again. Better to have a shard of something dirty or rusty stuck on the sock than stuck in your foot.

Her backpack drooped with extra weight, taking it far below the small of her back. She had dumped out the water as best she could, and adjusted the straps until they tugged at her shoulders, but nothing would fully compensate for a cheap backpack, soaking wet and filled with equally wet nails, not to mention the hammer. Her lower back ached, and her knees regained the rubber texture they had acquired earlier.

As she walked, she composed the passing scenery in her mind, painted it in as a Group of Seven or an Emily Carr. It was easy enough to do in this landscape. The sun glinting off the river, the strange, otherworldly shapes of the pines as they clung to spindly life off rocks caught in the torrent, the hulking mass of the granite hill to her left, purple and blue and punctuated with the rust-orange detritus of seasons past. The granite hill would take up the left third of the painting, looming like a sublime omen over the sun and the growth and the eccentric freedom of the trees and water.

She knew how to paint it all. She knew how to draw, what steps to take to transform a pencil line into a living, breathing being that would make people laugh and cry and learn. And yet, the execution failed her. Everything she had ever put out limped along for a while before dying in her waste basket or being imprisoned in a cupboard that she never intended to revisit. She could never put *herself* into her creations, not the way she wanted to.

She had come to animation school to be successful and cool. But she had realized halfway through their third-year business class that she did not want to 'market herself'. She wanted to market an image of herself that she thought people would find palatable. Back in the days of TV and newspapers, perhaps that was possible. Certainly, lots of movie stars had managed before the advent of the Internet. But in these glorious new days, everything about you had to be shown or people would grow suspicious. The technologies of this glorious new future demanded nothing less than full and total transparency, and anything less than full authenticity, full *confession*, gave off the scent of blood to the hounds that ran the world. And she couldn't be herself, the slut, the bisexual sex freak that it would be so easy for everyone to snicker at and hate.

Kenzie sped up, forgetting to watch her step. Her backpack smacked against her rump with the clink-clink-clink only a bag full of nails can manage.

It was on days like this, when the sun was shining and the wind blowing and the river flowing, that some of the clouds blew away from that time at Hallidan, and she wondered if perhaps she could do better now. When the landscape inspired her like this, she wanted to pick up a pen and start sketching it out, and the world be damned.

The world was a pretty heavy place to lift on your own.

The Log Palace came in sight around the bend of the hill. Almost there.

The shame began to burn in her stomach and at the back of her neck as she trudged across the bridge. Every moment, she anticipated a car full of tourists driving up the road, wondering who that dishevelled homeless person was that had managed to find her way all the way up from Hillscroft. My goodness, they're everywhere these days. The government needs to do something about re-funding the long-term care homes! Mommy, she's not even wearing shoes! I know, honey, try not to stare.

A car zoomed by, and she could see the passenger twist its body around to look at her. The car stopped with a crunch and a squeak of brakes, then slowly backed up. No, no, just go on to the museum and let me get cleaned up so you won't recognize me if we bump into one another...

A cute guy leaned an elbow out of the window. Really cute. His bicep bulged just the slightest bit out of his tight cycling shirt, which was a lovely shade of blue. He had the tan of an outdoor labourer, and a couple of tattoos floating around near his elbow and the lower part of his neck. One was a Canadian flag overlaying the map of Canada, and the other was a beautiful outline of a winter tree with a moon behind it. He smiled, and it was a working-class smile, full of snark and mischief. He had dark hair, and a well-defined yet sweet face. Probably some Italian blood there, Kenzie thought.

"Hey, you okay?" he said, the trace of a laugh on his lips.

Oh boy, a car full of jokers, thought Kenzie, I sure needed frat boys today. Oh yes, I did. That's just the thing to make it all better.

Kenzie took a deep breath.

"I'm the curator," she said. "I was putting up some signs across the river, and my boat got away from me. Along with my boots. As you can clearly see."

She smiled, just a little. Now that she could see herself from outside, she would have to be a true dumbass not to see that it was a little funny.

"Oh, you're Kenzie," said the guy. "I was wondering when I'd meet you. I'm Anthony. They call me in when there's landscaping work or handyman stuff that needs doing. This is my dad. He just drives."

The older, heavyset man behind the wheel raised a hand and nodded.

"Get in," said Anthony. "You can't mess up that back seat any worse than my tools do."

Anthony's dad shot him a long-suffering look, then nodded. Kenzie got in and buckled herself to the back seat. It was a boxy, older car with flaking, grey paint. Inside, the upholstery was the kind of brushy, high-pile stuff they didn't use anymore. It prickled on the backs of her arms.

Kenzie hadn't realized how much she needed to sit down. She felt drowsy almost as soon as her butt hit the seat, and when they arrived at the museum it took all of her mental effort to peel herself out of the car. Early morning plus shocking ordeal equals one hell of a long day.

Kenzie hoped she wasn't blushing when Anthony got out of the car to face her, standing up to his full height of six foot two or so. He had a lot of lean muscle on him, and Kenzie noticed that he also had a series of hoop earrings running down the back of his left ear. He wore a paint-stained T-shirt and cargo pants, but that only made her wonder how sexy he would look in one of those utility belts or a safety harness. Like a male stripper in the making, probably. Just add a little sheen of sweat...

"Thanks for the ride, you guys," she said, realizing that she hadn't the faintest clue what to call Anthony's dad besides 'Anthony's Dad.' "Anthony, I'm sure I'll see you around."

"I'm sure you will," he said, with a smile and a wink. "And call me Ant. Everybody does except the government."

Kenzie smiled, and the blush crept over her face without her permission. Stupid capillaries.

By the time she got to the door of her dad's office, Ant's chainsaw was already buzzing away in the background. Kenzie entered the office to find the whole gang crunched in there like a bunch of mismatched socks in a drawer: Mum, Dad, Ms. Winter. Dad sprang to his feet.

"Where in the hell were you? When we looked out and saw that the dinghy had gone, we were beside ourselves. I was just about to come look for you."

"The dinghy is gone," Kenzie said, watching Dad's face go from concern-rage to disappointment-rage in the second it took for her to say it.

"The water in the river rose while I was putting up signs, faster than I expected. I'm not sure if we still have spring melt running down at this time of year from the high places, but there must have been a flash rain upstream, or something, because one moment I was hammering up a sign, and the next, the dinghy was off the riverbank and floating downstream. I tried to catch it, and I fell in. The current took my boots. That's why it took me so long to get back."

"Excuse us," Dad said to Ms. Winter and Mum. They left the room, Mum last, her expression indicating that she did not believe Kenzie in the least and that Kenzie would hear about it later, at length, whether she liked it or not.

Once the door was shut behind him, Dad placed both palms on the desk. He had a pair of very unbecoming sweat stains spreading under the arms of his blue button-down shirt.

"You and I both know that it was too late for winter melt. What were you thinking, mooring the boat without a guy line? I bet you perched it about a quarter of the way in on the grass, didn't you?"

Kenzie's face got hot.

"No, I pulled it all the way up on the shore. I made sure I did. And the dinghy didn't have any holds for a guy line. I had a genuine accident here, and I'm noticing trouble with the river that may affect us. If it swells spontaneously, we'll need to keep an eye on it. And furthermore, I was across the river doing my job as curator of this museum. I made a decision to protect this property, and I noticed another problem that could potentially damage the building or the collection. But instead of having a conversation about it, you've chosen to dress me down like an unruly teen."

"Then stop acting like one. I told you we don't care about the opposite side of the river—"

"You don't care. Other people are concerned. I was following instructions from the police and the fire department, whom you had never even bothered to call."

"For God's sake, stop grabbing onto things and worrying the life out them. If I'd known you'd spend your time going on foolish side quests, tilting at windmills—you're as bad as your mother. Wading out into a dangerous river...it's just like the time she nearly got run over in Chicago, craning her neck to see the buildings. She just backed up into the street without thinking."

Kenzie let out a grunt of annoyance between clenched teeth. "You do not get to do this," she said. "You hired me to be a curator, not your daughter the puppet. I am going to care for this museum in the way that I was trained to do, and address the issues that I feel are pertinent to its upkeep. You have invested me with authority, whether you meant to or not, and what I did today, I felt was in the best interests of the museum. Now, you can either listen to my concerns, as a co-worker and a member of this team, or you can continue acting like this is your own personal sandbox and hoarding all the toys. I know you are better than this, Dad. I was in real danger today, and I know you want to do better than petty insults and politics."

She stood solid, not giving an inch, carving a mask of maturity and reason onto her face when all she wanted to do was scream.

Dad popped a big, goofy grin which was as close as he ever got to an apology.

"But, my deah," he said in a bad English accent, "I am so terribly, terribly petty. We mustn't let work get in the way of doing what we love."

Kenzie managed a weak half-smile back. She walked to the door, then turned back. She had to say it one more time, give him one more chance to listen.

"I was really scared today, Dad. I wish I could feel like you acknowledged that."

"Vell," he switched to an Austrian accent, holding a pen up to his face and pressing his lips together. "I can see you are craving validation from your father figure."

"Okay, I get it," Kenzie said over her shoulder as she headed for the apartment. "Obviously we're not going to have a meaningful conversation about this."

Dad's cackle rang out in the atrium, louder probably than he'd meant it to be. "Lighten up! You take everything so seriously. Your day will be bad because you've decided already."

"No, my day is bad because I fell down a freaking river and lost a good hundred dollars' worth of equipment and nobody seems to care unless they get to criticize," mumbled Kenzie under her breath. She would have said more, but she was approaching a clump of tourists gathered at the opening to the Folk Art wing. Bad enough she was in soaking wet clothes, with dirty stocking feet. Talking to herself would just add the cherry on top of the crazy sundae.

"'Scuse me," she said, shrugging an apology as she wedged her way through the group. The print dresses, sensible shoes and complete lack of anybody between the ages of fifteen and thirty-five marked it as probably a church group. She noticed a few quizzical glances.

"Sorry, fell in the river this morning. Got to go clean up!" she said, affecting her best chipper persona as she climbed the stairs.

She felt her shoulders relax a bit as she pushed the apartment door shut behind her, relieved to have gotten past the carvings without any more weirdness. Much of the oddity of the museum and its little corners and crannies had become more familiar over the last week, but those carvings, and the simulacra down the hall, never stopped making her feel watched and wary, ready for them to move or change or do...she wasn't sure what, and she didn't want to find out. But she knew deep down that they were capable of it.

She jumped as something moved past the kitchen area toward the front hallway.

"Oh my God, Mum, you scared me. I thought I was alone, finally." She hoped Mum would take the hint and get back to bustling around downstairs.

In Mum's arms were a big fluffy towel, a face cloth and a plastic mesh loofah ball.

"I thought that if I could speed up the process, you could be back down to work sooner," she said. "I've laid out some clothes for you in the bathroom. Feel free to change them up if you don't like them."

Kenzie felt the urge to snap at her, to ask why she had been in her room and why she felt she had the right to pick out her clothes. But after the walk, and the argument, and being seen by all those museum guests, she just did not have the energy.

"I'm sure they're fine," she said, taking the bath stuff and heading for the shower. "Thanks for the assist."

The hot water felt glorious on her cold and puckered skin. Kenzie hadn't even realized how numb her toes had gone until the hot water flowed around them, waking them up and warming them back to life. Steam filled the room, surrounding her with a visual white noise that calmed her mind and took her into a state of forgetting. She loved the suspended state of forgetting, of living in the moment and being empty of context or care. Sometimes she could escape to this place, and for a brief moment, lightness and relaxation consumed her.

The door clicked open.

"You've been in here an awfully long time. Don't you want to get downstairs?"

"Not until I'm clean," Kenzie said in her best 'what are you doing here' voice.

"Your father was very angry, you know," Mum said.

"You know, five minutes' peace would be nice. I don't barge in when you're showering."

"You used to," Mum said, a touch of nostalgia in her voice.

"Fine," said Kenzie, letting the last of her peace run down the drain with the last of the shower water. She turned off the water and groped for the towel on the hook, dragging it into the shower with her. "Dad was a total dick about the whole thing. He didn't listen at all, and all he wanted to do was criticize."

"Well, you have to admit your story sounded rather outlandish. Why would the river just rise like that? It *is* more likely that you just moored the boat wrong. You've always had such an imagination. Or perhaps you're just keeping more secrets and using your imagination to outwit us again."

Kenzie pulled back the shower curtain and scowled at Mum, sitting on the closed toilet. Mum handed Kenzie her underwear as if holding out a peace offering. She took them.

"Yes, Mum, I went across the river to meet with a cult and sacrifice goats. I lost my shoes up another cult member's ass, because we're crazy like that."

Mum handed her some socks.

"I'm not stupid, you know, as much as you and your father like to make fun of me. But anyone could see that there are parts of your story that just don't seem to add up. The river rising suddenly and then going back down, just in a few minutes' time...it seems too weird to be true."

Kenzie grabbed her shirt from Mum's hand before she had a chance to offer it. She shoved her arms through the sleeves in an irritable fashion, and shoved the buttons through the holes as aggressively as she could.

"Yeah," she said, "It doesn't make sense. On that we agree. But it doesn't make the story any less true. Believe it or not, I don't give a damn how weird it sounds."

Kenzie finished dressing, then left Mum behind in the apartment. Who cared what Mum did from then on, anyway? She was halfway down the hall to the Folk Art wing before realizing that she still wasn't wearing any shoes.

THE WITCH OF STONY FORKS

Kenzie sat in the same seat in the library, under the buzz of the fluorescent lighting. She pulled another newspaper from the stack. This one was from three months down the line: October 15, 1826. Someone had collected these papers as they pertained to the Stony Forks incident, she was sure of it now. Someone had stolen them from the library to stop people from talking. Perhaps Ettenby had had to quash revellers across the way, or some kind of coven. Clearly, someone had wanted to cover all of this up, perhaps even cover up evidence that Stony Forks had existed at all.

The front page beckoned her with an opening line that would have been at home in any gothic novel:

Rev. Dr. Davis Olbom Begins Séances at Stony Forks

Faithful readers of this paper will remember the announcement that Dr. Davis Olbom, foremost researcher in the spiritual realm, had volunteered his services in light of the recent occurrences at Stony Forks which have only grown in severity since our last report. Residents of the Hamlet report items having gone missing after mysterious floods and rainstorms, which now affect most families in town. All of the Iroquois traders in Stony Forks have, for the time being, taken their trading elsewhere, citing evil spirits after their medicine man was unable to effect any change. The pitiable Corkstones have found themselves the subject of much censure from the townspeople, who blame them for the occurrences.

Dr. Olbom has heard of the state of affairs in Stony Forks. In a statement to this newspaper yesterday evening, he confessed that he had already been interviewing some of the Iroquois people who had left the town and sought refuge in Hillscroft, along with white and black settlers. Dr. Olbom stated that "Enlightened people of the world should be looking to so-called 'savages' for answers when experiencing supernatural distress. The native peoples of this and many other lands are open to the spiritual realm, and often produce better answers than many a proper wife, or Reverend, for that matter."

The rivalry between the good Doctor and Rev. Smith has only intensified since his arrival. Rev. Smith invites all contrite worshippers to attend his daily services against evil, which he is now holding in protest to the happenings at Stony Forks.

With regards to his findings, Dr. Olbom, and his assistant Peggy Smith, the internationally acclaimed medium, have declined to comment overmuch at this time. His statement was simply:

"I have heard many tales of strange beasts and many nuisance occurrences coming from Stony Forks, but no scientist worth the name shall pronounce a conclusion before investigating the happenings in person, and at length. Tomorrow, with Mrs. Johnson's blessing and patronage, I shall make my first visit to Stony Forks and from there, if the Good Lord wills, pronounce my findings."

Kenzie scanned that newspaper as quickly as she could without tearing pages or getting things crooked. But each scan felt like it took an eternity. The tiny, rough-printed text crawled before her eyes as she tried to care about lame horses and upcoming sales of equipment and ladies' dressmaking services not being up to par. Someone's servant had run away. Someone's wagon had gotten stuck in the mud.

Finally, finally she could pick up the next paper. Ms. Winter approached her about lunch, but Kenzie said she'd catch up later. She pulled it from the stack, which had grown ever shorter; just a few more papers to go. The rest of the story must be in them somewhere. She had willed herself not to look at the front page of this one, lest it pull her away from her duties as a scanner. Now, she allowed her eyes to feast over the cover, drinking it all in.

A very strange etching graced the front cover, of a suited man and woman leaning away from a flapping goose in fright and alarm, while a peasant woman waved her arms as if to shush it. Somebody had put a lot of effort into this one. It looked as good as the prints in a Dickens book, and much the same style.

Stony Forks Woman Leads Renowned Psychic on 'Wild Goose Chase'

Renowned spiritualist and scientific investigator of all things 'beyond,' Dr. Davis Olbom, along with his assistant, the medium Peggy Sands, have been experiencing some censure and ridicule from the international press this past week due to some unusual and, some would say, discrediting circumstances at the Stony Forks investigation.

The good Dr. Olbom alleged last Thursday that a farm goose, which has been known to the community these past three years, is in some way connected to, or causing, the strange poltergeist activity which has plagued the Hamlet of Stony Forks. The incident began when, during a séance involving Miss Sands and the

Corkstone family, who are said to have initiated the haunting, Miss Sands produced the notion that the spirits were leading her to a grey goose 'of ill repute' in the town proper. She claimed that the goose, which roams the area after getting away from its owner, the widow Fenn, is possessed of an evil spirit, and that its owner can enter its body at will and spy on her neighbours, or cause mischief.

The widow Fenn, when confronted by the townsfolk, professed innocence of any knowledge of the goings-on. She is reported as saying "It got away from me. That is all," with a stern and dour appearance, which should not surprise anyone familiar with poor widows.

News of this incident has travelled already, reaching newspapers in New York, London and even Montreal. Members of the scientific community, who have long questioned Dr. Olbom's credentials and aims, were quick to scoff at the tale as an example of quackery. "Simply ridiculous," said Dr. Tertius Lydgate in The London Times, "is the notion that anyone should take Dr. Olbom and his dubious assistant seriously after this incident. He is taking advantage of a desperate community of uneducated farmers and labourers, and should be punished for leading them astray from the dictates of the Bible and of good sense. His 'assistant' is clearly hysterical and should be sent to an institution where she may receive compassionate care for her lunacy. This is the charitable explanation. If I were less charitable I would say that, given her background in Whitechapel, she is more likely to be a street charlatan than a madwoman."

Dr. Olbom maintains his faith in Ms. Sands' powers of deduction and prediction. "Not all prophets produce intelligible prophecy, even when they are correct," he said in a statement to the Gazetteer. "Ms. Sands is only beginning her work in the community of Stony Forks, and I have no doubt, with more time, that we shall be able to put the pieces of her revelations together, much like a puzzle. I ask that the public have faith in our work and allow us the time that we need to do our work, much as a fine carpenter needs time to produce a scrolled banister."

As to the claims made by some major metropolitan papers regarding the education level and credulity of our citizens here, the staff of the Hillscroft Gazetteer would like to remind all such columnists and commentators that we are subjects of the British Empire, recipients of the King's education, and inarguably the most advanced farmers and labourers produced by any Empire in the history of the world. We would refute the offensive notion that any of us have been taken in by a charlatan, and we would sincerely like to know what they would do if their neighbours' houses were being constantly flooded by a poltergeist or other such unexplainable phenomena. In our humble opinions as Editors of this paper, we think that they would be far less equipped by incredulity than we, who had attempted to consult someone seasoned in the investigation of such matters.

Oh dear, thought Kenzie, *a newspaper war, and country versus city at that.* She wondered, with a chuckle, if any copies of the Hillscroft *Gazetteer* had ever made it into the hands of the esteemed Dr. Tertius Lydgate. Perhaps, in their pique, they had taken the time to send him a copy. She certainly would have, in their shoes. Now more than ever, she wondered about the resolution of this case.

The goose she kept seeing had to be a descendant of the one that had lived in the village. That was the only explanation for a European goose still wandering the woods. But what had it bred with? Had there been more than one? Was there still? Surely someone would have noticed a flock of European geese veeing about the land, with all of the naturalists day-tripping to Algonquin and keeping bird books and helping with the annual counts. Such a thing did not usually go unnoticed in Canada.

There was no way it could be the same goose. And yet, had it not seemed awfully menacing? And the old woman's words that it had gotten away from her seemed strange. Why had she not tried to recapture it? Surely a normal domesticated goose would have clipped wings and would not be able to run that fast. Someone would have caught it. Maybe the widow Fenn had wanted it to get away.

And yet, Kenzie knew that the mainstream press's reaction at the time was logical. Who, indeed, pinned a series of violent hauntings and supernatural events on a plain farm goose? They honked, they walked funny, and honestly geese were probably the silliest, ungainliest creatures on earth. Perhaps the evil forces in the region were just using whatever they had?

Kenzie remembered the ingeniously patched-together simulacra, and suddenly the idea of an evil force that used whatever it had handy didn't seem so far-fetched. Things had been stolen from the settlers. Things like railroad spikes? Doll's heads? Butcher's papers? All of those things seemed likely to have been in some nineteenth-century cabins and workplaces.

She had a strange feeling then, like she had the image of a thing in her head that had not quite materialized, the outline of a thing that shifted, the shadows resting on the face of a person she had never met. She felt this way sometimes when an idea formed, a story or a picture, one that she knew was brilliant, would be brilliant, but that hadn't quite introduced itself yet. This idea was brilliant in a malevolent way, in the way it fit around the edges of the known truth, seeping into them like water encroaching on a surrounded spot of dry earth. Something that fit in all the right places but shouldn't.

She was getting more hysterical than Peggy Sands wailing about geese. She needed a sandwich. A sandwich was long overdue.

Ms. Winter stopped changing over bar code stickers when Kenzie plopped down in the chair opposite her, making a very library-unfriendly squeak. Kenzie hauled a PB&J made of lead out of her purse and unwrapped the plastic.

"Well, aren't you just a carnival of sounds that are not conducive to a reading atmosphere," Ms. Winter said with a smirk. "I should boot you out the door."

"Don't punish me. I've already starved myself half to death," said Kenzie, smiling. "And count your blessings that I'm not dripping all over the collection!"

Ms. Winter shook a long, manicured finger at her. She had painted her nails a classy, pearlescent peach colour. Or, someone else probably had. Home manicures never stayed that nice. She also pursed her lips and frowned. It was easily the most stereotypically librarian-ish thing she had done since Kenzie had met her. Most of the time, Ms. Winter looked like a sexy secretary from a 1940s film noir, twenty years past her prime but still with the perfectly coiffed blonde ringlets, the remains of a bombshell figure and impeccable makeup, and probably a lot wiser for the change.

"I don't even know what to say to you about this morning," Ms. Winter said. "The dinghy wasn't worth it. Don't you go chasing discount dinghies down the river and getting yourself drowned. I would never have told you about the trouble across the river if I had known you'd go around taking silly risks."

Kenzie chewed and swallowed a piece of her sandwich, feeling the lump of it all the way down, and then weighing on her stomach. One part of her felt the knee-jerk reaction that she always felt when admonished, to reach out and bite the finger waggling at her, and hard. But a much larger part of her quelled the urge to snap this time, because there was something soothing about the way Ms. Winter had said it.

"Geez, the way you say that makes me think that somebody actually cares about me around here, and not just about my reputation or a seventy-five dollar hunk of hollowed-out rubber. It's refreshing for a change."

"Everybody shows their frustration in different ways," said Ms. Winter, eyes downcast into the book she was labelling. Her hands worked like a mom putting a Band-Aid on a beloved child's knee. At least, how moms put Band-Aids on knees at friends' houses, and in movies. Kenzie had realized somewhere along the way, as she tried to pick up the pieces after animation school, that one of the reasons she had wanted to be a filmmaker so badly was because TV and film had often been the only places that had showed her what a functional life was supposed to look like. She had never behaved like the other kids. She didn't have the same expectations of how to treat people, or how to expect to be treated. Eventually, she had learned the rules from TV, films, and magazines. Without them, she would never have stood a chance of connecting with her peer group in any meaningful way.

The library's phone rang. While Ms. Winter took the call, Kenzie thought for a few minutes and ate more of her sandwich. She'd often wondered why strangers were so much kinder than the people she'd lived with.

Take her first boyfriend, Josh, for example. Mum had always handled the tragedies in her life with such *sensitivity*. That is, if sensitivity were synonymous with over-reaction and over-analysis.

Josh had dumped Kenzie in the middle of the high school talent show, of which he was the emcee. Kenzie had hidden in the bathroom, but when it became clear that everybody thought Josh a jerk and was on her side, even the skinny popular girls, she calmed down and determined to let it be.

She had gone home, and Mum could see that she had been crying. Mum had not taken 'I don't want to talk about it' for an answer. That day she had asked, and asked, and asked, and asked, and butted into every conversation and everything that Kenzie was doing until she was screaming at her, and Dad was yelling at both her and Mum (calling one an obsessive nag and the other rude and disobedient). Finally, realizing that Mum would not stop until she got the story, Kenzie snapped and told her.

That had not ended things the way Kenzie had hoped. Instead, Mum shifted gears. She bore into what Kenzie had done to lose Josh. Kenzie had no choice but to listen along like an exhausted rag doll while Mum postulated about why Josh did it (that was her fault) what he didn't like about her (also her fault; she slouched too much and had gained five pounds). It went on for days. When Kenzie got mad and didn't want to talk about it anymore, Mum would bribe her with desserts or clothes or a movie she wanted and apologize, and then go right back into it an hour later.

It was typical. Every friendship, every relationship, every job, every volunteer opportunity, every class where she got a B—every time something didn't go exactly Kenzie's (Mum's) way, Mum would obsess over every detail, to find out where Kenzie had gone wrong. Kenzie loathed it at first, but eventually, like a vine locked onto a trellis, she came to seek it out when things didn't turn out exactly as she had hoped. Because over time, dealing with the pain of blaming herself felt more active and responsible than dealing with the pain of rejection or failure.

One of the major things she had to re-learn with Dr. Maissen was how to just let things be. At least, she was in the process of learning that. The concept that rejection might not always be about her in some way—how she had held herself, some tiny thing she had said, her weight—had been a revelation, one that she had approached with much skepticism at first. One that still gnawed at her when she felt weak.

Maria had been a breath of fresh air for her. Maria. She would need to speak to Maria again tonight. She needed more of this compassion and care thing. She needed more people like Ms. Winter around, too. It eased her bruising from the fall.

Ms. Winter said, "Goodbye, Talynn," into the phone, unable to hide the hint of irritation in her voice. She strode back over to where they had been having lunch, lips pursed in annoyance.

"You know," Kenzie said, "Maybe it's pointless to argue, because everybody in this place seems to think I pulled a real boner this morning. And, I'll own the part about chasing the dinghy, but I was already pretty freaked out by that point. It's creepy over there, and there was this giant grey goose following me around and I was worried it would bite me or something, and who knew if there might be cultists or something roaming around, I mean, what do these losers even do all day when they're not trespassing and making up witches to invoke while setting illegal fires? I wouldn't put camping past them. Anyway, up until that point, I was really cautious. I swear to God, I moored that boat all the way up on the shore. The water level rose. That's the only explanation. Or maybe the goose nudged it, I dunno."

Ms. Winter arched a well-plucked eyebrow.

"You saw the goose?"

"*The* goose? I saw *a* goose. A very fat and well-feathered one, and brazen too, I might add. I've seen it a few times. It's some kind of European goose. Damned if I know how the stupid thing got here. Why, have you seen it too?"

"No, I thought that people were making it up, actually. That's the goose they say belonged to the witch. There's got to be more than one, obviously, and God only knows how they're breeding. But only a handful of people have seen it once, let alone two or three times. They claim it shows up before car accidents and baby deaths and all manner of ugly things that no one can substantiate. The more drug-addled of the believers even say it's possessed by a demon. Did you see any horns on it?" She gave a little, snorty giggle.

Kenzie felt a weight in the pit of her stomach but decided to play it off. Superstition was unprofessional. She felt her voice warble as she spoke again, but clamped down hard on the sound, her neck muscles constricting. She would not give in to ridiculous notions and become someone like that freak Talynn.

"Nope, just a really rude goose. Like many geese the world over. Maybe it was under the tragic assumption that I had bread in my pockets."

They both laughed, lightening the tension and reminding them on which side of these outlandish tales they stood, being curators of a factual museum and archive, and, you know, not on drugs and taking hallucinatory day trips out into the woods.

"I got mobbed by a swarm of geese at a petting zoo one time and you would not believe how pushy those things can get," Kenzie said. "And the ducks, too. I'd turn around, and the ones at the back of me would bite my butt when they finished their bread, so I had to keep turning like a bread-based lawn sprinkler until the food started to run out, at which point I chucked the last two slices in two separate directions and ran for my life."

Ms. Winter laughed again. "Clearly, you are equipped with all of the arcane arts and magical training necessary to face down even the most menacing of geese. I don't have to worry about you going across the river anymore."

"Not without a dinghy, you don't," said Kenzie, chuckling. "But seriously, we might think about bringing a decent ornithologist down here. We must have enough of them in the surrounding area. Maybe they could shed some light on where this colony of European geese is coming from. I'm surprised nobody has tackled it before."

"None of them probably took it seriously because of where the stories were coming from. That's what I love about this project. We're shedding so much light on local folklore and unearthing the facts on things that had previously been left in the hands of the ignorant. This is what historians are born to do," Ms. Winter said, glowing at her books.

"Well, then, I'd better get back to my illuminating," said Kenzie. "I'm already two hours behind."

The last newspaper sat on the shelf, soaked with age, the brown pages a solid reminder of a past that had long slipped through the cracks. Kenzie pulled it toward her, and read the headline:

Widow Leaves Town: Strange Happenings Continue

For weeks we, as the Editors of this paper, have received an unprecedented abundance of letters requesting news of the esteemed Dr. Davis Olbom and his assistant, Peggy Sands. This story has been, in our estimation, the most popular and intriguing story to the public imagination that we have ever run. Many have accused us of keeping you in suspense, but we want to assure the public that no news has been coming down the road from Stony Forks for the past few weeks. The good Doctor O. wished to conduct his experiments in relative isolation and without outside interference, and so he convinced Mr. Goody, the town's main trader, notary and default lawkeeper, to bar travel in or out except upon emergency and answerable only to himself. Even letters have been scarce, with many in Hillscroft visiting our office for news of relatives.

Citizens may now rest easy, as travel has resumed up and down the road from Hillscroft, and Dr. Olbom has concluded what has been described as a sublimely fascinating and eerie set of occurrences. The course of events is here set out for the reader as per a letter from the good Doctor which arrived yesterday evening.

The Prime Suspect Named

Although the widow Fenn at first professed innocence of any knowledge regarding the strange occurrences, Miss Sands at once saw through her. She sensed an evil presence, that of the Devil, around the Fenn cottage, and declared that the widow had once tried to buy a cow from Mr. Corkstone, which he had refused, the offered price being too low. She further declared that the malevolent and unwholesome goose that has been stalking the town for some time is none other than the widow Fenn's familiar, which contains the portion of her soul that she sold to the Devil. Astonishingly, when someone attempted to trap the goose, they heard a scuffle and a commotion at the Fenn cottage, and found the widow fled without a trace. She has not been seen nor heard from since, despite local dogs being sent after her whereabouts.

Evil Out of All Control

After the widow's sudden departure, a strange illness came upon Miss Sands, the likes of which she states that she has only known once before. She began speaking in tongues, and wandering when not watched. She was found in the widow's cottage, standing over a strange and open pit, which the good people of Stony Forks barred up at once, with strange trepidation. No one could any longer make any sense of her prophesying, so lost was she in the world of spirit. Strange figures scuttled around in the night time, and no longer would anyone venture out beyond sunset, even to follow the calls of nature. Residents of the town struggled to describe the figures, recognizing them as animals, but not any animal with which we are yet familiar. Some of them seemed to have human features distorted by some craft or other. Hails of stones buffeted the houses, their beginnings and endings happening at random. Pots were smashed by small bullets, the provenance of which is unclear. Doctor O. questioned the townspeople on this note, asking if perhaps they had run afoul of the Indians, but the townsfolk were unanimous in their reply that trade and sharing of the land had always been peaceable, and that they regarded the Iroquois as friends and necessary trade partners. The Indians themselves have not been seen in some weeks.

Stony Forks Dissolved

The good Doctor Olbom was unable to continue investigating the uncanny events at Stony Forks as of yesterday, October 30, 1826, when events took a startling turn. Mr. Corkstone, the center of all of the terrible events that have shook the nation thus far, awoke to find his entire herd of cattle, who had lived peaceably on the island for twenty years, drowned in the stagnant fork of the river which separates the two halves of Stony Forks. Despite the drownings being a recent occurrence, the cows, and the river, were in a state not fit to describe here, the water tainted for some time. A foul and sickening air was upon the place, which induced retching in many a citizen. Dr. Olbom himself was forced to admit defeat when he found Miss Sands lying in the putrid water, nearly drowned but for his expert ministrations. The poor woman had lost her senses and did not speak a word until that evening, and then only over and over the words "It got away from me." Doctor Olbom is praying that in time, she will regain her senses and return to a wholesome state of health.

Given the severity of these recent events, the good people of Stony Forks have moved to dissolve the settlement and move South at once. The Editors of this paper urge the good people of Hillscroft to remember Christian charity and to offer what shelter, food, and help they may to the poor unfortunates of Stony Forks, now without homes or land to call their own. The Reverend George Smith is offering up his church and his home for as many poor pilgrims as he can fit, with the admonishment that they should repent of their grievous sin and join him in daily prayer, and he is urging all faithful Hillscroftians to do the same. We are indeed in agreement with the Reverend once again, and glad to have healed the rift in our community. Pray for the safe passage of our Brothers and Sisters in Christ, and that this evil may wither and die in the light of the Lord's Prayer.

Kenzie finished the article and slipped into a little prayer of her own. Maria...it was time for Maria. She needed love. She needed sanity. She needed home.

She walked out of the library without preamble.

Ms. Winter called after her. "Are you almost done the papers? What did you find?

"Plenty," she said, "Read them yourself if you want to, but me, I need to process. Preferably with a fluffy blanket, some juice, and my best lady on the chat."

"The chat," she scoffed. "You say it like you're ninety years old."

"I feel ninety years old," said Kenzie. "Read the papers. I'm done for today."

DAY SLIPS INTO NIGHT AS GIRL SLIPS INTO DARKNESS

Kenzie took great pains with the set-up of her personal space this time, to keep it personal. She grabbed one of the high-backed chairs from the kitchen, the heavy ones that made a deep scraping sound on the ceramic tiles, and brought it into her room. Mum couldn't complain about that—there were four chairs and only three of them, and she would be in her room while she was using it. She wedged the chair under the door handle and tested the door a few times to make sure it was stuck solid.

She fished some tape out of her stationery box and taped a piece of printer paper to the door. She had debated herself about this one, but she didn't want to deal with Mum barging in simply because she wanted to claim ignorance of the hints in place. Kenzie wrote big letters, in ball point pen, every line scribbled over many times to make it as bold as possible:

PRIVATE TIME. VISITORS NOT WELCOME.

She felt like a stupid teenager having to do it, but knew that clear communication was the only way to keep Mum from exploiting loopholes and then claiming ignorance. She was sure that taping signs to the door would not help Mum's perception of her maturity any. Damned if you do, damned if you don't. She'd still err on the side of giving a warning. Then maybe, just maybe, Dad would see the evidence right in front of him as to why she lashed out.

With the door sign taped up and the chair in place, Kenzie put in her last safety measure. She pulled out her computer speakers, the portable ones with the extra-long cords, and sat them on the floor under the chair, inches from the door. She then put on her classical movie soundtrack collection, all brass and booming drums and bombast, and turned it up as far as it would go without harming her own ability to speak and be heard. With the speakers facing the door, she actually managed to crank them up pretty loud. And if Mum and Dad wanted to complain, there wasn't much for them to say. It was classical music, not death metal. And if they didn't want to hear the music at all, well, then they could stay away from her door.

She hadn't had time to text Maria earlier, but she knew her schedule. Tonight was a 'TV and dishes' kind of a night, usually. Dates tended to hover around the weekend, and she'd already had her radical knitting circle for the week.

The chat program rang once, twice, three times. By the time it got to five, Kenzie was hunched over, growing nearer to her screen, wanting to dive through. Should she text? She pulled her phone out of her pocket, ready to begin typing, when the calming blue of the night sky through huge rectangular windows popped up on-screen, with Maria sitting in front of it, wearing a towel, with water beaded up on her forehead. She smiled.

"Well, you've got timing. Why didn't you text first?"

Kenzie shrugged. "Sort of an impulse, because I missed you?"

Maria raised an eyebrow.

"How much you miss me? Because I only put on a towel thinking it could be anybody. I wasn't thinking you. My older relatives in Venezuela are actually getting really good at using chat programs." Maria tilted her head toward the screen. "What is with the music? I'd get it if you were trying to set the mood, but I don't think the Imperial March is really setting us up for lovin'."

"Yeah but it's loud," Kenzie said. "I'm trying to prevent that problem I told you about? You know, the one after our last chat, that weighs about two hundred pounds and wears running shoes all year?"

Maria's heavy brows made a line of disapproval.

"I can't believe she did that. You deserve to feel safe in your own home."

"This isn't home," Kenzie said quietly. "It's never going to be home. Perhaps more because my family is in it than if they weren't."

She angled the computer over so that Maria could see the chair barricade through the webcam.

Maria sighed. "They're exactly the same. And I told you they would be. Stop putting yourself through this. Either move out down to the town or come home. I'm worried about you. I remember the day you came home from the library and wanted to hide your books from me, because you thought I would make fun of you for reading inspirational and self-help books. I remember the look on your face when you admitted there were things you avoided enjoying, avoided knowing, because you feared being bullied for it. I see that suspicion in your eyes again. The one I thought we had gotten over. The look that you used to have when you thought I was out to get you or going to leave you for the next best thing. You're wearing down, Kenzie. Please, take care of yourself."

"I am. The best I know how. You're not going to like what happened to me today though. You'll probably tell me off like everyone else."

"Tell me," she said. "And if it has anything to do with your mother, I'll come down there. Don't think I won't."

"I would love it if you came down here. But no, nothing to do with either of them. Just me, a dinghy, a river, and a really strange goose…"

Kenzie told Maria the story, and she did indeed get scolded, all in good time. Then Maria filled her in on some happenings at work—one of the volunteers was ripping off pencils, and a lady had had a tantrum in the lobby when she'd arrived two days early for an event. Eventually, Maria made good on the promise to remove the towel. Kenzie double-checked the door and the chair before joining her, clothes off.

The ensuing session wasn't as good as going home and sleeping nestled into Maria's chest, but it did relieve a lot of tension. Whenever Kenzie talked to Maria, she could just feel the love pouring off her, even through a screen. She wanted so badly to kiss her again, to hold her. She would have to take a leave sometime soon and go back to the city and do nothing but gaze at Maria's radiance for the weekend until she stumbled home, glare-blind and dazzled.

They said their goodnights and sent many, many kisses back and forth. Kenzie even hugged the screen, which prompted a dirty joke from Maria. She lay down in bed and was most of the way to sleep before she realized that the chair was still up against the door. She'd let it stay there. She was too comfortable now, and if there was a fire, hey, she was sure someone would put up a sign to warn her. She chuckled at her own joke before sleep overtook her in earnest.

Kenzie woke up disoriented, standing, smelling dust and stone. She swayed in the manner of people half awake and yet somehow on their feet, her eyes not sure what they saw, baffled by the mostly-dark. She took a half-step forward and her foot struck a wall. The sound of ceramic tiles loose in their casings grumbled up from where her foot had struck. She put out her hands and they did not stretch out all the way, hitting dusty stone. Limestone by the feel: the material of graves, dusty and rough. Dirt came off on her hands. She was in a corner or a box, somewhere.

She looked up and saw dim, red light from the security system spilling through a square hole in the ceiling. It cast a strange, angular shape down part of the wall of the shaft, like a cubist curtain in a nightmare.

Heart now pounding, she ran her hands around the walls, grasping, searching for handholds that she knew weren't there. When she found nothing, she reached up above her head and jumped up, hoping to feel a rung, or a rope, some indication of how she had gotten down there that might also let her escape. She remembered the water...the stories of how it had flooded in unexpectedly and the rise she had seen in the river this morning, and her voice rose up into her throat unbidden, becoming a shrill scream.

A few screams and thrashes later, she realized what she should have known from previous observation. No one could hear her down here, and however she had gotten down the shaft, there were no handholds to take her back up. The stone was cold, cold as the early morning dew, as the breeze that blew in off the lake of an evening, when the day hadn't been quite able to decide if it was hot.

Kenzie hugged herself, shivering. Her feet were bare and she shuddered to think what might be under her toes right now. They had dug up the rusty remains of the simulacra from down here and who knew how many filthy old fragments were left?

A scuttling came from above, light and furtive. Hoping against hope that it was the door to the Folk Art wing coming open and that soon she would hear Dad walking down the stairs, she called out.

"Hello? Can anybody hear me? Is somebody there?"

Silence. The scuttling stopped. No footfalls. No door latches. No reply. Kenzie shivered again, afraid to look up at the red square of light. She gathered her courage and peeked at the top of the shaft, looking up so fast that her vision blurred a bit and all she got was an impression of a clear-cut square of light with nothing else in it.

The stone was getting wet…her feet were soaked in water. No, just cold. Just cold. Her feet were numb and it felt like a blanket of water, but when she moved them, no splashes echoed up the shaft, even when she kicked. No water. No water. Dry. No way for water to get in. And yet, how did water get into basements? It seeped, sometimes slowly and sometimes shockingly fast. Water was always seeping into places people thought it couldn't get to. Otherwise a multitude of hidden caves would not exist in the world. Water was insidious. It could get in if it wanted to, and not even prayer could stop it.

She thought she'd try prayer anyway. Perhaps the repetition would calm her. Muscles taut as a bow string and eyes shut, preferring darkness and disorientation to seeing what was above her right now, she started repeating the Lord's Prayer to herself, over and over, trying to draw meaning out of each phrase, really mean every word of it. In a way it was like counting sheep, but more protective. She also followed the tracery of the stones, logging their eccentricities and fixing them in her mind, correcting things for the stonemason of old so that the walls of the shaft would look more like a modern brick edifice than a country cellar. She had done that with ceiling tiles as a kid, whenever she was dumped off someplace to go to bed and couldn't sleep.

And then there were always those places. The ones where the lights went out and there was some shape. A shape you hadn't noticed when the lights were on. One that looked like a hunch-backed monster wearing a fedora, or a gravestone, or a noose hanging from the rafters. In those places, you needed to forget the details and keep your eyes screwed closed.

Something moved up there again. The same scuttling and a tapping, as if something were testing the floors, the glass, the drywall, with a hardened claw. This time, Kenzie remained silent, for she knew it was no friend of hers come to pull her out. In fact, it just might decide to descend on her, whatever it was.

Most people know what it is like to try to breathe silently, the terrible anticipation of curtailing your breaths while hiding in a shower hoping your friends don't find you, or while pulling a really delicious prank on someone who's about to walk through a doorway. Kenzie felt the terrible energy of anticipation: the lack of breath, the strange clarity and wooziness that comes from being frozen in place.

The scuttling would carry on, and then stop for a long time, and then come back as if from a long way away, growing in intensity. The movements, if she could discern them from this echoing hole in the ground, seemed exploratory, territorial, but almost aimless, with as much logic as a bug skittering around and around a light. After a long time hearing just one skittering, she heard others join in, starting and stopping seemingly at random, like a one-dimensional chorus of frogs on a hot summer night. The room filled with the chatter of hard points tapping on linoleum. Kenzie was covered in goosebumps, and could not say how long this had been, as her skin seemed to have gone into a default state of crawl.

My nervous system is going into safe mode, Kenzie thought. Much more of this and I'm gonna blue screen right out of this, and then who knows what will happen. She felt as if she were both there and not there, so surreal was this situation, this condition of her body, these noises all around.

Kenzie lost her balance, lost her focus a little with exhaustion and hyperventilation, and leaned on the wall. Just enough for her fingers to brush against the stone. Just enough for a sigh of dust to fall down behind her and for her to forget to regulate her breathing to keep the air from soughing in and out of her nose like a hacksaw. She let out a sigh and that was it. All of the scuttling silenced in an instant. All of the toys had gone back in their case. The dead returned to their graves at the approach of the living.

No, no, that wasn't right. They were watching. The scuttlers were watching now. They tensed around the hole; she could feel them sending a silent thought among themselves, like electricity through a rusty wire.

Something extended itself over the lip of the hole. It slid out, with the precision of a tool sliding out of a Swiss Army knife. Kenzie trembled and balled herself up, knowing that something was there but not wanting to see it, yet knowing that if she didn't see it, it could kill her or trap her or bite her or any other horrendous thing, and she would have no way of preparing for it.

Neck creaking with tension, chest vibrating with trembles and cold, so very cold, her skin turned to ice, she looked up.

A perfectly round, flat head stared down at her with empty eyes and a mouth frozen in a perpetual 'o.' The red light shone through the eyes, which contained nothing, and yet Kenzie knew they saw her. The head of this one had been made out of the hollows of a pulley mechanism of some kind, wood by the looks of it, and worn from use. Like many arresting images, the negative space held all the meaning; the eyes and mouth that were not there but were there all the same.

It stayed there. Kenzie could not move. It did not move. Behind the head was a webbing of some kind of mesh, old chicken wire maybe, arranged like a dog's raised hackles or perhaps a Renaissance collar. Its neck was far too long.

Kenzie imagined that terrible head detaching from the body and falling in with her. She stared and stared at it, for time without end, knowing that eventually she would lose the contest. She could not keep her eyes open longer than something with hollow eyes. Hours passed, in silence. None of the other things above moved again.

Kenzie awoke with the wall stones digging into one arm. One very cold arm; the rest of her was merely chilly. She leaned away from the wall, her arm slowly tingling its way back to life, and looked above. Pale dawn light filtered down through the hole, with only a pink trace of the security lighting from the night before.

The night before.

She checked around her frantically, terrified that she would find a heap of simulacra in the bottom of this pit with her. Nothing kept her company. She had fallen asleep against her will and they had left. She ran her hands up and down her arms, checking for injuries, then her legs. She was just as eerily whole as she had been when she woke up down here. If they had come down and explored her, nothing had changed—on the outside, at least. She pictured that grotesque thing with the hollow eyes ticking its way down the shaft, exploring her with its needle-like hands, and the shivers started up again. She wanted to throw up. But she did not want to throw up in this enclosed space. Besides, she would be the one figuring out how to get the puke out of the shaft. Can't have that smell wafting all over the Folk Art wing.

She gave a little gallows chuckle, half cough. Her voice. She could feel that her throat was rough from screaming and from the dust. She would save her energy until she heard movement. Her tummy rumbled. *Can anybody suspend me down some breakfast? Some bacon, eggs, and toast would be great, thanks. No canned peaches. My hands and arms are in no condition to be rubbing my face. That would just make it worse. Sticky peach juice and crypt dust. Mmmmmm.* More appetizing thoughts for a banner night. Breakfast of reverse champions. The ones that won the loser Olympics.

The light pouring into the mouth of the shaft intensified. Through the wall-sized windows in the gallery at the top of the shaft, Kenzie could hear traces of far-away birdsong. Somewhere nearby, a cardinal was getting very cheeky with its rival. A red-winged blackbird was staking out its territory and some little crumb scavengers, sparrows most likely but could be chickadees, peeped and cackled and jostled about. The light made things feel more normal, casting a bedsheet over the bizarre things she had seen last night. She sighed, finally relaxing a little. Relaxing made her whole body feel heavy. She just wanted to sleep again. She could sleep at the hospital.

All the world in this shaft was grey. The worst part in the light of day was that there was nothing to do. Hopefully Dad had a ladder long enough to reach down and get her out. She hadn't seen one in the utility room. He would probably have to call the fire department. She flashed back to an old episode of the Simpsons where Bart had pretended to fall down a well and remembered the end scene, where they had just hammered a sign into place saying 'CAUTION WELL.' That sounded about right for this fire department. Only this time, for lack of a ladder, they'd just make a sign saying, 'New Exhibit—Crazy Woman in Well.' Marvel at the way she lowers people's expectations! Be astonished at her rate of failure, so high that she was able to fall into a fifty-foot shaft while asleep and not be injured! Fans of famous losers the world over will not want to miss this!

Kenzie had even started laying out the posters and picking the fonts in her mind when she heard a sliding, dragging sound. For a moment she froze again, thinking that perhaps the creatures had invaded and now decided that they would take over. But when she heard footsteps, she knew the time had come. She screamed for help, as loud as she could.

"Dad!"

"Kenzie?" She heard his voice far off, and knew he must be at the bottom of the stairs. "Kenzie, where are you? Your room was barricaded but you weren't answering."

Kenzie felt all of the water in her body concentrate in her bladder when she heard those words. Her door had still been barricaded. She could not have replaced the chair if she had gone out that way. She had to go to the bathroom so bad...what was she going to do if the fire department couldn't get here for a long time? And thinking about the door to her room was making it worse.

"Dad, help! I'm down in the shaft! Call the fire department!"

Dad's face appeared over the lip of the shaft, his hair tousled, his normally 'thoughtful' forehead lined with even more deep creases. He swayed back and forth, then disappeared. She heard his footsteps and pictured him walking away from the hole and back toward it, circling. His face reappeared again.

"Good God. How did you get down there?"

"I don't know. I woke up down here. I don't think I'm hurt but I don't know how I got here."

"Hold on, Kenzie, I'm calling the authorities." He zoomed away from her line of sight, and then back in again, ducking back over the hole.

"You're not too cold, are you? Should we get blankets first?"

"I wore fleece. Get the ladders on their way. I have to pee!"

She heard his voice echoing back over his shoulder from somewhere in the atrium. "Well, don't do it in there! Lord only knows how we'd get the smell out of the Folk Art wing."

She couldn't fault him this time. She'd thought it herself.

At least there were noises now. She occupied herself playing noise-o-mancy, listening to the various footsteps and voices, trying to picture in her mind where they were, how they were standing, their expressions.

Mum came down and the sound of her voice when she called down echoed off the stones and rang in Kenzie's ears. Kenzie had to ask her to tone it down, which she did, for thirty seconds or so. She proposed nineteen different immediate solutions, none of which would work, and then set to work on the problem of how Kenzie had gotten down into the shaft, the topic that Kenzie had known she would turn to because a) there was no real way to know and therefore an answer must be worried out somehow, and b) it was the topic that Kenzie least wanted to discuss, especially while still down in the shaft.

The sound of a chair being pulled across the floor echoed down to her. Mum had grabbed the gallery volunteer's chair that sat between two of the large landscapes and pulled it up to the lip of the hole. She peered down at Kenzie, as if she were a problem to be solved, clearly fascinated and using the problem to stave off her panic.

"Can you remember anything from before you woke up down there?"

"I told you, no," said Kenzie, crossing her arms.

"Nothing? Not even a single little tidbit?"

"No," said Kenzie. "I don't suppose there is anything more useful that you could be doing right about now?"

"I am doing something useful. I am keeping you company. You know how you can work yourself up if you're left to your own devices."

"I like my own devices. And that hasn't been true for a long time."

"Oh Kenzie, just humour me. What else have you got to do?"

"Yeah, exactly," Kenzie said, frowning and staring at the wall. She could just choose to not answer.

"Do you know why the door isn't opening?"

"Yeah, I barricaded it. Then I forgot to take down the chair when I went to sleep."

"Well, it serves you right for locking the door. That's not safe, you know. Families should never have locked doors."

"Locked doors prevent killing sprees," said Kenzie under her breath.

"What?" said Mum. "Are you all right? Are you going to faint?"

"I said that makes no sense!" Kenzie yelled, making the walls ring and regretting the volume instantly. "If you're going to play Sherlock, at least use logic once in a while."

"I'll figure it out, just you wait," said Mum, that annoying tone in her voice like she was inspired by Kenzie's misfortune, like it was bringing the zest back to her life. "And you're going to help me. But later...I think I hear the fire brigade."

"Did they bring signs?" Kenzie called, weary to her very bones.

"What?"

"Nothing."

The sound of several booted sets of feet moving across the linoleum drifted down to her, along with the deep voices of strong men. Maybe the day wouldn't totally be wasted. Maybe one of the firefighters would think it necessary to come down and carry her. She'd always had a thing for firefighters and paramedics. For some reason, the people hiring those guys always seemed to pick the radiantly cute ones. She understood the abs. But you didn't have to be a looker or twenty-five to have abs. And yet, whenever somebody had needed a paramedic, the ones that showed up should have had their hair blowing in the wind on the front of a cheesy romance novel. The right look from one of those guys and she'd put fifty bucks in the boot at fundraisers.

So she was dirty and in her pyjamas. That could all work out. She had seen worse. And she had managed not to pee anywhere. Not the best circumstances, but maybe she could make do. Maybe her ankles were feeling a little weak, yeah.

The booted feet clomped to the edge of the shaft, sending down a little shower of dust. Kenzie dodged, but a little dust hit her face, causing her to shut her eyes. The grit burned in her eyes. She breathed in a hank of spiderwebby stuff and coughed, reaching for a piece of clothing that wasn't filthy, because her hands were filthy and she needed to wipe her eyes. She squinted down at her shirt until she spotted a respectable-looking patch of clean pink pyjama top amid the grey pseudo-colour of dust-covered fleece.

As she bent to wipe her eyes, she spied a familiar pattern on the stone.

"Canooie," she said, almost a whisper.

"Hey, are you all right down there?" came a familiar voice—and not familiar in the way that random hunky guy number six was sometimes familiar, you know, because you'd seen fifty of him on TV.

Kenzie felt another wave of surrealism wash over her, as it had when she had first become trapped in that shaft, as she stopped herself on the verge of saying, "Wait a moment, I'm not quite ready to come up yet. I've just seen something and I want to get a closer look."

There, drawn on the stone in what looked like white chalk, was a perfectly rendered drawing of Canooie, the heroic duck from her final film project at Hallidan College. She must have drawn it, but even she had never drawn it that well. She wanted to kneel down and marvel at it. Canooie was exactly as she had pictured him in her head, not the broken and warped way he had come out every time she had tried to put pencil to paper. Somehow, she had finally drawn him last night while trapped in the shaft.

She squinted back up into the light, saying nothing. Everyone was obscured by shadow now, as the outside light had shifted and so had the light within her. Somehow, down in this cave that wanted to kill the child in her, dry the life from her, drown her in mysterious rising water, her inner pilot light had re-lit. Since it was nothing she could explain to anyone else, she would take the ladder and keep silent. She would need silence to protect the small and delicate flame, anyway.

NO SIGNS

The light shifted again, and the face that came into view smiled the familiar smile of someone who had just found a friend in a pinch.

"Kenzie," said Ant, now wearing the white shirt and suspenders of a fireman. "We keep meeting in the most interesting ways. If we ever run into each other in the produce section at Wal-Mart now, I'll be shocked as shit." He popped a wide grin with well-defined corners that led to well-defined dimples. Still wore the earrings, though. Good. A guy could be too clean. Or maybe it was just the guys in the middle that were boring, because Captain America was pretty hot rocking that whole Boy Scout routine.

Kenzie shrugged. What did one say to that? "It's gross down here. I'd like to get out, if you don't mind."

Ant motioned to someone beyond the lip of the shaft, waving them over. He lay on the ground, balancing on an elbow. His posture, and his attention, felt a little bit like a teasing boy on the playground, looking for a chance to get at her pigtails. Cheeky. She liked cheeky. She remembered how gross and smelly she probably was, but at least she had worn fleece and not cotton so she wouldn't be showing her nipples off. That was a bit fast, even given her current thoughts.

"We see a lot of falls around here with all the drunk hikers and kids trying to climb the cliffs. You're really lucky you didn't break anything."

Here came the crazy.

"I don't think I fell," she said. "I just kind of woke up in here. My room is still locked, apparently. It only locks from the inside."

Ant screwed up his face like a little kid or a drunk had just told him the capital of Tanzania was the moon. A mixture of patronizing good humour and sheer what the fuck. He snorted.

"You fell in there. We just don't know how because you were sleepwalking, I bet. Here's the ladder." He slid backwards, disappearing from the lip of the hole. "Come and debate me up here."

The ladder inched down into the hole, slowly crushing Kenzie's space until she had to back into a corner to allow them to angle it in. Even then, it poked her in the shoulder, and it was hard, and weighed about forty pounds, and had a corrugated plastic nubbin on the end of it to make it hold to the ground. She climbed on at an awkward angle, but there were guys up at the top holding it steady so she managed to get some momentum going, one shaky bare foot after the other. The rungs felt funny too on her bare feet, ridged for her discomfort. The ladder sagged a little as she crossed the midpoint because they had rolled it out all the way and there was no overlap to keep it rigid. She continued, pretending it was one of those dodgy rope bridges at a water park.

Finally, she emerged again into the world of the living, breathing a deep breath as though she had just come from under the sea rather than from a dry-as-dust crypt for creepy dolls. She peered back over the lip, trying to find Canooie again down there, on the wall. But it was too far, and too dark, and her eyes had already adjusted to the morning light.

A strong arm wrapped around her shoulders, pulling her away from the edge of the hole and into a hug.

"Now that's enough of that," Ant said. "Stay away from there from now on. We'll have it filled in and sealed by the end of the month. As soon as we can budget for the materials."

Kenzie felt tears well up in her eyes, unbidden.

"Okay," she said, knowing there was nothing else she could say.

"We should take her to the hospital," said Ant over her head. "It beats waiting for the ambulance. They'll be another half hour at least."

Kenzie pulled back a little and smiled up at Ant.

"Don't they need you somewhere else? I mean, I know Lassie came and told you Kenzie was stuck down a well, but surely there's a kid out there playing with matches, or a hat-wearing bear that needs help with his marketing campaign. I mean, we're an hour from Algonquin. There's got to be at least one hat-wearing bear."

"You need sleep," said Ant. "But no, we're the volunteer auxiliary. We mostly go places with ladders. When we go places. So we can pretty much see this through if you need an escort."

"I'd feel better if we did," said Mum, hovering anxiously behind Ant.

"You two go," said Dad. "Someone has to stay and open the museum, and we're understaffed today as it is."

Oh boy, hours and hours of Mum's fussing and meddling, in a hospital waiting room, no less. Kenzie would keep Ant with them as long as possible just to keep someone between them.

By the time she returned to the office, the chipper light of early morning had become the brassy, dying light of afternoon fading into evening. The museum had about three hours of operations left, and she knew she should probably suit up and do what she could for the rest of the day, but the hospital had been exhausting. If she had been alone, it would have merely been boring, nerve-wracking, a little wearying, but ultimately a motivator to get back to the Log Palace and get on with her work. Now that the scanning was done, the reading room needed a refresh, and she needed to sit down on her own and start strategizing inter-facility co-operations and a social media program for the next year or so. She needed to figure out what meetings to have, and with whom, and schedule those. It was going to be a lot of desk work, but mostly creative desk work, and she liked the excuse to get creative even as it made her a little (a lot) nervous.

Today, though. After a night in that godforsaken pit she'd spent most of the day sitting in a waiting room with bad lighting, listening to feverish toddlers howling for caramels. Her mother, worse than the toddlers, had blathered on at a constant rate, afraid of the silence, punctuating long soliloquies about nothing with the most pointed questions she could devise regarding how Kenzie had got in the hole, how she had slept, what she had eaten, what had happened down there, all of which Kenzie refused to answer beyond her first 'I don't know,' her anger rising with every new volley.

Ant had sat on the other side of her, patiently nodding along with Mum, but his face when she walked away to get a chocolate bar or a can of pop said, 'you live with this all the time?' Kenzie sat like a conduit between them, the awkward electricity of wanting to make something happen with Ant but wanting her mother not to be there, or at least not be so bloody embarrassing all the time, making her feel much like young boys must feel when they pop a boner and still have to be 'it' in dodgeball.

Now Kenzie opened her phone again, to the contacts. There it was, still saved.

Ant had held out his hand for her phone while Mum was in the washroom and put it in there.

"You actually want to hear from me again?" she said.

"You're my boss. Think I could avoid you if I tried? Besides, I know you've got the Internet and all, but you seem like you could use a break from that." He nodded toward the bathroom. "In meatspace. How the hell do you do it? How does *she* do it? I don't think I saw her take a breath in twenty minutes."

Kenzie raised her eyebrows and shook her head.

"She's...unique."

"Text me later today and let me know how you're doing. It's not every day that an acquaintance of high esteem gets teleported into a gross old shaft."

Kenzie smiled.

"Ah, prurient interest. Now I get it. Inquiring minds want to know. How does Kenzie, the amazing teleporting curator, fare today? Rumour has it she has used her newfound notoriety to start a parasailing business. Just another strange tale from this crazy old world, folks."

"No," said Ant, "I just have a burning curiosity to see what you're like when you're not in a totally bizarre situation. I'm thinking it'll be this delicious fish-out-of-water thing, but the jury's out until it actually happens. So, what do you say? Wanna shock the shit out of me and grab a coffee sometime? I know a great little place down here in Hillscroft that bakes all their own stuff. Best date squares in town."

"*Date* squares, eh? I can see you've used this on a few other ladies."

"Is that a problem?" he said with a grin. "Some might say that makes me more exciting. Everybody loves a bad boy."

"If you find me having a girlfriend exciting—"

"I might," he said with a lascivious eyebrow wiggle that would have been unseemly on anyone else.

"Then we might just be square for date squares," she said, grinning, the excitement bubbling up in her like carbonation, swirling through her like milk in coffee. "The only problem is, now I kind of want those date squares.

That weird wrap Mum got from the cafeteria just isn't sitting right. I need some sweets to wash it down."

"Well, if it's sweets you want, I know for a fact they have this dodgy chocolate pudding in the cafeteria, too."

Kenzie made a face and they both laughed. Mum emerged from the washroom and asked what was up. Kenzie made up a story that some kid had almost pulled his mom over in front of the gift shop trying to get to the stuffed animals.

Back at the museum, Kenzie found Dad waiting for her at the information desk, his favourite haunt when he was directing the volunteers and watching traffic flow. The piece of masking tape on her arm that held on the little cotton ball itched and she pulled it off. It left a pair of square welts with a bright red dot in the middle, like a really bad version of the Canadian flag.

Well, now Ant and I match, sort of, she thought. She leaned in a number of different directions, trying to find a waste basket, until Dad held one up. She tossed the ball of tape like a basketball player doing a lay-up and it pinged in on the first try. The success felt good after the fail day she'd had, all the setbacks. It made her smile.

Dad did not smile. His skin looked overly wrinkled and sallow, the way it had when he had needed his heart operation but not known it.

"We've got a board meeting at the end of this week," he said, like someone who had just gotten out of bed, or perhaps needed to go back there. "What did the doctor say? Will you be well enough to make a good showing there? We have to start discussing strategy and I know you haven't gotten there yet, between the incident with the river and now this. Better to postpone the meeting a week than to embarrass ourselves."

Kenzie held her arms out.

"The doctors gave me a clean bill of health. They even took blood, although I'm not sure what blood has to do with any of it. No broken bones, no cuts, no scrapes. I was just really dirty and tired. I'll be up and running tomorrow, and I'd like to take the car into town and return the newspapers to the Hillscroft library. It will be a great start to our outreach with other facilities, and we can discuss what events they might be interested in co-running. I can also pick their brains on networking and on upcoming government funding initiatives."

"Okay," said Dad, "it might be a good excuse to get out of the house, as well. You probably need that after everything that's happened. You should go upstairs and get some rest. The firefighters that stayed behind were kind enough to get your bedroom door back open. The chair got busted, but it's nothing a couple of screws and some glue can't fix. I expect you will not barricade yourself in like that again. We don't have the budget for more doors, or for another curator, for that matter."

Kenzie felt a wave of weariness run through her. So much for that solution.

"How am I going to deal with Mum snooping, then?"

"I'll keep an eye on her," he said, as if a long argument had just ended. "Come here, I want to see you right here."

Kenzie moved around the desk, and he got up and gave her a tight hug. She hugged him back, tears standing in her eyes.

"I'm sorry, Dad."

"I know," he said. "I had to tell the volunteers the truth, and it will get back to the board. We'll weather this but please, Kenzie, from now on, be careful. Both around the museum and with your mental health. I want success for you, and for all of us. You know how much this place means to me."

Kenzie felt stories rising up in her that wanted to escape. She wanted to tell Dad about her suspicions about the water, and the goose, and the shaft, and the horrible things that had happened to the tiny hamlet of Stony Forks on this site so long ago. She wished she could tell him and be believed. She wished that he would listen. But she had heard his reactions to the stories before. He wanted all traces of the witch legend buried, even the truthful parts.

I was transported into that shaft, she wanted to say, by something that has been stalking me. Something that feels my weakness. Something that revels in my aloneness. There is something in the water. I don't know what it is or what it wants, but it thinks. And the simulacra do its bidding, those evil little things that I bet even burying would not stop. Maybe pouring cement over them would stop them, or fire. I think we are all in danger. No, I feel it, and my feelings are right more often than you think, Dad. I may not have a brain that works in a popular, socially-sanctioned way, but it works. By God, it works.

What she said was, "I know, Dad. I will get some rest and be as good as new in the morning. You'll see. Can't argue with the doctor."

"That you can't," said Dad. She knew he watched her go, and she could see the worried expression on his face without even looking back. Time to close the door, lie down on the bed, and forget.

As soon as her head hit the pillow, she was back home in the shaft. She'd had the foresight to bring a piece of chalk with her this time, though. She wondered where she got chalk, but at the same time knew that this visit was not like the last time. She would not need a ladder to get in or out because now that she had been down there, she could visit anytime. It was burned in her mind, in the way that surroundings often burn into the minds of the spatially and visually inclined. She had done this before, constructed whole buildings she had once known inside of her head, and walked around them, warped them in plausibly implausible ways, a playground for her mind and an architectural carapace for her feelings.

159

As her eyelids fluttered, she drew on that wall, masterpieces that no one would ever see unless they climbed down the godforsaken hole with her. She sketched, she shaded, she made things and creatures and clothing that in real life would make her a millionaire. The cave paintings at Lascaux had been reborn for a new generation, the primal expression of one girl's humanity amidst the cacophony of digital media and the narcissism of modern life that accompanied it; the expression of a core human being, a soul, in a world whose center had disappeared, where most people's centers had disappeared. She felt meaning again. She felt connection again. It would all dissipate into a depressive haze when she woke up, she knew, and she would find herself scarfing down tasteless canned peaches and moving around this museum, and life, as if pulled along on a track. Her life was *Pirates of the Caribbean*, not the story behind the ride but the ride itself, robots doing the same thing, over and over and over, and herself in the car being pulled along, the expectation being that she was entertained.

But tomorrow she would do something to leave the ride. She would wake up, and somehow remember this, even if she did not remember it. Tomorrow was the first new day.

OFF THE METAL TRACK

Kenzie pulled out onto the road, feeling a thrill rush through her as she skirted the cliff's edge and drove on down the sloping, curving road by the river toward Hillscroft. The sun was up, almost at high noon, and a beautiful breeze made the trees sway, the poplars turning their leaves over and over in the wind like the hands of a graceful dancer. Sun glinted off the river beside her and, although she could not stare the way a passenger could stare from the backseat, she felt the presence of the twinkling light and it lifted her mood.

As she often did when she visited a place and nature sung to her, she wondered what it must have looked like when the first settlers came here, before modern man had insisted on a straight, flat path carved out with dynamite and diggers, and the larger animals had been chased into the deep woods. She wondered what it would have been like for the people of Stony Forks, travelling this great and powerful wilderness, through blocks of sandstone so large and heavy, broken by tree roots and slowly sliding downhill over hundreds of years. Someone had told her once, on a hike, that great blocks of stone travelled over time and she had always found it fascinating, always wondered where they were going in such a hurry. Well, a hurry for stones.

In this place, even seemingly dead rocks had life, covered in moss, filled with bugs and small animals, trees coming along for the adventure. It was like a very slow fantasy epic that humans could never understand. The quest of the stone and the tree and the beetle...very experimental. They'd eat that up with the new lit-snob fantasy genre being so in vogue. She thought perhaps she would write that book on a lark, and make it as strange and inaccessible as possible, and watch people trying to decipher it. She'd invent a whole new strain of scholarship and become world famous. There it was. She smirked and gave a chuckle. If only it were that easy.

Another car passed her, piled high with camping gear and bikes. She smiled again, thinking about the fun they were going to have on this sunny day, putting up their tent and exploring this beautiful wilderness.

Perhaps, though, the part of the wilderness that inspired awe in her would have been the very thing that inspired terror in the Stony Forks settlers. She imagined being part of a group having left their homes and land, unsure of their future and now travelling in the claws of nature, a force so large and daunting in those days before tarmac and helicopters and antibiotics that even the rocks seemed to live and to overshadow humans like a fern overshadowing a small dandelion. The abundance of life and the scale of it all must have filled them with more terror, for if the river could rise up and drown a whole herd of cattle, just pull them right in, and if a goose could be a tool of the devil that had stolen a woman's soul, what then could the trees do? The rocks? The moss?

The nightmares on the trail, the sense of mistrust, must have been overwhelming. The land that had welcomed them, sustained them, given them a chance to reverse their fortunes after being born poor in overcrowded Europe had turned on them, and not just in the way of a drought or a frost or even a normal flood. The water had risen up to annihilate them.

Or, something in the water has risen up. A spirit, a monster, a creature no one had yet discovered. Something had made the water misbehave.

Kenzie whistled a little to the radio to bring her focus back to her driving. Mum had been persuaded to let her take the car and not come along, but she had not been happy about it. Kenzie had left the apartment to Mum wringing her hands with worry, a literal caricature of a fretful mother, calling out safety tips even once she had shut the door. Dad had gone to bat for her. She would not let Dad down by bringing the car back with a door dent or worse, a crumpled bumper. She focused back on the road, the sunlight, the signs along the way. No car, no escape. No escape, no dates with Ant. And she hoped there would be more after this one, the way things were going.

They had been texting for the past few days, just chatting back and forth about work and life and things on the Internet. Ant loved tattoos and Kenzie loved art, so they sent a few photos back and forth of lovely body art. They liked some of the same bands and a lot of the same movies. He had sent her a shirtless pic yesterday, and she had saved it. She wondered if the rest of him looked as good. Hell, she wondered if the rest of him *felt* good, too. Another little thrill ran through her.

She would meet up with him while they thought she was at the library. They could call the library too, and they would say she had been there. The work would get done. But hopefully, she would also get done. She wondered what turned her on more, that she was doing something her parents would hate or that she was doing it on the clock. She'd put in overtime tonight to make up for it. What else did she have to do? She lived at work, after all.

First stop? Praiseville. She had been waiting for this day since she had found those newspapers with Ms. Winter. Ms. Winter should really have come, but there was nobody to watch the library today with the short-staffing situation, and Kenzie would have advised against it anyway, whatever the staffing level. She wanted this date too much, and bringing the newspapers was the only way to get her hands on the car and cover her tracks.

Kenzie eased the car down a little bumpy hill, past the 'Welcome to Hillscroft' sign that marked the road's descent into a little bowl-shaped valley. The bulk of the town sat in that valley, with some of it stretching out to the left of the road, out to the banks of a small lake formed by a dam in the river. She had checked the library's location on her phone but had not turned on navigation. She wondered why she had decided to wing it, considering she had been to the town all of once and had never visited the library. Oh well, she would head in the right direction and stop if she got lost.

Three wrong turns later, including a stop at a convenience store where Kenzie was convinced the cashier couldn't tell left from right, she finally pulled into the ample, empty parking lot. A few seniors and stay-at-home moms ambled around the parking lot and in the foyer, but on a weekday during the school year she could probably shoot a cannon off through most of the building. This time of day, this time of week, the library was for people without jobs and for other librarians. Time for meetings, and workshops, and frantic shelving and re-displaying of all the materials they didn't have time to deal with on evenings and weekends. Also time to browse for new and interesting titles, a fun spelunking expedition if ever there was one. Kenzie looked forward to doing that, if ever the Log Palace's archives budget was increased.

Kenzie got out of the car, pausing to let the wobbly 'still driving' sensation clear out of her legs. The roundabout route to the library had left her pretty frustrated (especially that interlude with the hand-signals at the convenience store) but she had only herself to blame for that, and the sun was shining so brightly now, with only small puffy clouds floating through a sky that couldn't hope to cover up its gaudiness. Kenzie felt like the sun today, out there, shining, being herself and doing her own things and screw what anyone else thought about propriety. If she worried forever about propriety, she would lose all of the pleasure in her life, and who did that serve? No one. She was going to live in full colour, grab life and squeeze it for all it was worth.

The Hillscroft Public Library was a square, grey-on-grey, ultra-modern cube with large windows running in a stripe around the center, connected to a slightly shorter grey-on-grey, ultra-modern cube that was mostly windows and a significant number of sliding doors. It looked a lot like the newer libraries in major cities to the south, rather than the slowly crumbling, 1970s brutalist brick things that sat in most smaller and worse-funded towns, waiting for their ugly promenades and awnings to fall in. Dad had told her that Hillscroft consistently won Ontario's 'Best Arts Town' designation, and a lot of funding flowed their way for various community projects each time they won. In 2005, it had been the library.

A chunky woman pushing middle age, wearing a floral shirt and a complicated bun, sat behind a librarian's desk. She tapped away very slowly at something on her computer, making Kenzie wonder how someone who works with the written word had never learned how to touch-type. Oh well. Kenzie stopped at the desk. The woman stared at her computer, fingers tap-tap-tapping in a leisurely manner.

Kenzie placed the box on the desk. The woman blinked, and said, "Yes? Can I help you?"

"Hi, I'm Kenzie Glaston? The curator of Ettenby's Log Palace? We talked on the phone, I think."

"Oh no, I never talked to you. That was Linda." Her gaze slipped back to her screen for a long moment before returning wearily to Kenzie.

"Okay, is Linda here? She said to come down today. There is some information on these materials that I wanted to give her."

"You can wait over there. I don't know when she'll be back. Maybe an hour," said the assistant. She pointed to an uncomfortable-looking square chair at a pencil-grooved wooden table. As Kenzie stalked over to the chair, she generated evil nicknames for the assistant, Chunky McFacebook chief among them.

She had just released her jaw for perhaps the nineteenth time, to keep herself from grinding her teeth, when Linda walked in. Kenzie recognized her by her name badge, her crisp appearance, and the fact that all of the reference patrons today seemed to be over seventy-five, with mobility issues. Linda was much as she had pictured her on the phone: a heavyset, dark-skinned woman with well-coiffed black hair, middle aged, wearing a stylish, one-piece mod dress.

Kenzie stood up, schooling herself into a fresh smile and hiding any trace of her earlier frustration with the assistant. At least she hoped she did.

"Linda? Hi, it's Kenzie, from the Log Palace Museum."

Linda smiled. "Kenzie, yes," she said, coming over and shaking hands. "It is so good to finally meet you. Please, come into my office with the materials. I'm sure we have a lot to discuss."

Linda's office reminded Kenzie of a bank office, with glass panels covering the front, cinder block walls at back, and long louver blinds to make privacy when needed. Right now, the blinds were half-open, which was probably how they stayed most of the time. No sense in employing a head librarian if no one ever knows if she's in or she's out. Kenzie sat down in the visitor's chair, also very bank-like, and put the box on the desk as she did.

Linda opened the lid.

"May I?" she asked, before scooping the papers out.

"They belong to you now," said Kenzie. "For their age, they are in remarkable condition. They don't seem fragile at all. I can't think that too many people have handled them over the years."

Linda removed the papers from the box with great care, nonetheless.

"Wow. Most of the ones we still have on file of this age are between sheets of plexi, or permanently retired from the public collection," she said. "You say these were found in a crawl space at the mansion?"

Kenzie nodded. "We found them with a lot of other papers that we're in the process of scanning, and some weird folk art dolls that we've got on display now. It seems as though Ettenby's heirs just left or packed away anything they thought was worthless or eccentric. Dad had to barter the art back from a number of different collections after it had been sold numerous times."

Linda nodded. She seemed like a thoughtful woman, and practical.

"So, you've had the first look at them. What's in them? We can always use fodder for a new newspaper article, get some butts in the seats. And you know the *Gazetteer* is going to want to cover their own history."

Now it was time to go in for the kill. Here was where people would start flocking to Ettenby's Log Palace (and hopefully the library). She could see the Halloween tie-ins right now, between the dolls and the poltergeists. People would be swarming up here within a few years.

"I'm sure they will," Kenzie said, "You might want to start planning your media strategy for the fall now. These papers contain evidence that the Hillscroft witch legend was actually real."

"What?" Linda's face grew wary. She picked up the first paper and studied it, as if looking for a hoax. "You're kidding me. Why would the *Gazetteer* cover something like that?"

"I'm assuming because something was happening," said Kenzie. "And apparently it happened at Stony Forks, the hamlet that used to be on the Log Palace's property. Check the stories. Local residents reported poltergeist activity and it drew the attention of a spiritualist and his assistant. They travelled all the way from England to come and see it, and then they couldn't solve the mystery. It's *still* a mystery. Just think how much tourism this could bring in per year."

Linda leafed through the rest of the newspapers, stopping once or twice to skim the headlines. She was silent for a moment, then raised her upper lip. "No offense, but this library doesn't have a security budget that's worth much. I'm thinking of how many crazies this will bring in per year when people find out. We're lucky already that we're a small town and don't have homeless guys peeing in the stacks. We don't have the staff to deal with that. I mean, the building is nice and all, but that was one-time government money. We still have a small-town budget and we have to roll with that." She nodded at the stack of newspapers. "I honestly think these papers would be safer with the Log Palace. We'll be more than happy to have the digital files in the system, though. Not a lot the crackpots can do on a locked computer."

Kenzie tilted her head a little. Why couldn't one day go as planned in this job?

"So, I understand that your budget may not cover security, if security is needed. I'm truly sorry to hear that. But, as you may know, I'm not from around here, and from my point of view it seems like I've been hearing a lot of hype about this witch legend and the people who believe in it. People seem really freaked out in a way that I'm not quite getting. I mean, Salem, Massachusetts makes a pretty penny every year off of the witch legend, as do several other small towns in the States. Down there it seems like the Wiccans and the town officials get along pretty well and work together to bring in a lot of tourism. They get to educate about a dark time in history and teach people not to hate minority religions. What's wrong with that?"

Linda folded her hands in front of her.

"Nothing at all. Trust me, Kenzie, I'm as enlightened as the next person, but these people that talk about the witch, that want proof of her existence, they're not Wiccans. We don't talk about it much around here, because we like winning our awards and the wealthy residents that the awards attract, but there's an underbelly to this town. We get a lot of people fleeing the city because they can go out into the woods and do whatever they want and there's not enough police presence to catch them. And even if there were, they couldn't be patrolling every square meter of undeveloped forest. There's a reason so many people go missing up north and it's because forest like this swallows a lot of back-door doings. You've got your druggies, your radical hippies, and a lot of people that just don't fit in down south. Most of them are harmless, but a significant portion of them are suspicious, at the very least. You don't go wandering the woods in these parts unless you've got a buddy. Preferably a buddy, a dog, and a gun."

"I see," Kenzie said, her unease growing as she remembered the party she had seen across the river. She wondered if the papers would be safe at the Log Palace either, once word got out. Especially since whatever lurked around the building did not seem to have any particular respect for walls or the regular laws of physics.

"We do have a more secure facility at the Log Palace. If you think it best for us to keep them, we can do so for the time being, but let's get it on record that I consider this a loan. It's your property, and we are protecting it as a favour to you. I also understand your concerns about the local community, but we are in the process of dealing with any trespassing on the property, and hopefully whatever investigation we get going will trickle down to more safety in the community as the bad eggs get rounded up. I took some pictures of vandalism on our property the other day and submitted them for investigation. If there's one thing I know about small-town cops, it's that they're very convincing when asking troubled folks to leave town."

Kenzie heard Linda let out a sigh from her nostrils that perhaps she had not been conscious of, either in holding it in or letting it out. "Kenzie, I appreciate this, and I know that this is only the beginning of a long and happy collaboration with the Log Palace on many projects."

"One last question," said Kenzie. "Will the library be okay with the Log Palace seeking publicity for the papers? I think it would dovetail nicely with some of our other folk art collections, and we are thinking of rebuilding the ruins across the river as a historical village display. If you did not want to be mentioned as collaborator, we could leave the library out of it entirely."

Linda contemplated for a moment, mouth on fist. "I think that will be okay, as long as we're not mentioned. Be careful, though. I mean it. This community has worked long and hard to get that museum off the ground and we would be devastated to see it go down in flames because someone on the slow boat to crazy-town got too interested in the legends."

"I assure you that I have nothing but the museum's best interests in mind and, if we do decide to go in this direction, it will be approached from an academic and upscale standpoint. The way we would go about it, I doubt the crackpots will even hear about it, unless they have season passes or a PhD."

Linda laughed at this, and Kenzie was glad of the lowering tension in the room. First dance, complete. Now on to many more with the other museums, galleries, and universities.

"Thank you so much for coming in today, Kenzie, and I'm sorry to have wasted your time, really I am," said Linda, standing up and putting the newspapers back in the box.

"It's never a waste of time to come and catch up with a valued partner in history," Kenzie replied with a smile. She picked up the box.

Linda saw her to the elevator, Kenzie carrying the box. This was going to make pitching her marketing plan to the board much, much harder. Without the possibility of cross-promotion, and with another, well-funded institution having actively turned the project down, the board would come into the meeting skeptical, demanding a lot of answers she didn't necessarily have at the outset. She would push on though, because what else did she have?

The lady in the elevator speaker system announced the ground floor and Kenzie got off. Through the sliding doors, the day was getting a little warm, that strange combination of crisp air and sun heat that only May can manage, that makes it impossible to dress for anything.

Her phone rang. Dad.

"Yeah, I just finished at the library," she said. "I'm going to take my lunch hour in town and then head back."

That was fine. She knew it would clear all of his scans. Time to blow off some steam.

"I have to try one of these date squares, if only for the irony," said Kenzie, as she and Ant lined up beside the counter at Bean and Bar. The combination of coffee shop and homemade soap and bath products store seemed odd to Kenzie at first, but at least the place smelled nice on two separate fronts. Hillscroft was just full of quirky little places like this. It even had its own independently run adult store, which she and Maria would have had a blast in, had Maria been here.

She still wished Maria would just come up and visit her spontaneously. Having someone else to enjoy didn't make her miss their connection any less. She wanted Maria to be able to share in all of these explorations too. Hopefully in time she would be able to. In the meantime, she and Ant would scout everything out so by the time Maria arrived, she would be an expert about the best places to go in Hillscroft.

And he was cute. Tall, with just a hint of cologne whiffing off him, he ordered a salad bowl and a large coffee. Kenzie got the date square, a grilled cheese, and an apple cider, because how many places had hot apple cider in late spring? Not many. Maybe it would get her into the fall mindset and help with her musings on the marketing plan.

"So how many women *do* you bring here, or have you lost count?"

"Just a couple of friends. They've moved away now for school so I only see them every few months, and usually they're so busy with their families we don't have that much time to catch up. So I guess right now, none. I fully expect they're going to get boyfriends in college and forget about me, and that's probably for the best. We were just having fun. And you?"

"I have one girlfriend back in Toronto whom I love very much. We see other people and we always have. I highly dislike the girl she's seeing right now, but she has a right to be happy and have company while I'm gone."

"Uh-oh. What's wrong with her? Is this one of those lesbian feuds I've heard so much about?" he said, mischief written all over his face.

"Not really. I'm not lesbian enough to be a stereotype, after all. I'm bi. That might be the issue, I'm not really sure. She's just always treated me like I don't exist because I didn't burst from the womb with a rainbow flag between my teeth, ready to take on the world."

Ant nodded. "I'm really glad that I don't have to deal with that. Girls are hard enough to understand sometimes. Gay girls? It just seems to add another layer on that I don't get at all."

"Welcome to the club. I'm certainly not in *their* club...most of them just think I'm a straight poser, or gay and too afraid to commit."

"Well in that case, you should stick with straight men who think your orientation is totally hot," said Ant, taking a bite of salad.

"I hope you know that won't work," said Kenzie, "I'm society's worst nightmare...sexually fluid and non-monogamous. I don't even need a fright mask at Halloween. I'll just go as the media boogeyman."

"Okay, I'll try it this way then," said Ant. "I think you're really hot, I think we'd have fun together, and, when we're done here, I want to find a little out-of-the-way place I know of to work out some stress. What do you say?"

Kenzie blushed so hard she imagined even a beet would look less purple. She paused for a moment, unable to look him in the eye.

"I would say that I was thinking the same thing all morning."

Once they settled their bill, they went back to Kenzie's car. Electricity ran through her as she anticipated what they were about to do. She wondered what he looked like under those clothes, especially what he had in his pants. Now that everything was out in the open between them, she could lust openly. It had been so long since she could express this part of herself—for weeks she had been playing the perfect, sexless daughter, the librarian, the intellectual with no other interests besides the preservation of history.

They stole hungry glances at one another as Ant guided her along a winding road through a small subdivision that dead-ended at a clearing in the woods. It looked like an abandoned construction site where they had thought of expanding the housing. Of course, someone who worked in contracting would know about a place like this.

They parked at an angle at which no one walking by from the subdivision could see them. There was no trail head here, no good entryway into the forest, so the dog-walking crowd would stay out, and the joggers. She was surprised that the town would keep such a place open without putting up a gate or turning it into a park with lots of flood lighting, but then again, this was Hillscroft. Up here there just seemed to be more leeway.

The minute the car stopped, their energy unleashed on one another. They flew to each other's lips, licking, sucking, exploring. Their hands explored too. Ant's hands squeezed her boobs, and Kenzie's travelled to his chest and down, further and further. Her fingers brushed his hard cock. Jackpot. She could tell already that it was long, and thick, and going to feel good inside her.

Ant drew back with that trademark smirk as soon as she touched him there. He undid his fly.

"I know you want to suck this in public. This is your parents' car, isn't it, you naughty, little slut."

Kenzie licked her lips and dove onto his cock, taking it as far back as she could and sucking on it with vigor. Ant moaned. She loved this. She lived for this. Imagine how angry her parents would be if they found out she was out on a work day, in broad daylight, sucking a guy off in their car. She moaned too.

Ten minutes of sucking and Ant's hand on her head, and his moans, and they were both ready.

"Let's get in the back," he said. "I know you want me to cum inside of you."

"Oh, fuck yes," said Kenzie, opening the door.

Ant lay down in the back and opened his jeans. Kenzie slid down onto him, without even giving condoms a second thought. She wanted to feel him inside her and have him spurt his warm seed into her. She wanted it inside her when she went back to the museum, to know it was there. She'd probably have to take care of herself again tonight just thinking about it.

She slid down onto him, and he was huge, filling her up in the most delicious way. She rode him slowly at first, and then faster and faster, until she was in a frenzy. When she thought about where she was and what she was doing, she came so big that she screamed, not caring who heard her, and Ant came not long after. She wanted to do this again and again, in the worst possible places.

In fact, Ant was hard again a few minutes after they had caught their breath. This time, he took her doggy style, rough and grunting, and she came over and over again because this time he lasted forever. She hoped someone saw them. She hoped everybody saw them.

THE UNFINISHED DRAWING

K enzie's phone buzzed against the desk. She shoved it into the bottom of her purse, under a pack of tissues. There. Nothing to vibrate against now.

Returning to the desk, she re-read the paragraph she had just crafted. Outlining a marketing strategy was a lot like making a full business plan. Every word had to sell the idea or someone would hook onto the tiniest loophole and make it about their own benefit or pet project. Perhaps a truly seamless proposal was impossible. After all, get a group of people together with the intention of organizing something and factions will form. Everyone has an agenda, and not everyone stops to think if their agenda is really helpful to the overall goal. One thing that she had learned in art school was that people could find fault with *anything*. There are people in the world who would call a dog fake when it was biting their leg. That was how conspiracies got started, how truly great and timeless art fell out of fashion, how empires fell.

But she had been pleasing people all her life and this presentation would be pretty damn smooth. No handholds for bullshit and one-upmanship. It was all in the wording and the order of presentation. Start with the big goals. The successes. The strengths. The promises. Then bring in the expansion, and the witch, and the papers. It would be harder to say no if she hit them with the big gains first. How to describe the materials? Lots of adjectives would do the trick. How about...these mysterious, no, these profound and priceless artifacts (scary knife dolls) and historic edifices (terrifying witch ruins with pit) that will draw scholars in from around the country and, hopefully, *the world*.

Kenzie's phone buzzed in her purse. Her nerves tingled, electricity running through her body like it had a few days ago. She had slept soundly. No spooks. No sleepwalking. Just sleep. But he would ruin it all if she went back for more. The electricity made her sick now. What she had done the other day in the car didn't fit here. That was city Kenzie. Not even city Kenzie—somebody entirely different, somebody under pressure. It didn't fit and she would pretend it hadn't happened. Ant had lots of women. He would move on soon. She would forget about it until the next time she slipped up, and then next time, she would forget again. She had to fit right now, to make the board love her so that she could keep this job and get her damned reference. She'd already managed to get swept down a river and trapped in a pit. She didn't need 'carrying on with the maintenance man' added to the list of crimes. Maybe after the board meeting she would see if he was still interested. In secret. If she could get around Mum and Dad.

She tried to go back to the pitch document. The sketchbook she'd bought in town stared her down, along with the set of coloured markers and pens. Her first paycheque had been less than she would have liked (missed hours and all) but hey, she didn't have to pay rent here. The pens had made her happy. The colours had made her happy. Even sitting on the shelf at the store, they glowed at her. They felt like protection, like joy.

Colour swatches. That's what she needed. She would need a colour scheme for this whole thing and why not experiment with real media? It would help her sort out her thoughts. Then she could just pick the closest colour on that little RGB wheel later on. No good to pick templates. Templates were for curators who hadn't been to art school. She'd save everyone a bundle and there would be no need to hire a graphic designer.

She thought of the colours around here: the warm brown-grey of the stones; the orange brown of rust, almost neon in its own way; the deep green of the trees and the intensity of the new leaves. The leaves were still pretty new up here in May, and there was an intensity in the green that was hard to capture. Now she turned to a new page in the sketchbook and laid down a few greens, layered a few, but none of them seemed quite right. None of them were that true green. She suspected that it had something to do with the sunlight that streamed through new leaves. That ineffable colour when light hit leaf...she tried leaving some of the white page showing through, and adding yellow around the edges. That almost did it, but still not quite.

The colours and shapes that spilled onto the page were a diary of her feelings and impressions since first crossing that bumpy wooden bridge a few weeks ago. She drew the pine cones that she had thrown, the old ruin, even the case with the simulacra in it. She drew rudimentary frames around all of them, trying to hem them in, but they spilled across the page anyway. If only people could visit a museum of what was in her mind, she was sure they would find it fascinating and haunting and all of the other adjectives that had rolled around in her brain to tempt the board into accepting her marketing scheme. She imagined she would find other people's mind museums just as fascinating. And yet, at one time hers would have been empty. Even now, it had had some landscapes and minimalist abstracts on the walls, none of the rich history and authenticity of a hundred-year-old palace with Old Masters and gilded cornices.

For all its age, this house felt the same way. She had been to the historical wing, seen the fireplaces and the overstuffed horse-hair chairs and well-worn hardwood floors with their black dings and scrapes like cigarette burns after years of re-waxing. In her mind, she knew the age of this place. But in her heart, the Log Palace felt barer than she did inside, as if it had never even begun to have an identity of its own.

She felt a sudden urge to draw the water, to pin down something that she had seen, or maybe felt. She started with the grey stones, putting down a dove grey that would darken with a layer of light blue put over it. She carefully placed her lines, suggesting the light and dark playing off the stones with dark grey-blue fine-tip pen. She rippled the blue layer for the water, thickening it with extra applications and time to soak into the page here, and thinning it out there. She left space at the top for copious water lilies, a honeycombed space that turned into green, the lily pads like bees' honey chambers and the flowers a stark white that needed no colour, only shade.

It was beautiful, but it was wrong. She flipped a few pages over until she lost the bleed-through. Maybe just freestyle marker would get it. The shape of the river as it bowed around the island, the vertical lines of the tree trunks, maple and birch and ash, the shadows between everything and the glint of light off the water...

Still not right. Not exactly a crappy sketch day, where nothing could come out. The line drawings looked like the thing she pictured, and she liked the lilies at least. But liking them and the drawing feeling *right* were two different things. The water was not right. She had not gotten the shape of it at all. There was something about the negative space that tugged at her.

A knock on the door jolted her out of her fascination with the page. She blushed, remembering what she was doing. She must look like a total dabbler. She had sworn she wouldn't waste any more time on this, but after seeing Canooie in that hole, she had just become...curious again. Hunger had returned. She quested after that feeling that for a brief moment had re-inhabited her body, filled her up, and left her bright and energized.

Ant opened the door and leaned in, smiling. "Busy?"

"I was, um..." Halfway into the sentence, she couldn't really remember what she had been doing. Maybe she would just plug the presentation into a template after all.

Ant gave the sexy grin and Kenzie knew she was in for it. He leaned on the door.

"The eaves are clean," he said. "No more baby maple trees popping up on the roof." The flecks of dirt and leaves on his tanned skin, and the fact that he was still wearing his work gloves, spoke to the fact that his visit wasn't totally a ruse.

"Too bad," said Kenzie. "I know they're a pain in the butt but they're kinda cute."

"And who else do I know like that?" he said, holding his trowel up to his chin.

Dammit. She could ignore the texts. It was fifteen million times harder to ignore people. Cute people. Funny people with good chemistry and big...trowels. She smiled, all the while knowing that her plan to take a step back was well and thoroughly fucked.

"Why haven't you been answering my texts? I thought we had a good time the other day," he said, lowering his voice.

Kenzie sighed.

"I've just been...trying to concentrate on work. I've got to come up with a convincing strategy for my tenure here by Friday for the board meeting, or they're going to skewer me. It hasn't been the smoothest transition and I have to make sure they know that I've got the training to keep working here. Maybe if they see that I have good ideas, they'll forget about the accidents."

Ant glanced behind him, probably to make sure Mum was still in the gift shop and not wandering around.

"I'm pretty sure this place functions in spite of the board and not because of it. That's why they hired your dad as director. He's known all of them for years and can play the neutral party. Whatever they say, don't take it to heart. Half the time they're just looking for blood in the water to have a good fight. Nothing better to do up here when you're rich and bored and live in an air-conditioned mansion set up to look like a cottage. Everybody's got to have something that gets their blood pumping," he added with a lascivious smile.

"Well, at least I know what gets you going," said Kenzie, folding up her sketchbook. She'd made enough progress for today. Time to go check in on Ms. Winter in the library.

Ant stayed in the door when she approached. She could feel the warmth pouring off him, smell his sweat and his soap. Her lips met his almost automatically, sucking in his sweetness and anticipating their next meeting. Hopefully their next meeting would be soon.

She pulled back, worried someone had seen them. "Okay, you've gotten your kiss. Now let's both get back to work before someone raises a fuss."

"Your parents are going out tonight, right? To the concert series in the park?"

"How did you hear about that?"

"Your dad told me. How about I come over?"

"I can't wait," Kenzie replied, and to her surprise, found that she couldn't.

Ant pumped into her hard as she lay on her back, a sheen of sweat breaking out on both their bodies. He'd been fucking her for a long time and they were both close. She came, and then he wasn't far behind, spurting into her, driving deep, panting. He collapsed on top of her and held her a long time. They cuddled, and talked for a while, and then cuddling turned to wrestling, wrestling turned to dirty talk, and his cock was in her again. He didn't take it easy on her the second time.

"How am I going to pretend like nothing happened when my parents get home?" she said, knees buckling as she struggled to put her clothes back on, "The room smells like sex, it's a hundred degrees in here, and I'm trembling with every step."

Ant did up his fly, his face shadowed. Still, she could see the outline of a momentary hurt in his jaw and brows. Men never hid it as well as they thought.

"You could let me stay and introduce me," he said, his voice vulnerable.

Kenzie raised an eyebrow and made a playful expression.

"Oh, I see. So, is someone contemplating making me head wife in his vast harem?"

"I'd like to see where things go," he said. "You know I don't care if you have other partners. I've got other things going on too. Not just partners, but sports and hobbies I don't want to give up or pare down. I want to start a furniture business and that's going to take a lot of work on top of my regular schedule. I just think this could be something special, is all, and I don't want to let it go unsaid."

Kenzie put a hand to her forehead and pushed back a clump of sweaty hair that had been clinging to her brow.

"This...it's very complicated. I like you too, and if we were in the city I would bring you home to Maria, we'd all have dinner, and you'd be part of the group. But my parents...they don't get bisexuality. If I tell them I'm dating a man, they'll try to wear me down. They'll round me up to straight and then try to force me into a box that I'll never get out of. I don't want to give them another reason to nag me. You have no idea how awful they can be."

As she spoke, she gently ushered him toward the door. He went, slow and stubborn. They travelled down the hall. Kenzie felt the presence of the carvings just beyond the door in a way that she had not since her arrival. They moved. They stirred.

"So, you've got to be gay just to spite your parents? That doesn't sound like you're getting to be bi either," Ant said.

Kenzie sighed. "No, being bi is weird like that. I'm bi no matter who I date, but whoever I date makes people assume that I'm either gay or straight. And society just isn't at the point that I can walk around all the time with a guy and a girl on my arm. And most of the time, attraction doesn't even work like that. I'm as likely to fall in love with a big pile of girls or a truckload of guys as I am an equal number of both. It's all about who's around, who's available, and who's compatible."

Ant bent down to put on his shoes.

"So, I'm not seeing the problem here. You're bi no matter who you date, so date me."

The statement was so blunt, and so, well, *Italian*, especially with the little hands-out shrug he gave with it, that Kenzie had to giggle.

"All right, big Tony," she said in a put-on Brooklyn accent. "Watch it, I'm datin' here!"

Ant cracked up too. He stood up, and pointed a finger at her. "Don't call me Tony," he said. "That's my drunken uncle who makes an ass of himself at weddings."

This only made Kenzie giggle more. She kissed him again. "Okay, no more big Tony," she said. "Seriously, though, this is kind of complicated from my end. Give me some time to figure it out?"

Ant blew an audible breath out of his nose. "Yeah, but only because your mom drives me nuts. I don't know what the hell I'd do if I lived with her."

"*Thank* you," Kenzie said, letting her hand slap down on her thigh. "Sometimes it's just nice to hear that someone else notices."

Ant went to the door on his own. As soon as he touched the handle, she didn't want him to open it. And yet, she didn't want to say anything either. They'd had enough wacky adventures for at least a year of relationship time. The carvings were probably just the same as always.

Orange-blue, late evening light spilled down into the corridor, giving it that strange feel of having a filter put over it. One of those lighting gels they used in theatres. A wedge of pink dwindled in the corner, splayed across the wall like a stripped bone.

The orange on the carvings stood out even more in this strange contrasting light, and the blue made the bone whites of the eyes stand out even more. There were so many eyes...the waterlilies had turned into faces again. The simulacra was back at the base of the tree. She noticed that now it was not as much of a shock, that it did not look like any one simulacra that she had seen. It had the body of one and the arms of another and all were blurry. The portrait of the house itself was gone, and in its place was a brick shaft with a woman at the bottom of it, staring up with dead eyes. She was old and wearing 1810s-era clothing. Nothing was left in the portrait of the man and the lady rising from the water but a gun, some ripples, and a giant goose, staring at them with one dead eye.

Ant froze.

"You see it?" Kenzie said.

"Yeah, I fucking see it. How did this happen? These aren't the carvings that were in here when I came in. Is somebody playing a sick joke on us?" He called loudly, "You can come out now, it was really fucking funny, you sicko."

Kenzie heard a dry ticking coming from the walls. Anyone would think it was the heater.

"This doesn't make any sense. The sun is still up..." she said. "I've seen these before, but I thought I was dreaming."

"I don't know what you know about this, but I'm out of here. I can show myself out," said Ant. "You gonna be okay?"

"Yes," she lied, tears standing in her eyes. "I'm the curator. I'll deal with it. Just go."

Kenzie locked the apartment door behind her, heart pounding, praying that the locks would work. She had no reason to believe the locks would work. She ran into her room and turned on all the lights, then curled up in a defensive position on her bed. She kept her body turned toward the window, and when she saw the lights of Ant's utility van shine through the window and the sound of the engine pulling away, she breathed a sigh of relief. They had let him get out.

She had no proof that anything in this building would kill. Even the horrible, ticking monsters the night she had awakened in the shaft had not done her any harm and she had been trapped. And yet, she knew that they could. Something she had done had kept them away. Perhaps something in her kept them at bay. They had not been able to pass the mouth of the shaft.

Perhaps the witch had jumped into that shaft in the floor of her home or tried to climb in and could not climb out. That would explain her disappearance, but not the existence of the shaft in the first place. Why had she dug it and how?

She dug it so the water could get in, Kenzie thought with a shiver. Just like the water comes in through the shaft on the ground floor. Ettenby must have dug that one, because there is no record of it existing during the first haunting, which would mean that he was affected by whatever stalked the land here as well. Perhaps his heirs had stolen the newspapers from the library to avoid scrutiny. Perhaps Ettenby himself or one of his servants had stolen them.

A rattling sound jolted her out of her thoughts, adrenaline coursing through her veins. She looked around for something to grab but there was nothing sharp. Only a fine-tip pen. She grabbed it anyway, holding it like a really pathetic horror movie victim. She wouldn't underestimate herself though. She had seen a film once where Rachel McAdams shoved a pen through a guy's trachea.

"Hello?" came a voice that grated against Kenzie's nerves in a different way. "Why are all the lights off in here? Kenzie, are you awake?"

Kenzie set the pen back down on the nightstand, hands trembling.

"I'm here, Mom," she said. "I just found it more relaxing with the lights off."

"You missed a good one," Dad called through the door. "Holiday Road had this guy playing the tabla that you would not believe. The beats he was playing were just unbelievably complex. I was spellbound! And they had this woman, Montana LeBeau, and she sang the most amazing blues tunes about her life. What a storyteller."

"Great. I hope you picked up some CDs," Kenzie said, her pulse slowing, breaths deepening. With the board meeting on Friday, none of them could afford any more incidents. She would let this one slide, and hope—no, pray—for the best. Maybe these creatures only wanted to menace her. Maybe their bullshit could stay her little secret, just until everything got smoothed out with the board.

With Mum and Dad home, and the carvings back to normal (at least, she assumed), Kenzie went to the dresser and got into her PJs. She collapsed into bed, the feel of the flannel soothing her, warming her. She sunk deeper and deeper into the soft mattress, a fuzzy haze settling in around her. It was still pretty early but she didn't care. She'd had more than enough of today.

The buzz and the light of her phone zapped her out of sleep as fast as she'd fallen in. She grabbed the phone from the nightstand. The screen, distorted with bleary eye gunk, showed Maria's picture in a little icon.

Where you been? Miss you. Want 2 chat?

Kenzie felt a pull toward the computer. She would love to chat. She would love to have a heart-to-heart talk and tell Maria everything that had been happening, from the shaft onward. She wanted to tell her about Ant. She wanted the support that Maria gave so easily, the sage advice that flowed from her like some ancient mountain guy who'd given up everything but grasshoppers and meditation. The danger held her back. The danger of her mysterious flight down a fifty-foot shaft, the danger of her falling afoul of the board. The danger of Maria finding out about Ant, which Kenzie felt the slightest bit of hesitation about, even though she knew she shouldn't. Maria would flip her lid. Maria might come down here. After their conversation, things would go from bad to worse, because Maria would force herself into this world and fuck it up even more than it already was. Those two parts of Kenzie's life were separate and would remain separate. It was in everyone's best interest right now that nothing blow up, and her girlfriend showing up would certainly blow everything up.

She still wanted to chat. Her heart ached to see that smile on Maria's face when she popped onto the screen. More than that, Kenzie wanted to hug her, to sleep with her again. She felt her absence physically, every day.

I'm so sorry. Everything's been crazy. The board is upset about the direction we're going with the museum and I have to make a pitch on Friday, plus there's just been a lot of weird shit going on that I've had to deal with as the curator. I was actually in bed, if you can believe it. I'm completely exhausted. Talk tomorrow night?

Kenzie waited for the response, her eyelids drooping as she did. At least that part was the full truth.

KK, 2morrow night. No excuses! :P came the reply. They exchanged I love yous and then Kenzie went back to the flannel and the warmth and the soft mattress. Hopefully tomorrow would be better and she could summon the strength to have all of the hard conversations.

THE INAPPROPRIATE DRAWING

Kenzie woke up and felt a flake of something drift onto her cheek. She swiped her hand across the offending substance without opening her eyes. The thing crumbled under her hand, like dirt. Not an eyelash, or a skin flake, or even a spider.

She opened her eyes and squinted at the daylight flooding her room. Bright orange rust smeared across the back of her hand.

Kenzie froze, unable to scream, afraid to move, all of the breath temporarily gone from her body, as though she were suspended underwater.

The thing that had stared at her in the well, all empty eyes and spindly spider's legs, hung over her now, inches from her face. The rust that had touched her face vomited from its mouth and down its jointed chest, where a soup can cut in half made hinged shoulders. Its arms, made of twisted knitting needles, spread over her, sharp and delicate like the many arms of a millipede or the soft, membranous wings of one of those strange green things that hovered around lights in the summer.

Kenzie didn't move. The creature didn't move either. It was totally frozen, not even vibrating with the footsteps from the hallway outside her room. Kenzie trembled, feeling like she had to get away from the monstrosity before she was discovered. After what seemed like ages, Kenzie slid over a little, sweat streaming from her pores as she anticipated the rusty needles jabbing into her arm, drawing blood, turning her into a foaming madwoman with their dirty tips.

The door clunked open.

"Kenzie, I just needed to get your laundr...aaaaaaaaaaaaaaaaah!" Mum wailed, backing into the far corner. "What is that thing doing here? That's not one of the ones from the display. Daniel? Daniel!" Mum still wore a muumuu and no bra, and the gown twisted around her as she contorted herself. Her glasses slipped down her nose.

The thing remained stiff in its pose of menace over the bed, even after Kenzie slid the rest of the way out, the comforter held to her like some ancient talisman.

Mum inched toward the door. "Come on, Kenzie, we'll block up this room until your father decides what to do."

She stopped.

"Oh, Jesus Christ there's another one. *Daniel!*"

Kenzie rounded the bed. On the floor lay another simulacrum, but this one had died. A smaller one with a cast-iron skillet (no features) for a head and what looked like gardening forks for hands lay stretched out on the floor, (debatably) face down with one arm stretched out like a dying man searching for water. Its joints had all separated, turning it back into a collection of misshapen tools rather than a dirty little copy of a human. A small amount of water had soaked into the carpet, causing the dirt and rust on the dead one to bleed into the carpet.

The one above the bed wasn't dead though, just frozen. It still somehow held that pose. It hadn't been allowed to move. Perhaps it was the sunlight that froze it, but she doubted it.

Mum reached around Kenzie, pulling her back.

"Come on, Kenzie, get out of here. Why are you still clinging to that blanket? Here, give it to me."

Mum tugged on the comforter. Kenzie held firm. She felt like something terrible would happen if she let go. The thing would move. It would crawl on its spindles, quick as a wink, up her body and gouge out her eyes, enter her mouth, stab her throat.

Mum's hand came away with black on it.

"What have you done to that blanket, Kenzie? This smells like permanent marker."

Kenzie held the comforter up in front of her, trembling. On it, scribbled in with the jabs and lines of something drawn on flimsy fabric that folds as you make the stroke, was a perfect rendering of the dead simulacrum. Its frying pan head was shaded and textured to perfection, and its forked hands menaced with a gesture that made the drawing look almost as if it could move. You could look at it and see the next move—the hallmark of a well-trained animator's posing. It was coming in for a strike.

Kenzie looked around for the marker and found it on the floor by the nightstand, cap off. Water from her fallen glass on the nightstand had gotten on it too, making a large black ink spot on the carpet.

"Oh Kenzie," said Mum, still following her despite her avowed terror. "How are we going to explain you destroying all the carpets and linens? We just put these in and they were expensive."

Kenzie trembled with rage now, instead of terror.

"Is that all you've got to say? We've got some weird fucking, Dario Argento-level shit going down, and all you can think about is the carpeting? Congratulations, Mom, you just won the award for the most short-sighted, banal, small-minded..."

"Good God!" Dad exclaimed, stomping into the room with work boots on. "What the hell is that thing doing here? It's out of the display case!"

"It was never in the display case," said Mum. "It's a new one. Two new ones."

"No, the second one is dead," Kenzie said, feeling even loonier as she said it. "Bury it, burn it, but it won't go back together again. At least not as the same creature. You have to keep it from being reassembled into something worse." She wondered how she knew this, but she knew. She knew from the same place that you know yourself.

Dad scowled at her. He strode over to the simulacrum hanging over the bed.

"Dad, no! Don't go near it," Kenzie said, still clutching the comforter to her even though her hand was sweaty and probably very inky by now.

Dad put a hand around the thorax of the thing hanging over the bed. It moved and Kenzie screamed. Then it collapsed into a waterfall of loose joints and rust flakes, folding itself over Dad's arm.

"Kenzie, I don't know how you did this, but you need to get your head straight. If that means going back to the doctor, so be it. Our jobs are hanging in the balance and you're playing out some psychodrama with the exhibits. You had better not fail me. I don't know what you think we did to deserve these pranks, these cries for attention, but you're nearly thirty! It's time to leave it in the past."

Kenzie hugged the comforter to her tighter, bringing it up to her chin. Despite her best efforts not to show weakness, a tear escaped onto the fabric, spreading like ink. What would be the use of telling them what she thought? She couldn't tell them anything important without them blowing up.

"Is that all you think of me, Dad? Then why did you give me this job? So you could shake your head and act superior when I failed? So you could both prove to me how much I needed you? You're both sicker than me but you're too cowardly to get diagnosed."

"I'm going to put this doll in the case, where it belongs," said Dad.

"I'm going to bury the other one," said Kenzie. "We've still got two more hours until opening."

Kenzie felt her growing calluses grinding against the pen, on the joint of her thumb, the outside of her index finger, and the middle pads of them all. She had been drawing without end, after all, even in her sleep. And digging. And writing on this yellowing notepad the things that she found in the stacks of books she had been through, both from the Log Palace and the public library.

Her hands, dirty now with stains of permanent marker and dirt and pen residue on them, reminded her of her first few years in animation school. When things had been fresh and her calluses had developed the first time. She hadn't known about the calluses that you can't see. She was developing them on her hands but she'd had them for many years on her heart, wearing her into a trade far more sinister than children's cartoons. She had been worn into a pattern not her own, poured down moulds that she hadn't carved, and expected to cool.

Her hands and wrists had ached constantly in her sleep when she drew. They reminded her that she still wasn't that good, that she was destroying herself for something that would likely never pan out anyway, and yet she could not stop doing it, because the drawings were hers. Canooie was stiffer and less well-designed than anybody else's character but he belonged to her.

She had dreamt of work. She had eaten work and not much else. She had breathed in work and exhaled disappointment.

Why had she done it? Because somewhere, far off, she had the fantasy that perhaps one day she could make a drawing that would express her real life. Maybe she could put something down on the page that would make people understand. Maybe she could put something down on the page that could ease the suffering of another girl like her, so that she didn't have to live in hell for years on end, knowing who she was and yet never being able to breathe a word of it for fear of losing everything. Maybe one day, if she got tired enough, if she wore that bitch in her brain (her mother's copy) down enough, she could force her pen, her tired callused hands, to tell the truth. Just once. Tell it to everyone and let them see. Hopefully they would forget and leave her alone. That was the best she could hope for.

She had twisted in jealousy of the other art students. Maybe they could see it and that was why they kept their distance. She had thought it was just the school but then it had happened again in archival school. Everything the others did brought fresh hate, especially the talented ones. She said bitter and untrue things just to bring them down. At the time, she heard the things coming out of her mouth and couldn't understand why they spewed out of her like garbage water from a punctured bag, but now she knew. All they had to do was be themselves. All anyone had to do to succeed in art school was to be themselves, aggressively and without apology. She had hated them because being themselves was easy and innocuous. One loved fashion, another retro-style art, another gross-out humor. She had tried all of these on, thinking she could craft a persona that would be marketable but, as every experienced artist knows, shallow work doesn't bring the dollars.

She hated them because she could never be them. She wasn't marketable. She was too sexual, too queer, too outside the box. No coalition of concerned parents would ever want her drawing for TV, even if it was an adult show.

Who would hire her if she pulled out her flag and waved it as high as the others? She was dirty, and weird, and upsetting. She wanted to draw things that represented life in all of its complicated, full-colour glory. The nuance. The sex, in all of its spectrum. The violence and depravity. She wanted to tell the truth. Her truth.

But her truth tended to scare people. At least, it would if she ever let them in.

In the museum library now, finger joints aching, leg joints aching with the addition of high heels to her day, seeking and seeking under the buzzing yellow lights, she combed through book after book. She just needed a few definitive texts on othering, scapegoating, and group hysteria, and she could paint a picture for the board of the witch's life. The museum could stand as a lesson, a monument to a time when chaos descended upon an otherwise orderly colony and bigotry killed. It was a conversation that needed to happen. The witch was a person. The people displaced from Stony Forks had never been heard, their narrative covered up. Their pain still lingered in the air. Perhaps that was what fuelled the simulacra, the strange events with the water.

She wrote frantic notes, digging into the page. The digging and tearing added finality and seriousness. She needed to take herself seriously. Page numbers and APA-style references scrawled down the sheet. The next sheet carried the bumps of the first. The bumps on each successive page added to each other, like each successive year had pressed its marks into her. Her soul must look like a pile of mud covered in pine needle marks by that measure.

She stopped when the page swayed and she woke up, having forgotten where she was for a good few minutes. Where had she been? Page fifty of *Scapegoats Among Us*, or page 174 of *Witches Through History: A Feminist Perspective*? She had to stop staring at this notepad. She pulled her sketchbook out of her bag, along with a fine-tip marker.

This time, she sketched the river from the top. She felt like there had been something she was missing, something in the negative space. She drew the shape of the water lilies, relishing the easy feeling of looping in loose circles with open ends. Imperfect circles felt so good. There had been a hierarchy in school, and one of the criteria for membership was perfect circles and lines. Everybody learned the tricks to some extent, but Kenzie's circles would never be perfect. Maybe her circles were just meant to be waterlilies and leaves rather than doorknobs and buttons and can lids. She liked making the little internal tails that implied veins. Whatever she was drawing, the river, the plants, it had veins. Veins like hers.

As she sketched in the strange honeycomb shape of the plants sitting on the surface of the water, a feeling of deep satisfaction washed over her. Now she was getting to the truth of it, the thing she wanted to convey. Fuck you, Hallidan College. She pulled a small box of coloured markers out of her bag and layered greens on top of the lilies. She knew better than to render one object in a drawing so completely, but she was in a groove. The lilies were speaking to her. This was a study. In the back of her mind, the relevance of this during the work day popped up for questioning, but flitted away as soon as it arrived.

A shadow drifted in between her and the yellow lighting. She had forgotten about Ms. Winter, so engrossed was she in the research, the exploration of the lilies.

Today Ms. Winter wore a brilliant blue silk blouse and matching knee-length pencil skirt with blue piping. She pulled out one of the loose-jointed wooden chairs and sat in it.

"Kenzie, how are you?" The statement sounded casual but her posture, the folded hands that said 'I'm not going anywhere,' conveyed the rest.

"I'm fine," Kenzie said, smoothing her hair back, wondering if she had brushed it this morning. "I'm just a little frantic about the board meeting tomorrow. Rumour has it they're not too pleased with my tenure thus far. I'm just trying to make sure I have all my ducks in a row."

Ms. Winter tilted her head.

"Well, ducks love water lilies. And ponds. It's a nice drawing, by the way. I'm surprised. I never knew you were so talented."

Kenzie covered up her drawing with her elbows, without even thinking of it, feeling the sudden urge to shift her weight.

"I'm not, really. Just picked up a few tricks while I studied with the really talented people."

Ms. Winter pursed her perfectly painted lips, lifting her folded hands to them.

"I'm worried about you, Kenzie. This place isn't good for you. And I'm afraid I made it worse by getting you involved in my little squabble about the ruins. For what it's worth, I like you. I'd like you to stay on and learn with us. I think we can all do better as a team. I'm worried, though, that maybe *you'd* be better off somewhere else. Maybe in the city, hanging out a shingle for creative services. You've got so many talents and none of them are going to help the world if you stay here, spinning your wheels and letting your mum and dad drive you crazy."

"They don't—"

"They do. It's obvious to even the most casual observer. You hate them and they don't get you. Just leave. Quit. Go home. Do something different. It's got to turn out better than this. And if you decide to stay, you're going to have to work through whatever is causing all this drama."

Kenzie's fingers pressed the table until they hurt, her pinky joint cracking. She wrapped her legs around the base of the chair, tensing her muscles until she could feel the tendons in her knees straining.

"Whatever is happening with me," she said, "it's not your fault. I consider you a friend and you've only ever tried to help me. Except, you've only known me a short time. It's been insufficient for you to see that I fail spectacularly at everything I touch. That incident in the river was just chapter thirty-something of a very long book. I'm not sure if it's a comedy or a tragedy but it's plenty ironic, whatever it is. It wouldn't matter what you told me, I'd go find it and fuck it up."

Ms. Winter shook her head. "Sorry, I just don't see that in you," she said. "In the city, I've seen lots of jumped-up little morons living off of Mommy and Daddy's reputation, failing upward at every turn, but you don't strike me as that at all. I can see that you've worked extremely hard for very little applause. I can see that you've developed multiple skill sets that you can use simultaneously, that no one seems to appreciate the way they should. You don't strike me as a loser. You strike me as chronically unlucky."

Kenzie sighed, willing back the tears again. "In the end, isn't that the same thing? Loser, unlucky, both end up in the same place."

Ms. Winter got up from the chair. She placed a perfectly-manicured hand on Kenzie's shoulder. "Nope. Luck is just a stat. It's probabilities. If you keep playing the numbers, no matter how unlucky you are, something is bound to turn up. You just have to keep playing the numbers, girl, and I think you'll do just fine. Because the difference between unlucky and loser is that when your number finally comes up, you'll have something to show for it. You'll have the spark to put behind the bullet, the weight behind you to knock 'em dead. You have to stop thinking of new ways to fail and start brainstorming new ways to try."

"Thanks," said Kenzie. Her limbs felt heavy after all the sitting, and the frank talk, and the stress. Hours at an animation desk every day had taught her that when she felt like this, she needed a nice long walk, some scenery, and maybe some light conversation.

She rose and stretched. "I'm going down to the historical wing," she said to Ms. Winter. "Don't worry about this stuff. I'll file it all myself when I get back."

She found Dad in the parlour, chatting with some visitors. She stayed and listened to the story, one of the many quirky tidbits about the town of Hillscroft that he had picked up over the years. This one involved misuse of a shared town wheelbarrow and had even the teenaged son of the family that had come in seemed genuinely amused.

The parlour was one of her favourite places to visit during the day. She had not the nerve to visit it at night. The best preserved of the original rooms, it had once been Ettenby's entertaining space for intimate groups and business visitors. Dark, richly stained wood lined the wainscotting, the floors, the trim. All of the furniture was either dark wood or an odd lime-green velvet jacquard that no textile manufacturer had had the balls to produce since around 1920. Most days, when it wasn't too hot, the volunteers stoked a fire in the little metal fireplace lined with tiles at the end of the room, for the sake of realism. Today, as it was overcast and cloudy, a little pile of coals glowed and shimmered in the hearth. It smelled like wood smoke, old-fashioned wax and furniture varnish, and the peculiar sort of mildew that even clean old furniture collects when nobody sits in it.

After the group left, Dad beckoned her to the windows, the only place in the room pierced by any sort of weak light.

"Do you know where Anthony is? He hasn't shown up yet today and we need the garden beds edged. They look a fright. There's a pine down by the river that needs to be trimmed as well. The snow broke one of its branches and I'm afraid some kid is going to pull it down."

"He didn't say anything to me—" she caught herself before saying 'last night.' "Not yesterday, anyway. He seemed fine."

Lies. Why did it always have to come to lies? She hated them.

A tall, slim figure made a black shadow over all the dark browns and greens of the room. Ant stood in the doorway, sweaty and breathing hard. After years of being a nut, Kenzie had learned to distinguish sweaty working hard from sweaty scared. Luckily, Dad was just as tone-deaf as ever with that stuff.

"Anthony!" he said, smiling and opening his arms. "My goodness, did you run here? If you'd had car trouble, I could have sent Mandy to come get you."

Ant held out a wrinkled paper to Dad. The letter had wilted with humidity and probably been held in sweaty palms on the entire card ride to the museum. Dad read the letter. He looked up at Ant, his brows furrowed.

"But why? We pay you twice what you make doing odd jobs and we like your work. Please, I beg you to reconsider. There are only so many good handymen in town and we trust you. We don't want to have to go down to Lyle's Contracting. They'll hear 'museum' and think 'government grant dollars and solid-gold toilet seats' and we haven't got the budget for that."

Ant looked around the room, as if one of the shadows would leap out and bite him. She could tell the fireplace lighting was making him nervous, with the movements of the flames.

"I'm sorry," he said. "It's not an easy decision for me but I've made up my mind. I...don't think this is a safe workplace. We haven't found all of the weak spots in the building and anything could happen. I had an incident yesterday and...well, never mind. Get somebody with better insurance. It'll be better for everybody."

Dad's face reddened and his one hand clenched and unclenched. Kenzie could see the steam building for one of his classic tirades. Things had not gone as he planned and he was ready to burn bridges. She couldn't have him burning this one. She didn't want another possible partner running from her because of her family.

"Dad, what he's not telling you is that we're dating," Kenzie blurted out. Dad turned on her, his eyes echoing the coals in the fireplace for intensity. She continued.

"It's been going on for a couple of weeks now and we'd like to see where things go. Ant-thony," she tacked on, knowing that Dad would hate the nickname, "knew that things were shaky with the board and didn't want any potential rumours to muddy the waters. He's only trying to help. We have to appear as professional as possible tomorrow if we want to stay here, doing this work."

Dad changed gears. He raised an eyebrow. "Really? You two?"

"Yup. We didn't want to say anything in case it didn't work out. No need to upset the apple cart, right?" Ant said. His shoulders left his ears just a little bit, although he was still obviously unhappy to be in the building for any longer than necessary.

Dad put a hand to his mouth.

"Wow...this is not what I expected," he muttered.

Ant said, "Look, I can recommend a friend of mine. I've got a couple of buddies who do the same work for the same prices. We trade projects. I'll find somebody that wants to take it on. A couple of them owe me favours. You'll have somebody here in forty-eight hours, I promise."

Dad let a lot of air out through his nose. "Make it twenty-four and I'll give you a reference so glowing they can see it from space."

"Deal," said Ant. He made his excuses and left, much faster than he had come in and with far more confidence.

Dad made that face he made when he was struggling with a particularly difficult piece of furniture assembly. His brows pulled together and his face wrinkled pretty much everywhere. "What happened to your delinquent boyfriend in the city?"

"I don't have one. Mum made that up," she said. It wasn't a lie—exactly. "She didn't like the person I was talking to online and so she just assumed that it was some criminal boyfriend. You know how she is when she gets upset."

"Yes, I do," Dad said, disdain dripping from his voice. "And I can't say I'm disappointed that it turned out not to be true. Ant seems like a nice enough lad. You two should do fine."

He threw an arm around her. Kenzie felt sick. "You know, for a little while there I suspected your mother was keeping secrets for you. I had thought it was worse than I suspected, not better. I had even suspected you might be dating a woman."

Kenzie remained silent at that one. She had already been horrible enough today. She didn't want to compound it with more lies. She had finally made things official with Ant and therefore she would have to tell Maria tonight. Perhaps her honesty would ease her growing sense of dread that she was falling into her parents' world and moulding to their expectations again, whether she liked it, or not.

THE WORLD
SHIFTS AGAIN

Kenzie's eyes felt tired, squinting into the light of her laptop. She hadn't bothered to turn on any other lights and the fading sun outside offered little in the way of illumination. She felt the cold rays of the screen's light, blue-based like the colours of depression in a Picasso painting, play over her face. How could she feel light, she wondered, but she could. Ever since art school, she could feel it. Perhaps it was an old artist's trick, or one of those new senses that people pick up when immersed in a discipline for a long time, until it burns itself into them.

As the room grew darker, as she waited for Maria's call, she wondered if the simulacra were about. She heard no ticking, always a good sign. Nothing in the world had shifted. Her window still looked out over the parking lot and not the river. The simulacra, the goose, the witch in the carvings, they were all cowards. They only came around when her defenses were down.

Right now, Kenzie might as well have worn boxing gloves, so high was her guard. She had to tell Maria about Ant and she knew she was in the wrong. She had to find some way to spin it to make things okay. Technically, neither of them had rules against hooking up with someone without asking. Maria had done that with Lisa Callery and Kenzie had far more reason to despise Lisa than anyone that she could possibly pick up in Hillscroft. Stuck up little rainbow bitch. Even now she was probably filling Maria's ears with poison about bisexuals, and Kenzie specifically, gently and subtly outlining all the ways that Kenzie wasn't quite good enough, or worse, simply showing Maria by letting her into her shiny, perfect, out and open and proud and 'OMG aren't I amazing' life. Narcissistic bitch. Privileged little attention whore. Kenzie would bet that she even had a blog about her shiny life where she posted shiny perfect pictures and everybody praised her for how shiny and perfect she was, how pure a specimen of the perfect Lesbian™.

Maria's call rang through, the sound of the chat program's ring bouncing off the walls. Kenzie had left a fan on for noise this time, pointed at the door, but couldn't be bothered with the music. She was tired. Too tired to fight again. Mum could harangue all she wanted. Kenzie would just go to sleep and let her have at it without an audience.

Maria appeared, this time sitting in her bedroom, wearing a comfortable-looking velour jogging suit. Her curly hair was done up in a puff-ball bun at the back of her head. She wore no makeup and she still looked great. She didn't need to wear lipstick for it to be obvious that she had great lips. They were full and kissable and all of the things all those thin-lipped women who wore lipstick wanted people to think about them.

"Hey," she said. "It's been a few days."

"I know," said Kenzie. "I missed you. It's been chaos around here, setting up for the board meeting. I also had a really interesting run-in with the local library."

Maria raised both eyebrows.

"Oh really? Pamphlet-chucking interesting or something milder?"

"A bit milder. Let's just say that Toronto isn't the only place where people get handed jobs they don't deserve and can't possibly lose despite gross incompetence. Speaking of which, how is Lisa?"

Tension played out over Maria's features.

"She's fine."

A wave of nervous tension washed over Kenzie.

"Why are you so reluctant to talk about her? Did you guys break up?"

"No," said Maria, "we haven't broken up. It's complicated right now and I'd rather tell you after everything is said and done."

Trust, Kenzie, trust, she repeated to herself. The mantra did absolutely no good. What was Maria planning? Was she just waiting to break up with Kenzie when they saw each other in person again? Was she plotting her exit into the rainbow brigade, leaving Kenzie shivering and alone? Kenzie writhed internally. Outside, she knew exactly what to do.

"I've been spending time with someone here, too."

Maria cracked a small grin at this. It seemed more like the old Maria and less like this awkward, tired version that Kenzie saw before her tonight.

"Oh really? Who is it?"

"Well, I didn't plan it, but remember the cute handyman I told you about, Ant? I met up with him the other day for a date and we've had sex a few times since. Originally it was just a casual thing, but I'm thinking I might want to keep things going once I move back to the city. Even if it's just sexy pen pals. He's really funny and he's got a good capacity to handle the weird shit that always seems to crop up around me. I think you'd like him."

"Maybe..." said Maria, looking down.

Between the lack of sleep, and the hard conversation with Ms. Winter today, and the fights with her parents, and the confrontation about Ant,

Kenzie had left the energy to deal with this distance from Maria long behind her somewhere around noon. She had hoped, even though she was nervous, that Maria would meet her best expectations and not her worst. Maria often did things like that. She had hoped for some support after being attacked by Dad and questioned by Ms. Winter, not this lukewarm 'Uh-huh, yes dear' crap.

"What is wrong with you tonight? Was I not allowed to find somebody here, when you've found somebody there? I thought we had an open relationship on both sides. You're not the only one in a shitty position here. You know I blow off steam sometimes with sex. Ant treats me well and we have a good time, so what's the problem?"

Maria scowled, tears visible in her eyes.

"The problem is that you ran off for a year to be with your shitty, brainwashing parents after struggling for years with your sexuality, and now five minutes later you're with a man? When's the wedding, Kenzie, because I'm sure they'll be so happy you finally drank the Kool-Aid and did what they wanted! What the hell did I invest all that time and energy in you for anyway? For you to go back to looking hetero and hiding yourself for the rest of your life? Makes me feel really important. Monumental even."

Kenzie drew back, stung. The light from the laptop screen burned her eyes now, like staring at the sun, and she could see rays spilling out from it when she blinked. Maria's words hurt worse because they cut way too close to her own self-doubts, her inner criticism. That was why she had not brought up Ant before. That was why she had tried to hide him. Because she knew that even if she fucked him on the roof in broad daylight, her parents would be thrilled they were together because he was a man.

Stuck between not wanting to ignore her feelings because her parents might approve, and therefore letting them control her, and acting on her feelings and feeling like she had played into their hands, there was just no way to break the feeling of being controlled. She had done things they wouldn't like. She had repeated to herself over and over again that it was her choice, and her choice alone, and had nothing to do with Mum and Dad. But maybe she wanted to do it because it was comfortable. Maybe some part of her had done it because it longed for the security of a set world view, of having everything laid out for her. The idea that she could still want to go back to their world view disgusted her, but she knew in her heart that she could not rule it out.

"Wow, is that seriously what you think?" she said, giving a dry, humorless chuckle. "That I would get in a relationship with someone to please my parents? I can't believe you think that I came here to smooth things over. I came here to endure this so that I can get my reference. That's it, finito, the end. Ant and I connected. That's all. I needed company and he provided it. I'm sure there are lesbians in this town, but it's not like I can go out and find them. And besides, why do I all of a sudden have to date only women to make you comfortable? We both knew from the start that wasn't the deal. And you've been fine with my other boyfriends."

"Your other boyfriends weren't Joe country hick with all those weird traditional ideas. He probably thinks he owns you now."

"You know nothing about him! He does solo polyamory and, frankly, he's more interesting than a lot of the guys I dated before because he actually, I don't know, does something with his day other than sitting around pushing papers and discussing hypotheticals. What is really behind all this? It's Lisa, isn't it? Tell me the truth. She's been badmouthing me, hasn't she? Telling you I'm not good enough for you?"

Maria sighed. She pulled up her comforter, put it back down.

"Fine, if you want to push the issue, yeah, she's had a really bad attitude about you. Seems like you're determined to prove her right tonight."

"Seriously, Maria? What the fuck did she—no, never mind, I don't even want to know. Goodnight."

"Kenzie, I—"

"Goodnight!" Kenzie slammed the laptop shut.

Later, Kenzie wandered into the kitchen, eyes still stinging from the cry she had just finished. She pushed some bread down into the toaster and waited. Mum sauntered up from her place on the couch. Her face was bright, energized. Even her skin seemed brighter.

"Your father told me that you have a boyfriend," she said.

The toast popped. Kenzie grabbed it, not caring that it burned her fingertips. She opened the fridge door, grabbed the margarine, slammed the door. She did the same with the utensil drawer and butter knife.

"I don't want to hear it," she said, stomping to her room and slamming the door. She pushed a pillow over her ears until Mum stopped trying to call to her through the door. She wished she couldn't hear any of it but some got through. She didn't want congratulations. She didn't want her mother's admiration on appearing straight again.

She sat up, knees to chest, and ate the toast, grumbling internally about it having cooled while she waited for Mum to shut her trap. All she'd wanted was some nice melted butter and Mum had spoiled that too. She ate the bread so as not to waste it, with margarine spread on top but not at all liquefied. Disgusting.

Tomorrow, she would battle the board. As she curled up under the blankets, she thought with a smirk that none of them could be as sharp as the arms of that simulacrum, or as unsettling as the goose. And she was pretty sure none of them were having devil-worshipping parties across the river. Just humans. She could deal with humans.

INSULT AND INJURY

At first, Kenzie thought the dappling of the light above her eyelids was the sun moving through the trees. She waited to hear the wind outside, swooshing its way from spring to summer. But everything was still, including the light dapples.

She opened her eyes to find a sickly, dead tree of intertwining simulacra piled up over her in a nauseating organic latticework. The floor was littered with dead ones, their parts staining the carpet so that when they were removed, it would look like a randomized pattern, as if the carpet had been bought like that.

Kenzie didn't scream this time. She spotted an opening at the end of the bed and pulled herself through with her feet, trembling all over, arms crossed over her chest. After she had cleared all but her head, the far end of the pile trembled, clacking and squealing with rusty joints. She fell onto an empty place on the floor just in time to see the rest of the formation go down in a wave.

Their joints separated onto the soiled comforter. All dead, all gone. They could have decapitated her, or stabbed her with rusty knives, or any number of unimagined horrors.

She heard muffled footsteps.

"Kenzie," came Dad's voice, "what's going on in there?"

Kenzie saw the headboard for the first time. It was completely destroyed, gutted with a latticework of rough relief carvings depicting a nightmare tangle of faces and limbs, all blending into one another. She felt a weight in her pocket and pulled out the butter knife, the stainless-steel plating scratched to pieces, little bits of wood and stain still stuck in its teeth. It had bent a little, too, the slight curve of too much pressure applied at the wrong angle.

Mum and Dad burst in again, only this time the debris on the floor stopped them from coming in too far.

"They're all dead," Kenzie said to them. "They're not coming back."

"Dead?" her father said. "They're broken beyond recognition! Some of the ones from the case are in here. Kenzie, what are we...no, no, I just can't deal with this today. We'll keep the board out of the apartment at any cost, and tell them the missing dolls are just out for refurbishment. That's true enough. They'll need refurbishment."

Kenzie scowled.

"No. I won't let you put them back together."

Dad picked his way over an old tuning fork and a battered broomstick with the paint peeling off. He took Kenzie by the shoulders.

"Kenzie, this is the work of thirty years for me. I need you to pull yourself together today and pull this off. After that, you can have a mental breakdown if you need to and we can argue our way into the sunset, forever and ever. Just make this meeting work. For you and for me. Please."

The meeting. It hit her, its full weight pressing down on her shoulders in the way of early morning realizations, but doubly heavy because her mind had been blanked by the latticework of horror stretched over her bed. She was so tired that she could feel the lazy creep of adrenaline into her veins, her insides exposed for all the world to see. On the day that she needed vulnerability the least, she would feel it the most.

Forcing her brain to move forward on squealing gears, she tried to remember where she had left her presentation materials. She had set them all up in the office. Good. Nothing would be rust-stained or trapped under debris. Muffled through a sheet, she heard herself mutter reassurances to Dad. She stepped over the dead parts of dead things with cement-heavy feet, already struggling to push it all to the back of her mind. Her training, her inner businesswoman, normally so prominently worn on the outside of her, had retreated to some remote inner fortress, unwilling to be pulled out.

Kenzie left the room and headed for the shower. Perhaps the hot water and white noise would help her center herself.

"I'll get some towels," Mum said, going to follow her.

"I can get my own," said Kenzie. "If you want this presentation to go off, I need quiet."

Kenzie stood under the streaming water again and closed her eyes. She had turned the heat up too high, she knew it, but the sweltering steam-room effect was exactly what she wanted. Let the water burn all of the past away, leave it behind, flow it down the drain and out into that accursed river. Today, she had to forget her failures and project success. She rummaged around inside her for the artifacts of her training, determined to put them on display in an impressive glass case. She willed the water to wash away all but her professionalism, to make her forget that even her own parents thought she was broken.

Broken like the pieces of simulacra littering her floor.

She took a deep breath, let the tears well up, let the water carry them away, too. Everybody else in the world managed to succeed, at least some of the time. Today was her day. Today had to be her day. She was going to make it her day and damn anybody that got in her way. Today was the day that she proved everybody wrong and nothing would get in her way. Not terror, not despair, not other people's opinions. She would put on a crisp suit, style her hair, gird herself with expensive makeup, and play the professional.

But how did one play the professional when everyone was determined to treat them like a child? Was it a role you could inhabit without the buy-in of anyone around you?

She had to think that professionalism and adulthood lived in a world all their own, judged by autonomous criteria. Otherwise, she was doomed.

She turned off the water and stepped out into the steam. She could not see her face in the mirror. The steam had made it blurry, a puddle of colours rather than a shape. There were eye hollows and highlights, but no real definition. She could not have said as an impartial observer if it were her face, or her mother's, or the witch's etched long ago in a cursed piece of wood.

She tested her voice. At least that still worked smoothly. At least she hadn't screamed it all out.

"Today, I am a professional," she said, speaking softly with the tap on so that Mum and Dad couldn't hear. "Today, I do my best no matter what the cost and today, I succeed. I will make them love me. I have to."

The high heels felt like five-foot stilts today. She teetered as she walked, her tired knees protesting all the way. She gathered up the laptop, the USB key, the printed Bristol boards from the office. She practiced her pitch over and over in her head as she walked, as she and Dad waited outside the conference room, as she shook hands and smiled and forgot everyone's names immediately, because there was only one name and it was success and

212

its fuel was adrenaline and her burning nerves simply immolated anything else that touched them right now. The board reminded her of her professors and the parents of people she didn't like, all understated blouses and sensible, expensive haircuts. The uniform hands that gripped the world.

Dad stood beside her. Mum had stayed home, thank Christ. The conference room opened from a short hallway just off the bottom floor of the Folk Art wing. She had been to quite a few conventions, for academic work as well as for fun and fandom, and the conference room looked like every other conference room in existence. Tasteful, light-coloured wallpaper blended with tasteful, light-coloured wainscotting; for some reason, they always had Berber carpeting and, for yet another unknown reason, someone always decided to put in those God-awful square fluorescents that ensured that everyone in the meeting fidgeted uncomfortably for the duration without knowing why they were so unsettled. A small table in the back offered a tray of coffee cake, a coffee urn, cream and sugar, and several glasses of water minding their own business and not too full, thank you very much.

As they entered, the dry air hit Kenzie and she coughed, a respectable 'ahem' suitable for libraries and lectures. She wondered if she had already blown it with the cough. Her armpits were sweating, she could feel them. She wanted to look and see if she was getting a stain, or a smell, but could not think of a pretence to do so. She felt trapped in a box, an invisible hand over her mouth. Once it was removed, hopefully the right things would come spilling out.

Dad sat her at the end of the table, taking the seat at her left side. The puffy leather boardroom chairs made a hiss when Kenzie sat, their pneumatic controls sinking a little with her weight, adjusting.

"Now, I'm just here to support you today," Dad said. "You're the one with the plan and we'll make sure they know it. I'm an old grump, and things haven't been the easiest, but I've seen how hard you've worked and you've got a solid pitch here. I wouldn't have let the meeting go forward if I didn't think so. You're the one with the training."

Kenzie felt momentarily warm. As the board filed in, they brought with them a draft. All old and white as death, they looked anywhere but at her, busying themselves with the coffee and murmuring to one another in voices clearly designed to keep her out. Men, women, all of them over fifty-five, most by a mile. They sat down one by one, slowly rearranging papers and talking in scandalized whispers. With a few of them the stream of conversation never stopped. One woman's eyes bulged as she talked, like a spooked horse.

Once they had settled, like crows on a line, the folds of their casually expensive clothing yielding to gravity, the woman with the bulging eyes turned her neighing to Dad. Kenzie glanced at the agenda and the woman was not on it.

"Daniel, we want to know what has been going on. There have been too many accidents! People in town are starting to talk."

"Yes," chimed in a balding man in a golf shirt. "What are you *doing* up here?"

Dad blinked several times in quick succession. Kenzie had hated all of those historical society meetings he had dragged her to as a kid, but they had taught her just how much Dad hated it when people broke with the set agenda.

"We've already addressed this on the group email list, Terry," he said, face going pink. "We have brought in an expert—"

"Oh yes, your daughter," said the horsey woman. "And how much experience has she had?"

"Please let me finish, Evelyn. My daughter, who has just graduated from one of the best schools in the field, who has handled this sort of thing on internship already, decided that our safety measures and grounds security were not up to the modern standard and has been taking measures to rectify that. The amount we will save in liability is banking on this museum's future and she's right to do it."

"Certainly she's right to do it, *if* she could do it right, but all I'm hearing is about people falling into pits and getting washed away in the river. I know we're a small organization, but surely we can do better than this, Daniel," said another man with an age-creased face and a boutonniere from the local men's club.

Kenzie felt her face go hot. Dad was bursting out into a sweat, his skin beet red.

"I'm hearing a lot of opinions," he said, "from people who have not been here in a month or more. People who have nothing to do with the day-to-day running of this place, who I would challenge to pick up the task and try it themselves for a day. I have been working here on the ground every single day and I speak to the staff who are here, and not one of them has a bad thing to say about Kenzie. We all feel that she is moving this facility in a forward-thinking direction and her training is doing us good, and if you would kindly save the rest of the questions until after her *presentation*, which is, as you will notice, at the top of the agenda, I think you will be pleasantly surprised."

None of the board dared to contradict Dad—yet. She could see the weight of his years with them coming to bear. He had stood up for her, now she prayed that he would like her presentation. That they would like it, yes, but Dad was the only one she really cared about. She could see now how much he had put on the line for her. Now she was on the line, balancing, balancing, looking at the ground below, even though she knew she shouldn't, and hoping not to fall. She swayed like the tightrope walker in her mind as she pushed away from the desk and found her feet.

She flipped the laptop open. The click echoed across the room, silent, staring. She began the presentation. Okay, Kenzie, remember your timing, take deep breaths and just follow your instincts. You've memorized the speech. Whether they love it or they hate it, you've got to do it for you.

She trembled. She began anyway.

"Human beings are drawn to stories," she said. "In some ways, people come to museums for new stories, to hear the untold facts of places long ago and far away, or maybe a new take on what's right next door. History is made up of factual stories and we sell that to our guests every time they interact with us. I would argue that the best way forward for any facility focusing on history is to dig deep into our stories and find out what will make them compelling for a contemporary audience."

Horsey lady whispered to boutonniere guy. Kenzie flashed back to the catty bitches in her research methodologies class and felt a sense of defiance, a sense of anger that buoyed her. The quaver left her voice and she felt the words flowing from her core.

"The key to the story of Ettenby's Log Palace is mystery. Mystery is what pulls us along in a great story and what feeds our deeply human need for inquiry. While I was cataloguing and scanning some of the materials left in the Palace, I have discovered a mystery that defines all the others, an incident key to the history of this area and overlooked for two centuries. It is a story of the supernatural, of scapegoats, of mass hysteria. It is the story of the Stony Forks witch and the strange artifacts and accounts that surround her."

Dad shifted in his seat, starting to fidget and then folding his hands in front of him so he wouldn't be tempted. Kenzie knew the move well. She realized then that he had stood up for her despite not quite knowing if the proposal would fly. He had approved it out of trust for her. He had run with the way she had wanted to do it. A pilot light came on inside of her. The heat generated more steam. There was hope after all.

She narrated the papers she had found with vigor and enthusiasm, telling her own story in a way that would captivate any audience. She ended by emphasizing that the library had signed away ownership of the papers, leaving them the property of the museum. She moved on to the house across the river and the possibilities therein. She talked about the dolls, and although she faltered once, she hid it behind a sip of water. Here was professionalism, she thought, as she pointed and interpreted and outlined her business plan.

They would build positive press out of the mystery of the witch and the dolls, and use it to bring in major academic partners and grants. Better exhibits and major events would follow, and not only the museum but Hillscroft would become an academic destination. They would use the money to expand across the river and make a whole historic park out of the former Stony Forks settlement. The timeline, the numbers, the media strategy, they were all perfect. Well, as far as any business plan could be perfect.

The slides flew by and, by the time she reached the conclusion, the adrenaline could have had her talking for another three hours. She smiled and didn't care if anyone else smiled back.

"This museum could be a world leader in studying histories of early settlement, marginalization, and folk legends. We could be a haven for the hidden histories, the ones that no one else will engage with. Think of the possibilities with women's history, the Native community, psychology...the possibilities are endless, but they all begin...with this story and a big mystery. Let's be the ones to bring the facts behind that mystery to light."

Dad smiled back at her. He unfolded his hands in the crisp manner he used when he felt everything was in hand and he had won his point.

"Thank you, Kenzie, and now let the questions begin," he said, tapping the agenda.

The younger balding one raised his hand first. He didn't scowl exactly. No, it was more a self-assured disgruntlement that the status quo had been dislodged. It was the deadpan stare of the man whose order had been gotten wrong, who'd had the wrong colour of hydrangea planted in his garden and now it was all emasculating pinks and purples instead of whites and blues. He had been all handshakes upon arrival, but now it was clear that Dad was no more than an employee to him, the same as her.

"I think I speak for everyone," he said, "when I say that we need to stop and re-think things here at the Log Palace. We need change, oh do we ever, but this is not it. Daniel, we put you in charge because we thought that you were going to be sensible and reliable. Protect our investment."

"I'm trying to grow your investment and so is she," said Dad.

Baldy talked over him. "We are trying to preserve history here and provide a safe space for the community to come and learn. Not attract a bunch of loonies following a witch legend. You think you've got a problem with the partying teenagers? What's going to happen when the world-class freaks start rolling in? We're not equipped to deal with that and neither is Hillscroft."

"And what about the outcasts?" Kenzie said, loud, trembling, "What about the people whose story belongs here? Where is their safe space? You can't just walk onto a piece of land and decide what its story is. That's not history. That's colonialism. That's privilege speaking over the voice of those who came before. That's cultural murder. Do we want to represent some stereotypical view of the past, a polite place for people to drag their kids for the day to bore them to death, or do we want to expose people to something real that they could actually learn from?"

"Young lady, our money did not go into this place for you to turn it into some circus!" said horse face, her eyes bulging in righteous indignation. "In everything that we do, there is a high road and a low road, and the people you are talking about will lower the discourse here. There is nothing good or valuable in what you propose, just a bunch of misguided settlers who hit rough times and let their imaginations get the best of them. We must cast the low road aside, even if it's true, because we don't want people deciding to travel it for themselves."

"And what about the people that don't have a choice? The ones that get sorted onto your 'low road' no matter what they do? Where do they go to learn about themselves?"

"*Anywhere* but here," said boutonniere. "I motion for the dismissal of Kenzie Glaston as curator, effective immediately. All in favour?"

A chorus of angry ayes flew in her direction. Dad stood up, too.

"I'm begging you. Please don't do this. Give her another chance. This firing could leave a mark on her career that will never wash away. She might never get another job. Just because her work isn't to your taste doesn't mean she's bad at it. Have some compassion."

"Daniel," said Baldy, "we are leaving you out of this motion because of the length of time we've all known each other, but let me make this clear: if she is not out of this building by the end of the week, we'll have you both thrown out. Her presentation was incompetent, offensive, and completely out of touch with community needs. If she never gets another curator position, I'll consider myself as having done the industry a favour."

Dad put his agenda down, which he had been clutching to his chest like a shield. His hand flattened on the table, pushing out some of the deep wrinkles his fist had left in the paper.

"Then I resign," he said, quietly.

"Excuse me?" said horse face.

"I resign, you pompous ass! There must be a wind blowing, because the space between your ears sure is making a lot of noise. Expect my letter by tomorrow morning. I'll be gone by the end of the week as well, and heaven help you to find another director who will work for room and board. I don't expect Shelley Winter will be here much longer either, after I go."

He picked up the piece of paper with the agenda printed on it, now bent at all angles. He tossed it up in the air.

"Fuck the agenda. I'm out of here and you're on your own." Dad stomped from the room. Kenzie grabbed her papers and followed him, not caring who showed the board out, or if they decided to hang out in the foyer all night, whispering their funereal whispers until the simulacra came and cut them to pieces. Let *them* fall down the hole and then see how self-righteous they'd be.

Kenzie caught up to him halfway up the Folk Art wing stairs. She touched his elbow and could feel the damp of his sweat even through the thick material.

"Not now," he said, loudly, his voice echoing. He stopped on the stairs, breath heaving. "Not...now."

When the door to the apartment was shut behind them, Kenzie pleaded with his tension-hunched back.

"What happened?" said Mum.

"Never mind," Dad replied, falling onto the couch with a couple of recoil bounces that he didn't even bother to steady against.

Mum walked between him and the TV.

"Daniel, I'm worried. What happened?"

"Would you shut up, woman!" he bellowed. Mum sniffled and Kenzie felt even more uneasy than she had before. She could count on one hand the number of times Mum had cried in front of anyone.

"Stop yelling at me," she said.

"Then stop being such an abominable nuisance!"

Mum looked at Kenzie, her face streaky and crumpled up, and Kenzie felt hollow.

"I got fired, Mum. Dad quit," she heard herself say from a long way away. "We've all got a week to get out."

Mum shook her head like someone in shock, denying what they saw over and over.

Kenzie continued. "I don't know if you've ever met the board, but they're a bunch of pompous jackasses and they're going to mismanage this place into the ground. We're better off without them."

"And what would you know about it?" Dad snarled at her over the back of the couch. "Those people have ten times the experience you do and triple the sense."

Kenzie took a step back. She wanted to retreat into her room, but remembered what was in there.

"Dad, where is this coming from? I thought you supported my presentation."

"It was a risk, Kenzie, a risk that cost us both our jobs. You took thirty years of my work and just threw it away after I gave you a chance. I had thought—I had wanted to think—that you just had bad luck and a little bit of a depressive disposition. I thought a good job would turn it all around for you. But I see it now...all the weird stuff going on around here, all the accidents, all the losses...the common denominator is you and it's not random at all. You're self-sabotaging, Kenzie, over and over, and you don't care who goes with you."

"You're upset," Kenzie said, the words squeezing her chest empty, pinching her spine. "You're saying things out of anger but deep down I know you understand that this was the board's fault, not mine. All of the accidents...I didn't do them on purpose! I don't even know how they happened."

Dad's face had gone from red and sweaty to white and too calm.

"Then I'm sure you won't mind if I pull all of the security tapes in the building. I don't know why I didn't think of that before."

"Because you're a decent human being and I'm your daughter," said Kenzie. She wanted to throw up, but there was nothing there. She hadn't eaten.

Dad got up from the couch, weary, like an old man needing a cane. Mum supported his elbow.

"The daughter I knew would have cared about my legacy and my work. If I see you so much as opening a cabinet out of turn, I'm giving you two choices: check into a mental hospital until they deem you fit to leave, or take bus fare back to the city and shack up with whoever you can, because you've lost our support."

"Daniel," Mum said, rubbing his arm, trying vainly to soothe him.

"Don't argue with me, Mandy! This was her last chance and she threw it away. No, blew it up with all of *us* inside. Let's get out of here. She can sleep on the couch tonight."

Dad half-dragged Mum out the front door with a lot of clunks and bangs. After the door had shut behind them, she heard Mum's muffled voice before they faded away. "Are you sure we should leave her alone in there?"

Best question of the day, folks. Right there. She sure as hell didn't want to be alone with herself.

Sitting in the silence, with only the ticking of the kitchen clock for company, she stayed motionless for a long time, locked in a state of not thinking, not wanting to think or move or feel anything beyond the gnawing ache in her gut, which probably wasn't going away anytime soon, and her protesting ankles, still locked into her high heels. Eventually, she reached down and undid the clasps on them, pulling her feet out and stretching her toes.

Behind the bedroom door, something settled. At least, she hoped it was just settling, a piece of debris that had lain at a weird angle for too long, or something dislodged off the edge of the bed by all the stomping. She crept to the door in her bare feet, stretching over to put her ear to the door lest something knife-like shoot out at her from beneath. She heard the empty room sound like the sea in a conch shell and the echo of the ticking kitchen clock, but no uneven clicking of legs or the snicker-snack of bladed arms.

She went to the kitchen and pulled a set of work gloves out of the drawer under the sink. She couldn't sleep with those things in the house. She would have to dispose of them but no one could dig a hole deep enough for all that junk in half a day. Maybe if Mum and Dad had believed her, maybe if they'd stayed to help her—she wiped away a tear. This tear wouldn't have any brothers or sisters, as being alone, *feeling* alone, was something she had grown accustomed to over time. Not in the way that things sometimes grow on a person, like Brussels sprouts or peas, but in the way of a tolerated co-worker who never learns to cover their mouth when they sneeze.

Next she went to the shoe closet, where she had stashed a few Rubbermaid tubs from when she had moved in. These would do. She couldn't dig a hole but she couldn't have them re-assembling themselves in the middle of the night either. There was only one existing hole big enough and she was not looking forward to opening that again. Dad was going to kill her, but he'd find a way to hate her no matter what he saw on those tapes. She could even give the security camera the finger while she did it.

After tying a dishtowel around her nose and mouth, Kenzie took the tub into her room and got to work. She cringed as she opened the door but the room was exactly as she'd left it, bodies scattered, headboard mutilated. Gathering the pieces was surprisingly easy in the full light of day. As long as the board didn't come barging in again and pointing out her many inadequacies, she could handle a little bit of rusty crap on the floor. She tossed the pieces into the bins, only as much as she could carry in one load. Then, one by one, she took each full bin down to the shaft.

She emptied the last bin into the hole, listening to the clanging of metal and the ripping of ancient paper and the thud of wood all jumbled together. The simulacra jumbled up at the bottom too, becoming a warning to anyone who may want to venture down.

Kenzie wondered if Ettenby had thrown the simulacra down there originally. The hole must have kept them contained, because no one else had seen them before Dad had found the hatch. As she watched the jagged spikes for signs of movement, she realized that she could be in serious danger if she ever fell down there again. She pulled out her cell phone and dialled. She didn't let him finish his hello before speaking.

"Ant, I think you owe me a favour for springing your resignation on me like that. Meet me at the front gate of the Log Palace and bring your rivet gun. I'll do the rest."

THE SEALED HATCH

Mum and Dad came back wrapped in hush once the sun had set. They asked no questions. They disappeared into their room with the quiet click of the latch and then the apartment was silent again. Kenzie pulled some blankets out of the linen closet—at least these were not all covered in do-it-yourself sawdust from the headboard. She put on her heaviest set of flannel pyjamas and a fluffy blue housecoat. Now that her tension had subsided, she just felt cold. Especially her feet. She stuffed them under the blankets, hoping she might wake up with them warm.

As she settled into a cocoon of cotton on the couch, she felt like water displaced from a pool when someone has just done an enormous cannonball, suddenly much thinner than before and unable to find its way back to its source. Maria was gone. Mum and Dad were almost gone. She dreaded what they would find on those tapes, sure that there would be something there to indict her. Surely it was all her fault and whatever they saw would prove it.

Like many times before, Kenzie handled it. She forced herself to lie still for the count of one hundred: no fidgets, no opened eyes. She did it over again. She felt heavy as she started the third round, then the weariness made itself known, seeping out of her joints and bleeding through her muscles like watercolour travelling up a brush.

Kenzie was heavy and sinking. She tried to take in a breath and couldn't. Her skin was cold again. Where were her blankets?

She opened her eyes. Water pressed in on her from all around, cold water. She let out a startled breath that bubbled up, tickling her face. She flailed as she sank, feeling stone walls, a square shaft just wide enough for her to touch the edges with her arms out. She knew this place.

Panic gripped her as she remembered the riveted lid. Still, she pumped her arms and legs, pulling herself upward as her lungs burned. Metallic clouds drifted across her eyes, and her arms and legs felt like rubber, and still she flailed for her life, like an old 1930s cartoon. Her last moments would be utterly ridiculous.

Her hand hit metal and pain bloomed along her knuckles. She stretched up, face first, and reached a few inches of air at the top of the shaft. She gasped, struggling to catch her breath as she treaded water. She would eventually go under if she couldn't break the door down. She wondered if she could even get any force behind it when she was in the water. She'd have to try.

She banged on the lid. It didn't even vibrate much. Damn, she'd done a good job with the rivet gun. She braced her legs against the wall and threw all of her weight behind it, pushing with her elbows and locking her spine. Nothing.

She screamed. "Help me! Somebody please, help me!"

Something skittered over the lid. It wasn't human. Apparently, she hadn't killed all of them. Even now, locked in a losing battle against the water, she wished she had something, anything, to etch a picture on the bottom side of the lid. It might not work that way, but she'd take a chance. At least she'd take another few out with her.

She could see now. Why could she see? A bioluminescent blue glow had infused the water, settling on the creases in the bricks and making her skin luminous, like it had been one time when she went to a gimmicky black-light mini putt event in Niagara Falls. Down below her, the debris from the dead simulacra was still there, now outlined in all of its deadly splendour by the glowing particles. The glow started out dim, only bright enough to see because her eyes had been deprived of light for hours, and grew stronger, to the strength of a freshly cracked glow stick. Where it collected, it made little bug eyes as bright as an LED. They wavered in the water, slimy organisms watching her from all angles, floating by her at an uncomfortable distance from her eyes.

The water grabbed her right leg below the knee and pulled, hard and fast. Water flew up Kenzie's nose so fast that her sinuses burned like fire. She pushed a hand over her nose and mouth while she screamed out with everything she had. Her other arm grabbed for something, anything, to pull her back up. She was hurtling toward the rusty pile of monster bones that she had dumped into the pit. Her toes made contact and she braced for the end.

Then her toes were in soft sand. Soft, slimy sand with years of dead plant life collecting in it, and don't forget fish poop. She was still cold, and the water still pulsed with the little luminescent eyeballs. Her housecoat billowed around her in the calm waters. Here, the light was like day. She could see everything on the floor of the river.

She was breathing. At some point, she had started breathing with no resistance, as if the water was air.

The bottom of the river stretched out before her, rolling like the hills of some underwater esplanade. She almost expected to see walking paths running through it, with couples holding hands and people walking their dogs. Instead, there were only the paths of the water currents written in ridges on the sand and the shadows of a distant shoal of fish.

She felt someone beside her, saw them hovering out of the corner of her eye. She faced them, only to find that it was a swaying patch of seaweed, the delicate kind that lived in fresh water. It wandered slowly back and forth, once brushing her with a few errant fronds that felt like being lassoed with sewing thread.

She heard a ticking, muffled by the water. At her feet, a simulacrum crawled out of the weeds like a cockroach breaching a curtain. It was the child, the corseted tin can from the display case, with its cracked porcelain face and hands. It crawled to her on all fours, its cheap nylon curls moving very little in the current.

"Kenzie," it said, the word rolling around, echoing in its little drum of a head like a marble in a mug. It was thinking of her, but not just her: what she represented. Who she really *was*. The thing saw her.

"I like your neck. Can I take it?" the thing said. Its voice was like a cheap recording of someone playing a child, all innocence and syrup.

"No," Kenzie said, her hands rising to her throat. "Stay away from it. I need it."

Kenzie heard splashes from the bank, far away and behind her. Thousands of clicks and scratches and scuttles overwhelmed Kenzie's ears, as a wave of hundreds of simulacra blew in, like crabs migrating across the ocean floor. They scuttled around her, all in a hurry to get to a point about a hundred feet away, in the obscure depths where the little luminescent organisms formed a fuzzy blue wall with nothing beyond. She spotted one clicking by using her old pencil for a leg, the pencil she had thrown into the marsh. Her whole body shivered.

The child tilted its head at her. "Goodbye," it said, like a demented Cinderella. "Goodbye!"

It scuttled away with the others. They lined up around something that Kenzie could not yet see, forming an arc with rays like a stylized sun or maybe a really big eyelash. Something Kenzie could not see, the water itself perhaps, started to pick up the heads of all the simulacra. Row by row they rose into the air, their bodies falling into piles that the next ones scuttled up. Eventually, the water was a sphere of masks, of not-quite heads, like a sea urchin made of eerie, empty-eyed faces.

The luminescent stuff in the water drifted inward, toward the ball of faces, coalescing into a set of tentacles holding them up. Something that from this distance looked like weirdly shaped toothpicks rose up from the ocean floor in the center of the mass. Some were curved...bones. Legs, arms, ribcage: whatever it had been able to salvage from the shafts. There was more than one set of bones, more than ten. Who were all of these people? She had only read of one death. Where had all these bones come from?

Slowly, like a child putting together a set of Tinkertoys, the thing assembled the bones into a ribcage of sorts, made of far too many ribs facing the wrong way, a double row of them on each side. It stacked the leg bones on top of one another and used pelvises as platforms between them. The shoulder and arm bones it used the right way, only in the wrong place and too many, rotating the rib cage with the tentacles.

It had no skull. Instead, the luminous organisms coalesced once again, moulding themselves in and out of the shape of a face. First a screaming old woman with an unhinged jaw, then a young man whose face was a little too flat, then a goose. It finally settled on the old woman, but her jowls fluttered now and then, changing shape, boneless. The face sculpture tried to smile, but the thing could not smile. It grabbed a rib bone and pulled it in front of the face in a grisly imitation, like a really morbid happy face T-shirt.

The mouth moved. It was trying to form words. The face flickered and lost shape. Soon it disappeared. It shuffled a few of the masks from tentacle to tentacle. Finally, it shoved twenty or thirty with hinged jaws at her. They stopped only inches from her, their hinges clacking and chattering with no sound. Kenzie crouched low to the ground and they followed her.

The face swayed, as if the thing had tensed its muscles. When they spoke, they spoke in unison, an old decorative Japanese mask and a ma-ma doll among the more recognizable ones.

"You have to help me," it said, in a voice like dolphin-speak, high-pitched and warbling.

"You kill people," said Kenzie.

"Help me help me help me help me help me," the faces chattered, growing closer.

Kenzie screamed. Her feet dug into the muck as she cringed away from the faces.

"Stop it! What the fuck do you want?"

"I want Kenzie. I want George. I want Daniel. I want Mandy. I want Anthony. I want Maria."

"You can't have her!" Kenzie cried out, lashing out at a face made out of gnarled tree root.

"Stop," it said. "Stop, stop, stop, stop, stop, stop. You know my pain. I have no face. Never had a face. Want a face. Want a name."

"You're never going to have that. What in the hell are you? Not human."

"I could be...I just need more flesh, more bones, more to study from. I see you struggle with it too. You study, and you watch, and yet they reject you every time you try. They will never understand you. Why not give them to me? They're no use to you."

"Who?"

"Daniel and Mandy. I want them. Bring them to me. Drop one in each of the holes. I'll be your friend if you do. I'll never leave you, never hurt you, and you can give me anybody who stands in your way. We understand each other, we faceless ones."

"I'm not like you," Kenzie cried out. "You never knew who you were. I knew who I was, I just ignored and abused her. I made myself into someone else to try to gain acceptance, but it hollowed me out. I couldn't do it forever. I'm not some shapeless thing, just bent out of shape."

"One shell can tell another. I have seen the way you hide. You have as many masks as I. Would it not be simpler to rid yourself of the people forcing you to wear yours?"

"I'm not killing my parents!" Kenzie said.

"You force me. I wish I was not so alone. Always I am alone at the end. Bring them to me by sunset tomorrow, put them down the holes, or I shall take you in their place. You have such a pretty face. I will wear it until it crumbles, like the others."

"No matter what you do, you'll never be human," Kenzie said. The masks chattered at her in response. Some of them floated, dead. It was losing coordination in its anger.

"There are strange magics in this world, older than your petty race. You are so simple, so incredibly simple, and yet it has taken me so long to learn you...but learn you I will. And when I rise, I will rule from the shadows, a puppet master of all the things you throw away, including yourselves."

A jet of water struck Kenzie in the gut, and when she opened her eyes, the masks were gone. Her mouth was clamped shut and her lungs begged her for air. The water was water again and she could not breathe. She kicked up for the surface, emerging, gasping, from the water. She was near the shore. She could see the Log Palace, a blurred black hummock in the distance. She swam into the shallows, then crawled out on trembling arms and legs. Rocks bit into her knees as she crawled up the bank but she didn't care.

Once she had gotten under the pine trees, too far for one of those accursed tentacles to reach, she collapsed onto the grass and pine needles, staring up at the light. It was early morning already. Never had she felt more unprepared to face a day—and for her, that was really saying something. She lay on the ground, weak, cold, wondering if she could ever get up again. Maybe she would just freeze here. At least then nothing could hurt Mum and Dad.

But it would hurt them. The simulacra would hurt them. The thing in the marsh, the faces, could only control them so far. It had given the simulacra autonomy. They were made of pieces of it but it seemed to be a coalition of some kind of microorganism, and once on their own, the pieces had a will of their own. The ones she had killed had gotten hungry and tried to come for her. Something had stopped them. Was it the main organism or something within her?

Maybe it was trying to use her because it couldn't touch her. She wondered how long that would last. The drawings she'd done while asleep were so much better than anything she did while awake, and if she were awake when the simulacra finally came for her, she doubted she could defend herself. She wouldn't even know where to start.

She rolled over with a groan. Everything ached, like she had thrown up all night. The pine needles pricked her hands. She could still feel her hands. That was progress. She wanted someone to throw a blanket around her, give her dry clothes, help her into the shower.

She staggered to the building. The air system blew a gust onto her chest as she walked in, taking away her breath and causing another round of shakes. She steadied herself on the table that she had loaded her luggage onto on her first day. All she wanted was some understanding. She had no reason to expect it. She had gone into the river again. On top of everything else, she had gone into the river. She was unrepentantly haunted and no one would forgive her.

She paused at the foot of the stairs, fending off a bout of light-headedness. She swayed, then steadied herself, feeling like she was moving thousand-pound counterweights to keep her balance.

Step by trembling step, she pulled herself up, using the handrail for support, holding herself up with her arms. She pushed the door to the apartment open, hearing the drips she still left on the linoleum. Mum and Dad were there in the living room, hunched over a laptop on the floor, facing the door. They looked up at her, grief etched on their faces, tears streaming down.

"Oh Kenzie," said Mum. "We're so sorry."

THE TRUTH ABOUT HUMANS AND MONSTERS

K enzie stood there, silent, swaying in her fatigue and feeling like she was drunk and trying to put together a picture puzzle that didn't quite fit.

"What? Why are you sorry? I obviously just fell in the river again. Aren't you going to harangue me for it? You'll probably feel better."

Mum's face crumpled and she sobbed into Dad's shoulder. Dad motioned Kenzie over to the laptop, his hand motions soft and welcoming. He shook his head and Kenzie knew he was on the brink of tears as well.

"I can't even begin to describe what I'm feeling right now. You'll just have to come and watch, and I'll have to hope that you can forgive us."

Kenzie wobbled over, unable to forget her fatigue but not so cold anymore. She kneeled down on the carpet with Mum and Dad. The security camera software filled the screen. They had paused on a grainy, black-and-white image.

"I've assembled all of the clips together. We thought you should see it in order."

Dad played the first video. There was something wrong with the reception: a wavy, underwater effect distorting the image. She could just make out the Folk Art wing foyer, the security light, and the hatch in the floor. It was night time.

A human shape walked into the frame, then another. The image wavered and swayed, but she could tell by their walk, and by their pyjamas, which they'd had since roughly 1987, that it was Mum and Dad. Dad kneeled down and unlocked the hatch, letting it clang open with a sound that even the terrible mic on the security camera picked up. Mum and Dad backed up and waited, deadly still except for the swaying of the image on the screen. The simulacra ticked past them, just a few.

She recognized the third figure, even from the back. She staggered into view, sleepwalking, driven by some invisible force toward the hole. Mum came to her and put a hand to her lower back, guiding her to the hole. Kenzie kneeled down, lowering herself part of the way into the blackness. Mum took both her hands and stretched herself into the pit, lowering her as far as she could before letting her go.

A knot had formed in the pit of Kenzie's stomach. She already felt like she had spent the night throwing up. Now she might get the experience too.

Dad said nothing. A tear ran down his face as he played the next video. By the count on the bottom, it was two nights ago. He walked down the darkened gallery hallway, the bunching of keys visible in his hand. He went to the case containing the simulacra, undid the door and walked away.

"I have no doubt I left the door to the apartment unlocked, as well," he said, sadness permeating his voice, his posture, everything.

Kenzie felt like cold stone. Even the river water on her skin added to the effect, making her feel like a slick pebble on a shore somewhere. The questions poured from her.

"Do you remember doing this?"

Dad shut his eyes for a long time before answering.

"I didn't before I watched the footage but now...I have pictures that flit through my mind, like remembering a dream days later. I remember enough to know that it is not just some trick."

The next one was harder. The next one hurt.

"Did you have a choice?" she said, clenching and unclenching her hands, hating how the action tied her to Dad but needing to do it all the same.

"Some would say no," Dad said, sadly. "But I believe we did. It's just that the choice was made up of all the little choices we had made, for years and years, the ones that opened the gate for whatever monstrosity haunts this place. Our minds were open to it, because they were closed to you."

Kenzie felt tears rise in her eyes. She felt the betrayal of many years, not just a few weeks of being put down holes and running from terrifying junk dolls. It snaked through her like a wiring system just lighting up, but it had been her wiring system all along. She just hadn't allowed herself to feel it.

"Every once in a while," Dad continued, "I think we all see something distilled before us that shows us what we are. It may just be a part, but it shows us the whole. I saw myself on these videos and I knew that I had been doing this to you long before I was caught. I don't remember any of this but it felt so familiar that I suddenly felt the weight of everything, all of the things we've broken over the years. Including you. Why are we so cruel to each other, Kenzie? I have to think that we can all be better than this."

Kenzie closed her eyes. She had not been prepared for this. She had been ready for a fight. Perhaps that was part of the problem. But before she answered, there was someone else she needed to hear from.

"Mum?" she said.

Mum gave a shudder. She did not speak for a few moments, tears running down her cheeks. "I wanted to be the perfect mom," she said finally, "but I never realized until now that it was all about me. I was so focused on what other people thought I should be, I was never the person you needed me to be. It's like I was deaf and blind wherever you were concerned, just like I was in that tape. I want to listen to you. All I really want is to love you and have a relationship with you. I just didn't know how. I couldn't see you through my perfectionism. Please give me another chance to prove I'm not the woman on that tape. I'll never forgive myself for putting you down that hole. Never."

Kenzie dissolved into tears. This was the ending that she had always hoped for but never dared expect, and here it was, from the unlikeliest of sources and at the worst of times. As she softened, falling into her parents' arms, as they all cried together, she realized that there was a weight on her, too.

"I was always so intent on getting even with you for not listening to me," she said, "that I never stopped to ask if I was hurting myself. But now I realize I was just playing into the same hurtful dynamic that has kept all of us prisoner. We've all hurt each other and we do need to do better. All of us."

Dad pulled back from the group, his brows pulled together and the lines on his face standing out.

"What is happening here? We have to get away, today, and forget about our possessions. We should all pack our bags, get the most important things, and just leave. We've saved money. We can afford to start over someplace else. Let's just go and let the board deal with whatever monstrosity is here."

"More people will die if we do that," Kenzie said, sadly. "We could get away. They might not be so lucky."

"How do you know that?" Mum said. "No one's died. There have been hundreds of people in and out of here for months and not even an injury."

Kenzie heard it as a criticism at first, but forced herself to engage peacefully. She would break the cycle. Mum could not know what she had experienced.

"The dolls...they move around. They're dangerous. There's something in the water, in the river. It controls them but not completely. It's made up of smaller creatures, little microorganisms that band together to make one larger thing. I saw it last night. It pulled me into the shaft again and somehow pulled me into the river."

"But you put rivets in the lid. We saw them when we came in," Mum said, nearly crying again.

"I know. It doesn't seem to obey all of our natural laws. When it pulled me into the river, it did something to me. I could breathe underwater when it wanted me to."

"I want to believe you but this is all so strange. I would be calling the doctors and having you admitted if I hadn't just seen those tapes. But still, no one has died."

"They have in the past," said Kenzie. "The witch I've been reading about, the Widow Fenn...I think she fell under its influence. She was alone, and bitter, and friendless, and I think it got to her, or she woke it up experimenting with witchcraft, or something. How it started, I don't exactly know. But I know how it ends—with her melding half of her mind with a goose and jumping down a shaft of her own making—a companion shaft to the one in this building. That's why I think Ettenby was affected too. I think he stole the newspapers from the library to stop anyone from suspecting what he was doing. Dad, were there any suspicious deaths while Ettenby held the Log Palace?"

Dad put his hand to his chin.

"Not suspicious *deaths* exactly but he did have a rather odd policy regarding his servants."

"And what was that?"

"Part of their contract was that their funerary expenses would be covered by Ettenby, but they had to agree to be buried on his land. Nothing that would seem unusual until all the rest of it came up, but while we were digging for the renovations, we never found a single bone, let alone a body. We all just assumed that they had been moved eventually to another cemetery when burial plots on private land went out of vogue."

"That's where all the bones came from," said Kenzie.

Mum made a deep sigh. "I feel like I want to ask, but I don't want to know the answer," she said.

The sick feeling in the pit of Kenzie's stomach grew and a lump gathered in her throat.

"No, you should know the rest," said Kenzie. "The thing in the river...I don't know what it was, but it's old, and shapeless, and it wants to be human. It wants to be like us but doesn't understand what it means. It grabs body parts and bones and puppets them until they wear out, assembles them into monstrosities of its own vanity. It wants a face. It wants more bodies. It told me that if I didn't deliver you to it, one in each shaft, it would send the dolls to come and kill all of us."

"Good God," said Mum. "We have to leave, Daniel, we have to! We can't face something like this. We can't risk it."

"And what are we supposed to do?" Dad said, his voice rising again. "Just let it kill the next family that moves in or a guest? Or one of my friends?"

"Your friends that fired Kenzie and let you resign? Those friends, you mean? Send them a damn letter. I didn't come this far in life to become a Lego booster pack to a swamp monster!" Mum said, raising her voice too.

Kenzie suppressed a smile, knowing it was inappropriate but liking this new side of Mum.

What were they going to do, though? The logical thing to do was just to leave, but Kenzie had some reservations.

"It can teleport people," Kenzie said. "Maybe it gets in our systems from drinking the water and that's how it affects our minds, but I know it can teleport people too, because none of what happened last night obeyed the laws of physics. If we leave, there's a really good chance we'll just wake up back here, if that's where it wants us. And if it has to teleport us back here, it's going to be desperate and we're going to arrive on its terms. We could wake up in a shaft filled with water and no one around until morning. We have to meet it on our terms because that's the only way we can catch it off-guard."

Dad put a hand over his face. Mum's lip trembled. She turned her head away like Kenzie had a wound she just couldn't bear to look at. She looked up at the ceiling. "What are we going to do?"

"I don't know," Kenzie replied.

A buzz from the coffee table startled Kenzie, making her fall back onto her hands. A familiar tune filled the room. Her phone rattled against the table, dancing in a slow circle as the phone rang and rang. She picked it up.

"Kenzie?" Maria said. "Can you see the parking lot from your apartment there?"

"What?" said Kenzie, fear and vulnerability slowly filling her again like a balloon ready to pop.

"Come to the window," Maria said.

Kenzie moved on wooden legs to the bedroom window. Maria stood in the parking lot, a cab just pulling away. She saw her and waved. Kenzie waved too, tried to look happy.

"I've come to get you and bring you home," said Maria. "I love you and I want to be with you. You belong with me."

"I do," Kenzie said. "But you need to come in and talk to us. There's a lot that you need to know and you're going to find it completely unbelievable."

"Okay...what, are your parents being good to you all of a sudden?"

"That's not the weirdest part," she said.

DEFINING THE EDGES

Mum and Dad came with Kenzie to the door. First, they stopped in the office to print a sheet that said 'CLOSED DUE TO FLOODING.' Dad taped it to the museum's front door, then took the opportunity to go down to the driveway and flip over the 'closed' board on the main welcome sign.

Kenzie looked down to the river as they left the building. The water crawled by, moving with a lithe muscularity, like the workings of a large snake's belly as it slithers along a branch.

Maria waited for her in the parking lot, small and thin against the robust background of the trees, the rocks, the wide-open spaces, and the sky. But to Kenzie, she was the diamond sitting in the middle of a corn field. Her smile sent rays across the lawn that could illuminate a small football stadium. Kenzie ran to her, against all of her better judgement, like a little kid. She threw her arms around her.

"I thought you were done with me," Kenzie said.

"I'm never going to be done with you," said Maria.

Kenzie breathed in the smell of her shampoo. She had forgotten just how much she missed Maria's soft breasts pressed against her and the warmth of her, like a furnace burned within her, powering her to unknown lands and untold heights.

Mum waited at the edge of the parking lot, hands gathered sheepishly in front of her.

"So, this is your mom," said Maria. She managed to keep most of the unimpressed voice and body language in check, but some seeped out around the edges. "Hello, I'm Maria." She held out a hand, her tone suitable for an adult Kindergartner.

Mum came up, her steps and body language screaming awkwardness, but she took the proffered hand and shook it. "I'm Mandy," she said. "I've...behaved badly. I think you already know but I thought you should know...I know."

Kenzie nodded to Maria in response to her quizzical look.

Dad took that moment to arrive back from the sign. "So, this is what Mandy was hiding from me, is it?" he said, hands on hips. "Why do you have to be such a damned prude, Mandy? I thought she was on drugs!"

"Well, if you weren't such a hothead, maybe I could have told you."

"And drugs were better? Really?" said Dad, giving an eye roll that used his whole head.

Kenzie felt her face grow hot. They still had a long way to go before they weren't abjectly embarrassing. Who knows. They were family. Maybe they would never get to that point.

"Dad, Maria, Maria, Dad," she said. "Now can we save the rest for family therapy? *Please?* I need a moment alone with Maria before we go inside."

"Be careful out here and stay away from the river," Mum called as they retreated back into the building.

"Not an idiot, Mum. I'm twenty-seven!" Kenzie gave a sigh. "That's them. In all their nagging, bickering glory. Voila," she said. "I will never end up like that and if you see symptoms, I need you to promise to shoot me."

"Deal," said Maria. "Now why are we standing out here, exactly? It's a bit cold."

"I know how this sounds but I need you to call that taxi back, go down into town, and get a hotel room. If all goes well, I'll meet you there later tonight. If I don't show up, call the cops, and you can have my stuff. Distribute it as you feel would best aid humanity, especially my rubber duck collection."

Maria slapped her hands to her thighs. She gave the exasperated look she saved for burnt turkeys and long lines at the license bureau.

"Kenzie, what the fuck are you talking about? I've been getting this creepy cult vibe off you for a while now and you better not be telling me you're doing some sort of mass suicide ritual. The way you've described your parents, I might just believe something like that. *Man*, your mom is awkward!'

"She doesn't get better," said Kenzie. "But no. You're going to have to follow me a long way on this, so get ready. There is some kind of ancient evil here lurking in the water that is looking for a human face and has been manipulating my parents and trying to get to me in order to add to its body collection. It has an army of scary dolls that it put together out of junk to look like humans (I call them simulacra) and they don't always obey its commands because it's made up of millions of tiny microorganisms. It also travels through these weird shafts in the ground that it shouldn't be able to get into and teleports people when the mood is right. It's been killing people and cutting up their bodies for at least two hundred years that I can figure from the records and it is still no closer to getting a human face, but if it ever does I think that humanity may be in big trouble. Big trouble," Kenzie said, nodding at the end for emphasis.

Maria returned her nod, mouth wide open. "I'm not patronizing you, but I have to ask. Does psychosis run in your family?"

"No," said Kenzie. "And yes, I'm taking all my meds and vitamins. Mum and Dad are jerks but they've never been diagnosed with anything. We also have video tape of the simulacra from the security cameras. I'll tell you the whole story when we're all safe but right now you have to leave. The thing in the river wants my parents dead so it can try again to build a human body for itself. It pulled me into the river last night and gave me an ultimatum: either I deliver them, or it kills all of us."

Maria snorted. She placed her hands on her hips and squared her feet underneath her.

"Kenzie! If this is not some sick, twisted joke, you need to call the authorities."

"And tell them what? What would they do, exactly? And let me tell you, the police and fire officials around here are worse than useless. They'd just tell me to put up a 'Monsters Keep off Grass' sign."

Maria tilted her head. Oh boy. Now Kenzie was gonna get it.

"Okay, so what's your brilliant plan?"

Kenzie shifted her weight, and her gaze.

"Look, I don't know, but there's got to be some way to stop it. I killed a ton of the simulacra in my sleep. It had something to do with my drawings."

Maria dropped her chin almost down to her chest.

"Your drawings?" she said, as if that was the most fantastical thing Kenzie had said tonight. "You're actually drawing again?"

"Yeah...the only good ones are when I'm asleep, though."

"Show me," Maria said, walking past her. "This, I gotta see."

Kenzie threw up her arms. "Maria! You can't *stay* here. It will get you too and I couldn't live with myself."

"You're not gonna live with yourself if you're dead," said Maria. "And I'm not leaving you if I can help you stay alive. So, show me these drawings, and shut up and love me."

For the second time that day, Kenzie felt herself grinning in spite of everything that was going on.

K enzie and Maria stood in front of the mangled headboard, the dim afternoon light filtering through the windows, filling the reliefs with shadows and insinuations. The weather had grown overcast, the clouds pregnant with rain and threatening to go into labour with distant peals of thunder.

"Wow," said Maria. "It's really disturbing but I can still see it hanging on a wall in a museum somewhere. Why didn't you ever tell me you were this good?"

"I wasn't," said Kenzie. "Let me show you some of the stuff I did when I was conscious."

Kenzie went to the desk and unfolded her large sketchbook. She took Maria to her concept designs for the museum and the sketches she'd done of the river, the water lilies, and the negative space between them.

"Well, you're nuts," said Maria.

"You're just concluding that now?"

"Yup. The fact that you can't see that these drawings are just as good as the ones on the headboard proves it. I'll call the men in the white coats," she said, giving Kenzie a longer-than-average kiss.

"I'm not letting you hide this ever again," Maria said after they parted, tapping the page with her index finger. "Why couldn't you do this for a living?"

"Tried already," said Kenzie. "Failed spectacularly. What more is there to say?"

"I don't think it was because of you. That I think you just had bad luck and bad luck is a lottery."

Kenzie looked at the water lilies again. Maybe they weren't so bad after all. "You sound like another friend of mine," she said.

Maria ran her hand over the latest water lily drawing, the one where Kenzie had tried to capture the negative space.

"There is a weird composition to this one, though, like you were trying to depict something that wasn't really there," she said.

Kenzie frowned.

"That's weird that you should say that, because that's exactly how I felt when I did these studies. Like something inside me was trying to express something with no shape."

Maria put her hands in the small of her back, the look of thoughtfulness on her face that she got when putting a particularly difficult chair together from IKEA.

"Maybe it's about control, about definition. A lot of ancient cultures believe that if you create the perfect image of something, you control it. You understand it and own it. Some believe you can even kill it. Images have power. Maybe you do, too."

The light fell over Kenzie and she felt it, for the first time in so many years. It was the light that had illuminated the first tender leaf that she had picked up off the ground. It was the light that had bled into her soul when she first saw a forest and wanted to pick up a pen and record it for history because its beauty needed to be seen. It was the light that had flooded into her from a computer screen when she had first seen Canooie live and move and dance. She had created life that day and she had a tiny portion of the power of the Almighty God in her fingertips when she held that pen. Light expanded within her and she knew what she could do to give them their best and only chance.

"Maria," she said, "I want you to take a few hours and get to know my parents. They're fucked up but they're not bad people. They've proven that to me since I arrived here, despite everything we thought. Watch the videos with them if you're still doubting. As for me, I need to be alone, and quiet, and fruitful. I need my art supplies and my mind, and my memories. I want to spend these last few hours, at least, doing what I'm truly good at. If we fail, maybe they'll find the drawings and know what to look for. Maybe I'll end up in a museum and complete the circle of life."

Maria gave a nervous chuckle. With another long kiss and a lingering embrace, she left Kenzie in the ruins of her bedroom, at the desk by the window.

With the door shut, Kenzie reached for her markers, her pens, her pencils. These would be the weapons she brought to bear against the thing which had no face.

FACING DOWN THE NIGHT

The rain broke as the sun set, both outside and in. As Kenzie studied the drawing, feeling as though there were a few strokes missing but not able to decide where, a crack of thunder echoed through the building and a drop of water hit the desk.

Almost instinctively, she folded the drawing up and slipped it under her shirt. She ran into the kitchen as the downpour began, rain falling from the ceiling, soaking the carpets and making the linoleum treacherous and slippery. She dove under the sink and pulled out a garbage bag, then tossed the box to Maria.

"Quickly, rip some arm holes and put these on!" she said. Maria pulled out a bag and handed the box to Mum. Kenzie put two on herself, just to be sure, then her raincoat. She had to protect the paper. She ran back into the bedroom, skidding once on the wet carpet, and shoved a few markers into her jeans pockets, in the colours that she thought might be missing.

"What's that ticking sound?" Maria called from the living room. "It sounds like hundreds of rats in the walls."

A shadow crossed the window. It was a simulacrum, followed by many more.

"It's the simulacra," said Kenzie. "They're covering the building."

"Let's get down to the river," Dad said. "It's time."

Kenzie opened the door to the apartment, the others behind her. In the hall, the rain was even stronger, coming down in sheets almost too thick to see through. The floor was covered in water, which flowed around their ankles toward the main staircase.

All of the paint had bled off of the carvings. Without the paint, they were every carving Kenzie had seen and a hundred more, all jumbled up together, making her eyes play tricks as her mind put one together, then another. They became all of the images and strange twisted combinations between images, playing with the mind's natural inclination to assemble shapes.

"And I thought they were creepy when we came in here," said Maria. "Now I can't stop looking at them. Why can I see the hundred different things?"

"Keep moving," said Kenzie. "Everything in here was made or inspired by that thing and it will trap us if it can help it."

She took Maria by the elbow and tugged her. Mum and Dad couldn't leave the gallery fast enough.

Kenzie looked down the other hall and the case was wide open again. This time though, she knew Dad hadn't opened it. The painting at the end of the hallway had melted away to the underpainting, a hollow-eyed ochre madman sitting on a gravestone rather than an overstuffed chair. Writing coursed down the canvas in ink rusted out to a red-brown, looking like someone had written it in blood. Ettenby had written a confession under that painting. Kenzie sloshed through the water without even thinking about it, wanting to get a closer look, to get the real story and the last piece of the Ettenby puzzle. She had known about the witch but what had he done?

Dad pulled her back from the fire doors just as they slammed shut, so hard that the glass within them splintered. A few pieces flew at Kenzie's face. She shielded her eyes but one piece slashed the outside of her arm.

"Take your own advice," Dad yelled over the rushing of the water down the stairs. "You could have been trapped in there and stabbed to death by the dolls."

"You're the one who got me into research," she quipped as they faced the stairs.

The water was draining into the shaft. Kenzie had known it before seeing it, from the sound and the source, but when she looked over the banister and witnessed the whirlpool for herself, she shuddered.

"I don't want to go down there again," she said. "If the current catches us, it will take us right under that lid. I just know it will."

"Let's just stay together and hold onto the railing," said Mum.

They all went, step by step, calling to one another and holding hands. Everyone had one hand on the person in front of them, one hand on the railing. Dad got to the bottom. The water swirled around his ankles but he stayed up. Maria got to the bottom. She slipped a little but stayed up. Mum got to the bottom, and it was like she didn't have feet anymore. She flipped onto her side like a fish, pulled toward the hole faster than the amount of water would have made possible. Dad had her hand. It slipped but held fast after that. Maria grabbed for her other hand and caught it, but still Mum stayed flat on her stomach, pulled hard by the water.

"Kenzie!" she called. "Help!"

Kenzie completed the last few stairs as fast as she could, agonizingly slowly, and ran up around Mum. She stared at the horrible lid over the shaft, sucking in water that went who-knew-where. She planted her feet, and centered herself. She lifted Mum's waist. Mum found her feet again. They all kept hold of her until they reached the front doors.

Outside, the thunderstorm raged. They emerged onto the lawn to the glint of a thousand little eyes and hands and nasty can bodies crawling around, staring at them. The simulacra carpeted the lawn and the building, a continuous writhing mass of animate junk. At the sound of the door closing they parted, making a path down to the river.

They all went, as the water rose in a giant, unnatural hump from the river bed, and glowed that eerie blue-green from Kenzie's nightmare. It was a nightmare, even if it had really happened. They stepped sideways to avoid slipping on the grass and losing everything before the confrontation even began.

The simulacra rushed around them in a wave, to the shore. The thing rising from the river made its tentacles and picked up its disturbing faces.

"You brought them," it said in its terrifying dolphin-voice, "and one more. You can start over, blank, make a new self."

The thing rushed up the bank, around her, grabbing Mum and Dad and Maria, imprisoning them in pillars of water. She could tell by the way they struggled that the thing was suffocating them.

A wave of panic ran through Kenzie. She fumbled with dumb, numb fingers at the hem of her shirt, swiping a few times at the plastic before finally getting underneath. She yanked the drawing out from under her shirt and unfolded it, the rain spattering onto the page.

"You think you don't have a face, but you do," she shouted. "This is what you are and you are ugly."

The thing made a noise like a malevolent balloon letting out air.

"That is not what I am. I am everything and nothing. I have any shape I want. This is just the one I choose to live in."

Kenzie turned the drawing to her. Why wasn't it working? Mum and Dad clutched their necks, their faces masks of desperation. Maria struggled, trying to swim out of the column of water but remaining trapped in place. She didn't have much time. She didn't have any time.

She had no control because the creature didn't see itself in the picture. Perhaps she had to draw its own conception of itself before the magic would work. But how did it see itself?

It wanted a face.

Kenzie took out the lightest shade she had brought, the one used for delicate shadows, and in the center of the mass of tentacles and false faces, she quickly drew another face. It was a mixture of the witch and Ettenby, with bright eyes like a goose. This, this was how it saw itself. This would define, and kill, that which had no face.

"You want a face? You've got one. Look at the picture now and tell me what you see." She held up the page.

The thing screeched. The water rumbled and, one by one, all of the bodies of the simulacra blew apart like jangling metal popcorn. The thing in the water writhed and twisted, losing its coordination. Maria kicked free of her water column, which collapsed. Mum and Dad remained trapped. It was holding on to them like a clenched fist on a trembling water arm.

"I defined you," Kenzie yelled at it. "I own you, and I banish you from this earth, this dimension, this universe! Disintegrate, disperse, and let us never see your lack of face again."

The tentacles exploded. The columns of water did too, and Mum and Dad collapsed onto the ground, coughing and spluttering. And then, it was just water again. The water crept back into the river, where it would stay forevermore.

They stayed on the bank a while, arms around one another's shoulders, before travelling to the car and going to that motel that Kenzie had told

Maria about. None of them would ever cross that bridge, or enter that mansion, ever again.

EPILOGUE

Mum and Kenzie sat in a circle of other pairs, moms and dads and kids—young kids, but adults too. Many had found themselves later in life, as Kenzie had, but they were all on the same journey. Mum stood up and twenty vulnerable people watched, and listened.

"I didn't always understand my daughter," she began. "I think on some level, I felt like she was bisexual to punish me for being so critical of her. I wanted to be the perfect mum, but in the process, I forgot I had the perfect daughter, just the way she was, someone who could teach me things I never even knew I didn't know. Things got bad—I'll spare you the details, because most people that know us would find it unbelievable today to talk to us, but they got about as bad as they could get. Lives were on the line. I wanted to blame Kenzie, but then I saw a videotape of myself and I saw, right there on camera, how horrible I had become. We looked at each other then and we both knew that we could do better. And you all can do better too. All it takes is taking a good look at yourselves and an even clearer look at the people sitting across from you. Don't take them for granted. Don't feed into patterns of anger and hate. Reach out for help if you need to. We're sitting here in this support group to bring others to the place that we've gotten to. Because we've been to hell. We're the only ones that know how to pull other people out."

"Thanks Mum," said Kenzie. "And now, let's break for some coffee and cookies. Next week's family Pride meeting will be about healthy relationship choices and boundaries. There's a lot of material to cover, so arrive on time."

Kenzie got up out of the uncomfortable plastic chair, creaking her back forward.

"Ow, we have got to see if we can get a couch or two for these meetings," she said.

"We could have a fundraiser," said Mum. "Maybe some of the local businesses would chip in. You know how persistent I can be. The squeaky wheel gets the grease!"

Kenzie made her way over to the refreshment table. She poured an orange drink into a paper cup, and one for Mum. The church basement they were in had a lot of those inspirational posters all over the walls. She liked most of them but had a pretty constant reflex to rip down the one with a serene forest lake in it.

The museum had limped on after their departure, much as it scared Kenzie and the rest of the family to think of it. The organization had gotten a ton of insurance money and cleanup was underway. They had wanted to come after Dad, after her, but there was no way to prove that they had done anything. Inspectors had ruled the cause of the flood inconclusive. It had happened too fast for a few people to have filled such a large building, and all of the plumbing, roofing, and insulation was intact.

Ms. Winter had stayed on, contrary to anyone's expectations, and was leading the cleanup. Kenzie woke up worrying for her but contacting anyone still at the site scared her even more. She told herself the monster was gone.

She had seen it die. She repeated this to herself but the primal part of her, the part that wanted to live, knew that she would never touch that earth, that water, again.

The door to the church basement opened, letting in a whiff of crisp fall air. Maria walked in, her canvas jacket lined with lamb's wool bunching up around her face and making her look even cuter than usual. The nip in the air had put a healthy flush on her cheeks that went with her smile. Kenzie left the shadows of her memories and moved into the light and warmth of today.

"Hey, Lady, you went overtime tonight," Maria said. "I believe somebody has a deadline?"

"A self-imposed deadline," said Kenzie. "It's unpaid, remember?"

Maria came and put her arms around her.

"I'm not letting you quit on yourself. You've got a business plan and this time, it's going to work. You're a natural artist and people are going to be clamoring for your work."

Kenzie laughed. Maria was right. She had to finish anyway or she'd be working through Ant's visit this weekend.

"I'd give it six months," she said.

"Give it two years," Mum said, coming up and hugging both of them. "This time, we're seeing it through."

THE END

ACKNOWLEDGEMENTS

I come from a family of readers, and so the first people I need to thank for this book are my Dad, for reading to me every night for thirteen years, and my Mom, who always encouraged me to challenge myself and never forced me to read at my grade level. Nan, I can never thank you enough. You've been my biggest supporter and without you, Odyssey would still just be a dream. Pa, your sense of wonder, curiosity and inventiveness (not to mention your sense of adventure) have served me well.

Thank you to my husband, Robin McLean, the Most Interesting Man In The World, who never stopped believing that I could achieve whatever I wanted to, and who always calls me on my shit. I think we can both agree that the main weakness in this area is the lack of guards. Yeah I said it.

There are also some very specific thanks in order for Ms. Arkell, who tried to understand the teenage freak skipping class to read fantasy tomes in a deserted hallway, and Master Jeong, who gave me the discipline I needed to finish books in the first place.

Thanks to Jeanne Cavelos, Robert J. Sawyer, and all of the instructors and participants of the Odyssey Fantasy Writing Workshop, Class of 2006 and TNEO 2008. Without your critique and guidance, I would not have the commitment to craft and professionalism that I do today.

Thank you to Pat Dobie, my amazing freelance editor, who helped me whip the book into shape before submitting, and to Can-Con 2017, for providing a venue for me to pitch this concept. Thank you to all of my friends in the convention community, especially my writing colleagues who have been there for me every step of the way. Ira Nayman, Timothy Carter, Jen Frankel, Stephen B. Pearl, Karen Dales, JF Garrard, Catherine Fitzsimmons, MD Dragon, Victoria Feistner, JM Frey, and all of the wonderful authors I haven't met yet who are on this journey with me, you rock, and I look forward to our time together more than you know.

Lastly, and most importantly, I want to thank my publisher, Renaissance Press, for appreciating my vision and taking a chance on a queer horror concept that meant a lot to me. Special thanks to Marjolaine Lafrenière and Nathan Fréchette, whose hard work and dedication made this book a reality, and gave it a lot of style in the process.

Many additional thanks are due to my editors at Renaissance, Natalie Cousineau, L.P. Vallee and Vicki Martin.

That's all for the acknowledgments, but if I forgot you, please know that I am forgetful and it wasn't personal. I hope you enjoyed the book!

Renaissance.
Diverse Canadian Voices

Renaissance was founded in May 2013 by a group of friends who wanted to publish and market those stories which don't always fit neatly in a genre, or a niche, or a demographic. We weren't sure what we wanted to publish exactly, so like the happy panbibliophiles that we are, we opened our submissions, with no other personal guideline than finding a Canadian book we would fall in love with enough that we would want to publish and sell.

Five years later, this is still very true; however, we've also noticed an interesting trend in what we tended to publish. It turns out that we are naturally drawn to the voices of those who are members of a marginalized group (especially people with disabilities and LGBTQIAPP2+ people), and these are the voices we want to continue to uplift.

To us, Renaissance isn't just a business; it's a family. Being authors and artists ourselves, we are always careful to center the experience of the author above all else. We involve our authors in every step of the process, and trust that they know how to best market their labour of love, though devoted committees take on the difficult tasks of copy editing, designing and marketing to achieve professional results.

At Renaissance, we do things differently. We are passionate about books, and we care as much about our authors enjoying the publishing process as we do about our readers enjoying a great, professional quality and affordable product on the platform they prefer.

renaissancebookpress.com
info@renaissancebookpress.com

If you enjoyed this book, you will love these other Renaissance titles!

Find them all (and more!) at
renaissancebookpress.com

WE SHALL BE MONSTERS

Edited by Derek Newman-Stille

ANTHOLOGY

"It is true, we shall be monsters, cut off from all the world; but on that account we shall be more attached to one another." Mary Shelley, *Frankenstein*

Mary Shelley's genre-changing book *Frankenstein; or, the Modern Prometheus* helped to shape the genres of science fiction and horror, and helped to articulate new forms for women's writing. It also helped us to think about the figure of the outsider, to question medical power, to question ideas of "normal," and to think about what we mean by the word "monster." Derek Newman-Stille has teamed up with Renaissance Press to celebrate Frankenstein's 200th birthday by creating a book that explores Frankenstein stories from new and exciting angles and perspectives.

We Shall Be Monsters: Mary Shelley's Frankenstein Two Centuries On features a broad range of fiction stories by authors from around the world, ranging from direct interactions with Shelley's texts to explorations of the stitched, assembled body and narrative experiments in monstrous creations. *We Shall Be Monsters* collects explorations of disability, queer and trans identity, and ideas of race and colonialism.

With stories by Day Al-Mohamed, Lena Ng, Ashley Caranto Morford Cait Gordon, JF Garrard, Andrew Wilmot, Evelyn Deshane, D. Simon Turner, Kaitlin Tremblay, Lisa Carreiro Eric Choi & Joseph McGinty, Jennifer Lee Rossman, Randall G. Arnold, Alex Acks, KC Grifant, Halli Lilburn, Kev Harrison, Corey Redekop, Arianna Verbree, Max D. Stanton, Victoria K. Martin, Priya Sridhar, Liam Hogan, Joshua Bartolome

Parasomnia

by Éric Desmarais

Paranormal Suspense

At the Aux-Anges institute, nestled in the woods outside of North Bay, they study and treat parasomnias, or sleep disorders. Ashley suffers from night terrors, Terrance sleepwalks, Kiri sleep-eats, and Paul sets fires; they are there for treatment. Adelaide took the job as a counselor to discover why she still has an imaginary friend.

When they discover the secret hideout of an old club called the Dreamers, they are shocked to find that the five of them are connected through more than just the Institute.

"Parasomnia has a great plot and a diverse cast of well-rounded characters. I thoroughly enjoyed it!"
– Nathan Caro Fréchette, author of the *Family by Choice* series

"Éric Desmarais is a master of characterization. He creates unique, quirky and believable characters who I hope to meet again."
– Sue Taylor-Davidson, author of *To Pluck A Crow*

by Kaitlin Caul

Horror

**Die. Become a zombie. Get needled.
Do it all over again...**

In Redby, zombies weren't the enemy. They were just one step in a never ending cycle. Die, become a zombie, get a needle full of nanotech and live to die once more. Immortality. Or the next worse thing. But that was how life went in Redby, otherwise known as Zombie Hell.

Cassandra Saratores, former soldier turned zombie hunter (and sometimes zombie), lived in that hell for ten long years. Caught in the endless cycle of death, zombification, and resurrection, Cass became scarred inside and out.
When the walls came down and Redby became nothing more than a sensational news story, those scars remained.
Now she spends her days in a mental hospital, reminiscing on life as one of the undead.

Ten years in hell changes a person.
When news arrives that Almesa, the company responsible for the zombie virus and its cure, isn't as dead as they were rumored to be, Cass has to make a choice: remain in the hospital and work toward a normal life, or suck it up and reclaim her mantle as the last zombie hunter?

If Almesa's plans succeed, the world is going to need as many hunters as it can get.

"If you've ever wondered what happens to survivors of the zombie plague, and if they can ever truly rejoin 'real life' again, this is definitely the book for you! Fast-paced, insightful and layered, this book delivers something for every zombie story lover."
– Marie Bilodeau, bestselling author of *Nigh*

BONHOMME
SEPT-HEURES

by Evan May
Paranormal Suspense

The darkness with a smile in it

Something is killing the children of Lac de Thé, a tiny Quebec town. No-one sees it. It leaves no evidence. The only suspect is a character from a centuries-old folk tale, and the only safety appears to depend on following the story's ancient rule: all children must be indoors at home by seven o'clock.

Now, a mysterious government agent has summoned Adam Godwinson, former priest and book dealer, to help bring an end to the deaths, but the consequences of his last brush with the unthinkable lie heavily on him, and it may be Adam who needs rescuing most of all if anything is going to be done about Bonhomme Sept-Heures.